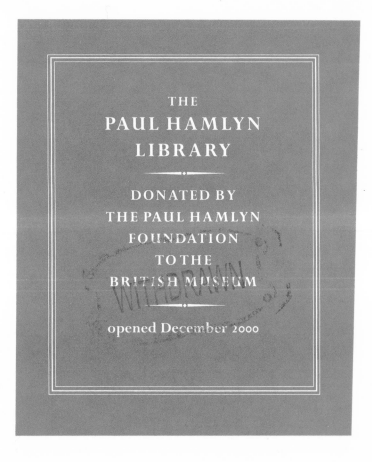

PICKING UP
Gold and Silver

PICKING UP
Gold and Silver

Stories by Rudyard Kipling
Selected and With an Introduction
by M. M. Kaye

St. Martin's Press
New York

Library of Congress Cataloging-in-Publication Data

Kipling, Rudyard, 1865–1936.
    Picking up gold and silver : stories / by Rudyard Kipling ;
  selected and with an introduction by M.M. Kaye.
        p.   cm.
    ISBN (invalid) 0-312-04686-8
    I. Kaye, M.M. (Mary Margaret).   II. Title.
  PR4852.K39   1990   90-36122
  823'.8—dc20   CIP

First published in Great Britain by Macmillan London Limited.

First U.S. Edition
10 9 8 7 6 5 4 3 2 1

Contents

Introduction

THERE used to be an old song, a nursery rhyme, that said: 'Here we stand on Tom Tiddler's Ground, picking up gold and silver.' I suppose we would all like to find ourselves on that fabled territory, but for me it exists in the many books of Rudyard Kipling's short stories— twenty-one in all. Because here is gold and silver in abundance, just waiting to be picked up. Some lead and copper here and there too, let's face it; but in very small amounts compared to the true coin— the golden guineas and silver crowns of yesteryear, which are still there and still untarnished. You only have to pick them up.

I can safely say that I have been a Kipling fan all my life. Well, very nearly all my life, since I cannot have been much more than five years old when my father read *The Jungle Book* to me, and from then on I have regarded RUDYARD KIPLING as a name of power. One that, like Keats' nightingale, can hand you the key to 'magic casements, opening on the foam/ Of perilous seas, in faery lands forlorn.'

The fact that the faery lands that Kipling wrote of were often Indian ones probably had a lot to do with my early fascination for his stories, because I, like him, had the good fortune to be born in that perilously magical country. To this day, whenever I feel homesick for it, I take down my old, tattered copy of his masterpiece, *Kim*—that marvellous love letter that he wrote to India—and read it again: perhaps for the hundredth time, yet always with as much delight as when, a homesick teenager who had been brought back to England to be educated, I found it in the school library and, reading it for the first time, was instantly comforted. For here lay all India, under my hand!

To anyone who has ever lived there, and to many readers who have never even set foot in that beautiful, bewitching, often maddening and sometimes terrifying land, *Kim* is strong magic. The same can be said of many of Kipling's short stories, but when I was asked to select a dozen of them for this book, I chose mainly those set in India because I always think of them as being, in Kipling's words, tales of 'mine own people'.

Among those I have chosen, four can be classed as ghost stories—one of them, 'The Return of Imray',[1] among the most spine-chilling that I have ever read. Another four are about animals, and four more are about people—a *Sunnyasi* (a wandering holy man); a British Chief Engineer in charge of building a bridge across the Ganges; Mowgli the wolf-boy, the child-hero of *The Jungle Books*[2] grown to manhood; and finally, the brief, bitter-sweet love story of an Englishman and a young Indian girl. Only two of these twelve do not have an Indian background: 'They'[3] being set in England in Kipling's home county of East Sussex and 'The Bull that Thought'[4] set in France, on the plains of the Carmargue and the Crau.

Hemingway lauded bullfighting as an Art with a capital A. And maybe it is; though personally it has always repelled me. As a spectator sport it is almost as unfair as matching those unarmed Christians against a pride

[1] From *Life's Handicap*, published by Macmillan, London, and Macmillan, New York.
[2] *The Jungle Book* and *The Second Jungle Book*, published by Macmillan, London, and Century, New York.
[3] From *Traffics and Discoveries*, published by Macmillan, London, and Doubleday, Page, New York.
[4] From *Debits and Credits*, published by Macmillan, London, and Doubleday, Page, New York.

of starving lions turned loose in the Colosseum in Rome. No hapless Christian was ever known to have left that blood-stained arena alive, and nor does any fighting bull leave the bullring save as a corpse on its way to be cut up and sold as meat. So the idea of a bull who can think, and who is just as much a cold-blooded killer as the men who not only bait him but also incite him into attacking and disembowelling sad, broken-down, blinkered old horses in order to tire out his neck muscles and make him easier to kill, is refreshingly original. While the way in which the story is told, by an elderly Frenchman, is Kipling at his best. Here are a few lines taken from a paragraph that describes Apis the bull, who, having created mayhem in the bullring, allows himself to be played by an elderly and undistinguished matador who had been a herdsman in his youth:

'He raged enormously; he feigned defeat; he despaired in statuesque abandon, and thence flashed into fresh paroxysms of wrath—but always with the detachment of a true artist who knows that he is but the vessel of an emotion whence others, not he, must drink.'

As in his *Jungle Books*, Kipling gives his animals human characters; something to which his critics have often objected. But then when has anyone who has ever owned and loved an animal or a bird—or even a goldfish—not thought of it as having the same feelings as we have, and credited it with being able to think as we do? True, Apis is a murderer. But he is fighting for his life against men who, having selected him for his fighting qualities, have driven him into the bullring to be killed for the entertainment of hundreds of blood-thirsty humans. It is salutatory to find him turning the tables on them.

I have included the other non-India story, 'They',

because it has to do with the greatest tragedy of Kipling's life; one that cannot have failed to affect his thinking and his character, and must have been harder to bear than the death in action of his only son, sixteen years later. He and his seven-year-old daughter, Josephine, who was the apple of his eye and the heart of his heart, both developed pneumonia as a result of catching cold and being severely sea-sick during an appallingly rough wintertime voyage from London to New York. Rudyard, who was then at the height of his fame, came so close to death that the streets outside the hotel in which he lay ill were strewn with tan-bark to prevent the noise of the traffic disturbing him. Hourly bulletins on his condition were issued to the waiting Press, prayers for his recovery were said in the churches, and groups of people knelt to pray for him in the streets and in the corridors of the hotel; while telegrams, cables and messages, several from the Kaiser, poured in from all over the world, demanding news and sending sympathy and encouragement. Had he been a reigning monarch or a modern film-star of the first magnitude, he could not have aroused greater global interest. In the event he recovered; but little Josephine, who had always been a delicate child, did not.

The death of his adored first-born was a blow from which he was never to recover, and it has been said that Rudyard left his original Sussex home, The Elms in Rottingdean, because it contained too many memories of her. This is not strictly true, for it was not the golden ghost of Josephine that drove him into leaving The Elms, but the fact that the house was too accessible to sightseers and tourists, who would gather outside to stare over the garden hedge at his front windows in the hope of catching a glimpse of the great man. However, it is certain that for him The Elms was haunted, since it is on record that he told his mother that he saw the child everywhere; running through its rooms, playing in the garden or sitting in an empty chair. Yet he did not leave her behind when, close on three years after her death, he acquired a more secluded house, Batemans, which was to be his home for the rest of his life. Sussex people say that in fact the reason he bought it was because he thought he saw Josephine looking down at him from one of the upper windows.

His cousin, the novelist Angela Thirkell, writing of the child's death, said: 'Much of the beloved Cousin Ruddy of our childhood died with Josephine and I feel that I have never seen him as a real person since that year.' Poor Ruddy! I am inclined to think that an incident he describes at the end of 'They' actually happened to him; probably at The Elms. But then I too believe in ghosts. You cannot have been born in India and spent the formative years of your childhood, plus a good slice of your adult life there, without recognising the truth of Shakespeare's famous dictum that 'There are more things in heaven and earth, Horatio,/ Than are dreamt of in your philosophy'. And Rudyard too was born in that enchanted country.

'By Word of Mouth',[5] one of his ghost stories that I have included in this book, was originally written as a column-filler when he was a young cub-reporter working for *The Civil and Military Gazette* in Lahore. A collection of these column-fillers, once intended to fill any space left vacant because of a temporary shortage of news items, formed one of his first books; he called it *Plain Tales from the Hills* and it made him famous.

My father—who for some forgotten reason I always called Tacklow—was only two years younger than Kipling, and, since his family had a tradition of India-service,

---

[5] From *Plain Tales from the Hills*. Thacker, Spink, Calcutta, Macmillan, London.

he too eventually came to that country; arriving at a time when young Rudyard's fill-ins had begun to appear fairly regularly in the columns of *The Civil and Military*. Tacklow was so fascinated by them that he took to cutting them out and pasting them in a bazaar-bought album which he treasured all his life. Only a very few of these were signed, and then only with the initials RK—one well-known poem, 'Paget, M.P.', first appeared in this newspaper signed 'An Englishman'. Tacklow therefore had no idea who had written them until Thacker, Spink printed the first copies of *Plain Tales*,[6] which appeared in paperback on every railway book-stall in India, priced at one rupee. Tacklow bought that too; as well as all the subsequent railway paperbacks of RK's books. Nowadays I imagine that their price would be above rubies. But alas, a year or two after my father's death, all his books, together with most of our household possessions, were destroyed in a disastrous fire that gutted the London warehouse in which they had been stored.

I have chosen 'By Word of Mouth' for two purely personal reasons; first for the sake of the verse that Kipling wrote to accompany it, and secondly for its descriptions of the forest road that leads out of Simla to Chini, and the bleak, wind-swept Dâk bungalow[7] on the hill-top at Bargi. My sister and I were both born in Simla, which in the days of the Raj was the summer capital of India, and we once had a house on a ridge of the hills just above that road. During the two years we lived there my parents would often take us out for picnics to Fargu and Bargi, which were then exactly as Kipling has described them in this story. (Nowadays there is a motor road in

---

[6] First published by Thacker, Spink, Calcutta. Later by Frank F. Lovel, New York, and Macmillan, London.
[7] Rest-house, Lit: 'Post Bungalow', since postmen and travellers put up there in the days when the mail was carried by hand.

place of the old, unmade track that was used for centuries
by traders from Tibet and Mongolia bringing their wares
into India.)

Like Somerset Maugham, Kipling had a habit of
collecting true stories and writing them as fiction. And
I have no doubt that the story on which he based 'By
Word of Mouth' was told him by some friend or chance
acquaintance who knew the real Dumoise. I have heard
stranger tales myself, and had no reason to disbelieve
them. Some of the strangest were about elephants . . .

In the closing years of the nineteenth century, when
Tacklow was a young man newly arrived in India, he
used a pad-elephant whenever he went on shooting-leave
in the Terai—a vast tract of jungle and tall grass that
used to stretch for hundreds of miles along the foothills
of the Himalayas, but is now, like the rain-forests of
South America, being systematically destroyed by man.
His pad-elephant's name was Pramekulli, and Tacklow
used to tell me endless stories about her wisdom, sagacity
and charming ways. He would have liked above all things
to own her; but unfortunately, no one other than a Raja, a
Forest Officer, or the owner of a very large estate, could
hope to own an elephant, since the amount of fodder that
they eat daily would ruin a townsman or anyone who
lived in barren country where there were no forests or
grasslands and where crops were hard to raise.

When I was a child in Old Delhi, at a time when
'New' Delhi was little more than a map on an empty
stony plain, my sister and I made friends with an elephant
that belonged to a travelling circus. We used to bring it
gifts of cakes and fruit and it had an endearing habit of
greeting our arrival with a loud and joyous 'Toot! Toot!'
Then one year, when we returned from spending the
hot-weather months in the hills, our elephant and his
mahout (handler) were not in their accustomed place and

no one knew where they had gone. They did not reappear for two years, but when they did, the elephant, spotting us from a long way off, hailed us with an enthusiastic flurry of welcoming toots—doubtless in expectation of more handouts! But at least it proves the truth of that old saying, 'An elephant never forgets.' That one didn't; and it is in affectionate memory of these engaging animals that I have included two stories about them in this book: 'Toomai of the Elephants'[8] and 'Moti Guj—Mutineer'.[9]

'Red Dog'[10] and 'In the Rukh',[11] are both Mowgli stories; Mowgli being the boy hero of the *Jungle Books* who was befriended and brought up by wolves. *The Jungle Book* and *The Second Jungle Book* contain between them eight Mowgli stories and seven other tales. Five of these seven are about animals, and two are more concerned with a person than a specific animal: 'Toomai of the Elephants' being mainly about a small boy, the son of a *mahout*, who hopes to be an elephant tracker when he grows up, and 'The Miracle of Purun Bhagat'[12] about Sir Purun Dass, KCIE, 'Prime Minister of no small State', a man who lays aside his honours and retires at the height of his career to take up the begging-bowl and become a *bhagat*, a wandering holy man. I have included both of these stories in this book because they have always been among my favourites; particularly the latter. The hill road that leads into the mountains beyond Simla is the same as that which the Civil Surgeon, Dumoise, took

[8] From *The Jungle Book*, published by Macmillan, London, and Century, New York.
[9] From *Life's Handicap*, published by Macmillan, London, and Macmillan, New York.
[10] From *The Second Jungle Book*, published by Macmillan, London, and Century, New York.
[11] From *Many Inventions*, published by Macmillan, London, and D. Appleton, New York.
[12] From *The Second Jungle Book*, published by Macmillan, London, and Century, New York.

in 'By Word of Mouth'; and I can picture every mile of
it as he and Purun Bhagat would have seen it, and
remind myself how fortunate I am to have been born
early enough to see it before lorries, buses, jeeps and
private cars roared along it!

In Rudyard's day, and in mine too, one could walk or
ride along that lovely, lonely road for miles without seeing
any sign of life save an occasional wood-cutter plodding
along with a load of kindling on his back, or, perhaps, a
flash of spotted yellow fur crossing the shadow-splashed
road ahead as a leopard sprang soundlessly across it.
Sometimes a troop of monkeys would hurtle rowdily
downhill; and always there would be a lone eagle, bal-
ancing on a wandering air current high overhead. There
was never more than one; but as Kipling says of the kites
in the plains, you knew that if any creature died 'that kite
would swoop down, and the next kite miles away would
see him drop and follow, and the next and the next, and
almost before they were dead there would be a horde of
hungry kites come out of nowhere.' It was probably the
same with the eagles. But the thing one noticed most
was the silence: something that is becoming rarer in
a noisy world that is criss-crossed hourly by scores of
jet planes—until even the polar bears can scarcely be
interested enough to look up as one of them flies over
the North Pole.

On windy days the forests were full of noise, and
during the monsoon the hillsides would roar with the
downpour of rain, while the din that a storm could raise
was truly awesome as the peals of thunder echoed back
and forth against the sounding board of the mountains.
In calmer weather the smallest breeze could set the pine
needles whispering, but on windless days the silence was
so deep that one could literally hear a leaf fall. Not
any longer though. Mr Henry Ford and the internal

combustion engine put a stop to that long ago. Yet I can still see, with my mind's eye, Purun Bhagat, wearing the orange-coloured robe of a *Sunnyasi* and carrying a begging-bowl, coming upon the deserted shrine on the crest of a pass and saying to himself: 'Here shall I find peace.'

I had been familiar with the early Mowgli stories from the time that Tacklow read aloud to me from *The Jungle Book*, but though I was almost within sight of double figures when I read the tales in *The Second Jungle Book*, I was still capable of being reduced to tears by the death of Akela, the lone wolf, in 'Red Dog', and by the final story in that book, 'The Spring Running', which I did not really understand but thought very sad because it tells how Mowgli fulfilled Akela's prediction that one day he would go back to his own kind. That story (which is not in this book) tells of how he was driven to go back to man, and how Grey Brother and the other three wolves who were his brothers in all but blood, went with him. It ends with Grey Brother sniffing the dawn wind and saying: 'Where shall we lair today? For, from now, we follow new trails.' Then there is a line of dots under which Kipling has written: 'And this is the last of the Mowgli stories.'

Well that, in one sense, was true. Though in fact there *was* another Mowgli story: 'In the Rukh',[13] which I have included in this collection because it reminds me of our Christmas-time shooting camps in India; and also because Tacklow knew and admired the real Inspector General Muller,[14] Head of the Indian Forestry Department, and used to tell me stories about him. 'In the Rukh' is a story

---

[13] From *Many Inventions*, published by Macmillan, London, and D. Appleton, New York.
[14] Not his real name. I presume I was told it, but if so, I have forgotten it.

about Mowgli, and his four wolf-brothers, when he is no longer a boy but a man, and it appeared in a book of RK's short stories called *Many Inventions*. I remember how delighted I was to find it, because it rounds off the Mowgli stories so well. And also because I hadn't really liked 'The Spring Running' and felt sad and somehow let down that the tales had ended so inconclusively. It was lovely to meet Mowgli and his four brothers again and to find that they were doing all right.

India is full of tales about toddlers being lost in the jungle and befriended and brought up by wolves (it is nearly always wolves!). During the late 1930s the Indian newspapers reported at least two cases of children who had been found in the jungle and dumped on the nearest Mission Hospital: one a boy of about six or seven years old, and then later on, two little girls, presumed to be sisters. Kipling must have come across a story of wolf-children (probably from the real 'Muller' who would have heard many of them) and filed it away for future reference. According to Carrington,[15] he used it for 'In the Rukh', one of the short stories in *Many Inventions*, which was published in 1893—a year before *The Jungle Book* and two years before *The Second Jungle Book*, which between them tell the story of the wolf-child Mowgli. So although it appeared first, it was in fact written after he had finished the saga of Mowgli; possibly while he was waiting for his father to finish the illustrations for those delightful books.

Of the other three stories in this collection, my favourite is 'Without Benefit of Clergy',[16] which is another story from *Life's Handicap*. It tells of the

---

[15] Charles Carrington, author of *Rudyard Kipling, His Life Work*, published by Macmillan, London.
[16] from *Life's Handicap*, published by Macmillan, London, and Macmillan, New York.

brief idyll of an Englishman who installs his enchanting Muslim mistress in a house in the Indian city. Their love story ends tragically: Ameera refuses to go to the hills for the hot weather, and when the temperature soars and there is cholera in the city, she catches the sickness and dies. That is all. I have always thought that this slight tale must rank as one of the most beautiful and touching of love stories, and that the dying girl's last words to her lover, when she changes the great Muslim affirmation of Faith 'I bear witness that there is no God but God' to 'I bear witness that—there is no God but—thee, beloved!' the most touching declaration of love that anyone could make.

'The Lost Legion'[17] is yet another ghost story that Kipling must have been told in his early days as a reporter, for it is based on a tale that has long been part of Frontier legend. Even as late as the early thirties one could find people in Peshawar, Nowshera, Rissalpur and Mardan—which were cantonment towns for the British–Indian Army—who had heard it from their fathers or grandfathers and accepted it as a matter of course. The Frontier tribes certainly believed it: this story of an Indian cavalry regiment (*Rissala*)—Kipling calls it a regiment of Indian Irregular Horse—that mutinied in the spring of 1857 and set off to march southward with the intention of joining the insurgents who had captured Delhi. However, they were forced to head north into the Kyber Hills where the tribesmen fell on them and hunted them to the death for the sake of their arms and accoutrements.

I once asked an elderly acquaintance of mine, a retired *Rissaldar* who owned an orchard on the outskirts of Peshawar, if he had ever heard this particular story.

[17] From *Many Inventions*, published by Macmillan, London, and D. Appleton, New York.

He nodded without much interest and said that all men knew it: his grandfather had told him the tale when he was a child, and even in his father's time it was known by everyone on the frontier. But when I asked him if he knew the name of the 'dead *Rissala*' he replied: 'Assuredly', but refused to tell me what it was, insisting that it should be forgotten. There was, he said severely, no profit in remembering shameful actions. And besides, all those who had betrayed their salt had paid a heavy price, since all had been killed and the very name of the regiment had been struck from the rolls. He had not heard about the incident that Kipling puts in this story, of a small force of British, Indian and Gurkha units being sent to arrest a well-known agitator and his friends in a village beyond the border. But when I told him about it he shrugged and said that the *Sirkar* (the Indian Government) was always sending troops across the border to arrest agitators or punish those who raided the villages and carried off women and cattle, so it was only to be expected that now and again some of them would see the 'dead *Rissala*'.

I like to think that Kipling's *Rissala*—'the very much alive *Rissala*' of the story—was the cavalry wing of my husband Goff Hamilton's regiment, The Corps of Guides. In fact, if that part of the story is not entirely fiction, it must have been his regiment—for two reasons. The Indian Officer who cries for mercy when he sees that the Afghan sentry in the look-out tower has spotted them by the flashes of lightning, is a Pathan, and the majority of Guides were recruited from beyond the border. Then, when the Mullah's men wake in the morning and come out of their huts, they see 'men in green, and red, and brown uniforms, leaning on their arms, neatly arranged all round the crater of the village of Bersund, in a cordon that not even a wolf could have broken.' Well, the green uniforms would be Gurkhas and the red a British regiment—for at that date (approximately 1890) the British army would still have been wearing the regulation scarlet uniforms. But the brown (khaki, actually) *must* have been the Guides, because at that time they were the only regiment to wear khaki uniforms.

The Corps had been raised in 1846, eleven years before the mutiny, by one of my favourite India-service heroes, Sir Henry Lawrence, who decreed that its uniforms should be khaki—which is the Persian word for 'dust-coloured'—instead of the far too eye-catching scarlet that made an advancing British Army visible from a range of several miles! Therefore the *Rissala* in 'The Lost Legion' could only have been the Guides, who would have mustered in the dark and ridden out as silently as possible from the little cantonment of Mardan which was their home-station for close on a hundred years. The same Mardan where Major Wigram Battye, whose body was exhumed from its grave near Jalalabad and brought back by raft down the Kabul River, lies buried for the second time. And from where my husband's kinsman, Walter Pollack Hamilton, VC, the first of three Hamiltons to serve in the Guides, rode out at the head of 78 men of the Corps to act as escort for Sir Louis Cavagnari, the newly appointed British Ambassador to Kabul. In Kabul Cavagnari was killed—together with his Military Secretary and 73 of the Guides, including their youthful commander and the Medical Officer, Dr Kelly—when an Afghan mob attacked the Residency and burned it to the ground.

The Cavagnari Arch, which was raised in Mardan to commemorate the hopeless but heroic defence of The British Residency in Kabul, still stands there, and in 1987 I went out to Pakistan for the centenary of the Guides Church in Mardan, taking with me a plaque

to the memory of my husband—the last Hamilton who
would ever serve with the Guides—which was dedicated
at the Centenary Service in the presence of many of his
old friends and comrades. It is largely because of Goff and
his beloved Guides that I have included 'The Lost Legion'
in this collection. Though I think it would probably have
gone in anyway: I always liked it.

The last story, 'The Bridge-Builders',[18] is another that
is taken from *The Day's work*, and has always appealed
to me as typically Kipling. Throughout his life he had an
enormous admiration for 'doers'—the men who did the
work but did not talk about it. Soldiers, sailors, airmen,
administrators, explorers, engineers... One suspects
that he would have liked to be one himself, and did not
consider that writing was really work in the true sense
of the word. But then he never wanted to do anything
but write, and had become hooked on journalism and
printer's ink at a very early age when the headmaster
of his public school, The United Services College, made
him editor of the school magazine.

Rudyard's heroes were people like MacAndrew of
'MacAndrew's Hymn',[19] who was Chief Engineer of a
merchant navy ship, or like Findlayson of the PWD (Public Works Department, India) the Chief Engineer of the
Kashi Bridge, who is a perfect example of the type of man
that he most admired and certainly envied. His 'Bridge-
Builders' tells of a flash flood on the Ganges, the greatest
of the Indian rivers, and of how Findlayson's bridge,
which has been more than three years in the building
and (except for a few weeks' work on the central piers) is
nearing completion, fares when the flood water hits it.

[18] From *The Day's Work*, published by Macmillan, London, and Doubleday
& McClure, New York.
[19] See *Rudyard Kipling's Definitive Verse*, published by Hodder & Stoughton,
London, and Doubleday, Doran, New York.

I have always admired and envied Kipling's gift for descriptive writing and his ability to put sounds, scents, heat, light and cold into words that make you able to see and hear and almost smell whatever it is that he is describing. An example of this is his description of the arrival of the flood waters on the hot sand of the shrunken river, where the coolies working on the new bridge had built a temporary village that now has to be hastily dismantled before the main flood reaches it:

'She moves!' said Peroo, just before the dawn. 'Mother Gunga is awake! Hear!' He dipped his hand over the side of a boat and the current mumbled on it. A little wave hit the side of a pier with a crisp slap.

'Six hours before her time,' said Findlayson, mopping his forehead savagely. 'Now we can't depend on anything. We'd better clear all hands out of the river-bed.'

Again the big gong beat, and a second time there was a rushing of naked feet on earth and ringing iron; the clatter of tools ceased. In the silence, men heard the dry yawn of water crawling over thirsty sand.

Who else but Kipling could have described so exactly the sound of rising water creeping across the hot silver sands of an Indian river? Or used the word 'mumbling' for the stealthy movement of an unseen current fingering a man's hand?

Findlayson and his foreman, Peroo, a one-time *lascar* (deck-hand) on the British–Indian Boats, are swept down by the flood water aboard one of the clumsy, flat-bottomed stone-boats, which breaks up, stranding them on a little island in midstream. Here, by the incessant flashes of lightning, they see a number of animals and two humans who have also taken refuge. 'The Gods. Who else? Look!'

says Peroo, who has given Findlayson a handful of opium pills to ward off fever, and swallowed the rest himself, certain that they are doomed when the rudderless boat is whirled away on the crest of the flood. Findlayson, crouched beside him in the wet grass, decides that Peroo must be right, since: 'After the Flood, who should be alive in the land except the Gods that made it—the Gods to whom his village prayed nightly—the Gods who were in all men's mouths and about all men's ways?'

Findlayson and Peroo think that they are listening to a meeting of 'The Great Ones', met together to hear the complaints of the River, Mother Gunga, who demands the Justice of the Gods on the bridge-builders who have harnessed her waters and made them run between stone piers. Kali, in the guise of a tigress, supports her, complaining that worshippers are deserting the Old Gods to follow after new ones. But Shiv, in the person of a sacred bull, says it is not so—that the new ones are only the old ones with new names. To which Krishna, 'the idol of dreaming maids and of mothers ere their children are born—Krishna the Well-beloved', replies that he, living among his people, knows their hearts and that it is they who are to be reckoned with, not the Gods of the bridge-builders. In time they will fall away from their old beliefs and change more than the names; but he alone they cannot kill . . . 'So long as maiden and man meet together or the spring follows the winter rains.' He urges the Heavenly Ones to make the most of the time that is left to them, to 'Take dues and listen to the cymbals and the drums . . . while yet there are flowers and songs. As men count time the end is far off; but as we who know reckon, it is to-day.'

Kipling wrote that story in the last years of the nineteenth century, when his country's Indian Empire looked set to last for another thousand years. Yet I have always suspected that he had a personal, private, crystal ball in his head which, occasionally, gave him glimpses of the future; and that this was one of them. Findlayson and his Indian colleague, Peroo, symbolise the companionship and trust that so often existed between the British and Indians in the days of British rule, and without which the Raj could not have lasted a year. It illustrates, too, their mutual dedication to the work on which both were engaged, and which they toiled at not so much for money as for the approval of their fellow workers, their equals. The talk of the Gods foreshadows the end, which was to come almost exactly fifty years later. Half a century! —that is a long, long time out of the life of a man '. . . but as we who know reckon, it is to-day.'

Now that day too is past and gone. But for very many of us, Rudyard Kipling illuminated it with his own, extraordinary light.

M M Kaye

Without Benefit of Clergy

Before my Spring I garnered Autumn's gain,
Out of her time my field was white with grain,
The year gave up her secrets to my woe.
Forced and deflowered each sick season lay,
In mystery of increase and decay;
I saw the sunset ere men saw the day,
Who am too wise in that I should not know.
Bitter Waters.

I

'BUT if it be a girl?'

'Lord of my life, it cannot be. I have prayed for so many nights, and sent gifts to Sheikh Badl's shrine so often, that I know God will give us a son—a man-child that shall grow into a man. Think of this and be glad. My mother shall be his mother till I can take him again, and the mullah of the Pattan mosque shall cast his nativity—God send he be born in an auspicious hour!—and then, and then thou wilt never weary of me, thy slave.'

'Since when hast thou been a slave, my queen?'

'Since the beginning—till this mercy came to me. How could I be sure of thy love when I knew that I had been bought with silver?'

'Nay, that was the dowry. I paid it to thy mother.'

'And she has buried it, and sits upon it all day long like a hen. What talk is yours of dower! I was bought as though I had been a Lucknow dancing-girl instead of a child.'

'Art thou sorry for the sale?'

'I have sorrowed; but to-day I am glad. Thou wilt never cease to love me now?—answer, my king.'

'Never—never. No.'

'Not even though the *mem-log*—the white women of thy own blood—love thee? And remember, I have watched them driving in the evening; they are very fair.'

'I have seen fire-balloons by the hundred. I have seen the moon, and—then I saw no more fire-balloons.'

Ameera clapped her hands and laughed. 'Very good talk,' she said. Then with an assumption of great stateliness, 'It is enough. Thou hast my permission to depart,—if thou wilt.'

The man did not move. He was sitting on a low red-lacquered couch in a room furnished only with a blue and white floor-cloth, some rugs, and a very complete collection of native cushions. At his feet sat a woman of sixteen, and she was all but all the world in his eyes. By every rule and law she should have been otherwise, for he was an Englishman, and she a Mussulman's daughter bought two years before from her mother, who, being left without money, would have sold Ameera shrieking to the Prince of Darkness if the price had been sufficient.

It was a contract entered into with a light heart; but even before the girl had reached her bloom she came to fill the greater portion of John Holden's life. For her, and the withered hag her mother, he had taken a little house overlooking the great red-walled city, and found,—when the marigolds had sprung up by the well in the courtyard, and Ameera had established herself according to her own ideas of comfort, and her mother had ceased grumbling at the inadequacy of the cooking-places, the distance from the daily market, and at matters of house-keeping in general,—that the house was to him his home. Any one could enter his bachelor's bungalow by day or night, and the life that he led there was an unlovely one. In the house in the city his feet only could pass beyond the outer courtyard to the women's rooms; and when the big wooden gate was bolted behind him he was king in his own territory, with Ameera for queen. And there was going to be added to this kingdom a third person whose arrival Holden felt inclined to resent. It interfered with his perfect happiness. It disarranged the orderly peace of the house that was his own. But Ameera was wild with delight at the thought of it, and her mother not less so. The love of a man, and particularly a white man, was at the best an inconstant affair, but it might, both women argued, be held fast by a baby's hands. 'And then,' Ameera would always say, 'then he will never care for the white *mem-log*. I hate them all—I hate them all.'

'He will go back to his own people in time,' said the mother; 'but by the blessing of God that time is yet afar off.'

Holden sat silent on the couch thinking of the future, and his thoughts were not pleasant. The drawbacks of a double life are manifold. The Government, with singular care, had ordered him out of the station for a fortnight on special duty in the place of a man who was watching by the bedside of a sick wife. The verbal notification of the transfer had been edged by a cheerful remark that Holden ought to think himself lucky in being a bachelor and a free man. He came to break the news to Ameera.

'It is not good,' she said slowly, 'but it is not all bad. There is my mother here, and no harm will come to me—unless indeed I die of pure joy. Go thou to thy work and think no troublesome thoughts. When the days are done I believe . . . nay, I am sure. And—and then I shall lay *him* in thy arms, and thou wilt love me for ever. The train goes to-night, at midnight is it not? Go now, and do not let thy heart be heavy by cause of me. But thou wilt not delay in returning? Thou wilt not stay on the road to talk to the bold white *mem-log*? Come back to me swiftly, my life.'

As he left the courtyard to reach his horse that was tethered to the gate-post, Holden spoke to the white-haired old watchman who guarded the house, and bade him under certain contingencies despatch the filled-up telegraph-form that Holden gave him. It was all that could be done, and with the sensations of a man who has attended his own funeral Holden went away by the night mail to his exile. Every hour of the day he dreaded the arrival of the telegram, and every hour of the night he pictured to himself the death of Ameera. In consequence his work for the State was not of first-rate quality, nor was his temper towards his colleagues of the most amiable. The fortnight ended without a sign from his home, and, torn to pieces by his anxieties, Holden returned to be swallowed up for two precious hours by a dinner at the club, wherein he heard, as a man hears in a swoon, voices telling him how execrably he had performed the other man's duties, and how he had endeared himself to all his associates. Then he fled on horseback through the night with his heart in his mouth. There was no answer at first to his blows on the gate, and he had just wheeled his horse round to kick it in when Pir Khan appeared with a lantern and held his stirrup.

'Has aught occurred?' said Holden.

'The news does not come from my mouth, Protector of the Poor, but——' He held out his shaking hand as befitted the bearer of good news who is entitled to a reward.

Holden hurried through the courtyard. A light burned in the upper room. His horse neighed in the gateway, and he heard a shrill little wail that sent all the blood into the apple of his throat. It was a new voice, but it did not prove that Ameera was alive.

'Who is there?' he called up the narrow brick staircase.

There was a cry of delight from Ameera, and then the voice of the mother, tremulous with old age and pride—'We be two women and—the—man—thy—son.'

On the threshold of the room Holden stepped on a naked dagger, that was laid there to avert ill-luck, and it broke at the hilt under his impatient heel.

'God is great!' cooed Ameera in the half-light. 'Thou hast taken his misfortunes on thy head.'

'Ay, but how is it with thee, life of my life? Old woman, how is it with her?'

'She has forgotten her sufferings for joy that the child is born. There is no harm; but speak softly,' said the mother.

'It only needed thy presence to make me all well,' said Ameera. 'My king, thou hast been very long away. What gifts hast thou for me? Ah, ah! It is I that bring gifts this time. Look, my life, look. Was there ever such a babe? Nay, I am too weak even to clear my arm from him.'

'Rest then, and do not talk. I am here, *bachari* [little woman].'

'Well said, for there is a bond and a heel-rope [*peecha-ree*] between us now that nothing can break. Look—canst thou see in this light? He is without spot or blemish. Never was such a man-child. *Ya illah!* he shall be a pundit—no, a trooper of the Queen. And, my life, dost thou love me as well as ever, though I am faint and sick and worn? Answer truly.'

'Yea. I love as I have loved, with all my soul. Lie still, pearl, and rest.'

'Then do not go. Sit by my side here—so. Mother, the lord of this house needs a cushion. Bring it.' There was an almost imperceptible movement on the part of the new life that lay in the hollow of Ameera's arm. 'Aho!' she said, her voice breaking with love. 'The babe is a champion from his birth. He is kicking me in the side with mighty kicks. Was there ever such a babe! And he is ours to us—thine and mine. Put thy hand on his head, but carefully, for he is very young, and men are unskilled in such matters.'

Very cautiously Holden touched with the tips of his fingers the downy head.

'He is of the Faith,' said Ameera; 'for lying here in the night-watches I whispered the call to prayer and the profession of faith into his ears. And it is most marvellous that he was born upon a Friday, as I was born. Be careful of him, my life; but he can almost grip with his hands.'

Holden found one helpless little hand that closed feebly on his finger. And the clutch ran through his body till it settled about his heart. Till then his sole thought had been for Ameera. He began to realise that there was some one else in the world, but he could not feel that it was a veritable son with a soul. He sat down to think, and Ameera dozed lightly.

'Get hence, *sahib*,' said her mother under her breath. 'It is not good that she should find you here on waking. She must be still.'

'I go,' said Holden submissively. 'Here be rupees. See that my *baba* gets fat and finds all that he needs.'

The chink of the silver roused Ameera. 'I am his mother, and no hireling,' she said weakly. 'Shall I look to him more or less for the sake of money? Mother, give it back. I have borne my lord a son.'

The deep sleep of weakness came upon her almost before the sentence was completed. Holden went down to the courtyard very softly with his heart at ease. Pir Khan, the old watchman, was chuckling with delight. 'This house is now complete,' he said, and without further comment thrust into Holden's hands the hilt of a sabre worn many years ago when he, Pir Khan, served the Queen in the police. The bleat of a tethered goat came from the well-kerb.

'There be two,' said Pir Khan, 'two goats of the best. I bought them, and they cost much money; and since there is no birth-party assembled their flesh will be all mine. Strike craftily, *sahib*! 'Tis an ill-balanced sabre at the best. Wait till they raise their heads from cropping the marigolds.'

'And why?' said Holden, bewildered.

'For the birth-sacrifice. What else? Otherwise the child being unguarded from fate may die. The Protector of the Poor knows the fitting words to be said.'

Holden had learned them once with little thought that he would ever speak them in earnest. The touch of the cold sabre-hilt in his palm turned suddenly to the clinging grip of the child up-stairs—the child that was his own son—and a dread of loss filled him.

'Strike!' said Pir Khan. 'Never life came into the world but life was paid for it. See, the goats have raised their heads. Now! With a drawing cut!'

Hardly knowing what he did, Holden cut twice as he muttered the Mahomedan prayer that runs: 'Almighty! In place of this my son I offer life for life, blood for blood, head for head, bone for bone, hair for hair, skin for skin.' The waiting horse snorted and bounded in his pickets at the smell of the raw blood that spirted over Holden's riding-boots.

'Well smitten!' said Pir Khan wiping the sabre. 'A swordsman was lost in thee. Go with a light heart, Heaven-born. I am thy servant, and the servant of thy son. May the Presence live a thousand years and . . . the flesh of the goats is all mine?' Pir Khan drew back richer by a month's pay. Holden swung himself into the saddle and rode off through the low-hanging wood-smoke of the evening. He was full of riotous exultation, alternating with a vast vague tenderness directed towards no particular object, that made him choke as he bent over the neck of his uneasy horse. 'I never felt like this in my life,' he thought. 'I'll go to the club and pull myself together.'

A game of pool was beginning, and the room was full of men. Holden entered, eager to get to the light and the company of his fellows, singing at the top of his voice—

'In Baltimore a-walking, a lady I did meet!'

'Did you?' said the club-secretary from his corner. 'Did she happen to tell you that your boots were wringing wet? Great goodness, man, it's blood!'

'Bosh!' said Holden, picking his cue from the rack. 'May I cut in? It's dew. I've been riding through high crops. My faith! my boots are in a mess though!

'And if it be a girl she shall wear a wedding-ring,
And if it be a boy he shall fight for his king,
With his dirk, and his cap, and his little jacket blue,
He shall walk the quarter-deck—'

'Yellow on blue—green next player,' said the marker monotonously.

'*He shall walk the quarter-deck,*—Am I green, marker? *He shall walk the quarter-deck,*—eh! that's a bad shot,— *As his daddy used to do!*'

'I don't see that you have anything to crow about,' said a zealous junior civilian acidly. 'The Government is not exactly pleased with your work when you relieved Sanders.'

'Does that mean a wigging from headquarters?' said Holden with an abstracted smile. 'I think I can stand it.'

The talk beat up round the ever-fresh subject of each man's work, and steadied Holden till it was time to go to his dark empty bungalow, where his butler received him as one who knew all his affairs. Holden remained awake for the greater part of the night, and his dreams were pleasant ones.

II

'How old is he now?'

'*Ya illah!* What a man's question! He is all but six weeks old; and on this night I go up to the house-top with thee, my life, to count the stars. For that is auspicious. And he was born on a Friday under the sign of the Sun, and it has been told to me that he will outlive us both and get wealth. Can we wish for aught better, beloved?'

'There is nothing better. Let us go up to the roof, and thou shalt count the stars—but a few only, for the sky is heavy with cloud.'

'The winter rains are late, and maybe they come out of season. Come, before all the stars are hid. I have put on my richest jewels.'

'Thou has forgotten the best of all.'

'*Ai!* Ours. He comes also. He has never yet seen the skies.'

Ameera climbed the narrow staircase that led to the flat roof. The child, placid and unwinking, lay in the hollow of her right arm, gorgeous in silver-fringed muslin with a small skull-cap on his head. Ameera wore all that she valued most. The diamond nose-stud that takes the place of the Western patch in drawing attention to the curve of the nostril, the gold ornament in the centre of the forehead studded with tallow-drop emeralds and flawed rubies, the heavy circlet of beaten gold that was fastened round her neck by the softness of the pure metal, and the chinking curb-patterned silver anklets hanging low over the rosy ankle-bone. She was dressed in jade-green muslin as befitted a daughter of the Faith, and from shoulder to elbow and elbow to wrist ran bracelets of silver tied with floss silk, frail glass bangles slipped over the wrist in proof of the slenderness of the hand, and certain heavy gold bracelets that had no part in her country's ornaments, but, since they were Holden's gift and fastened with a cunning European snap, delighted her immensely.

They sat down by the low white parapet of the roof, overlooking the city and its lights.

'They are happy down there,' said Ameera. 'But I do not think that they are as happy as we. Nor do I think the white *mem-log* are as happy. And thou?'

'I know they are not.'

'How dost thou know?'

'They give their children over to the nurses.'

'I have never seen that,' said Ameera with a sigh, 'nor do I wish to see. *Ahi!*'—she dropped her head on Holden's shoulder,—'I have counted forty stars, and I am tired. Look at the child, love of my life, he is counting too.'

The baby was staring with round eyes at the dark of the heavens. Ameera placed him in Holden's arms, and he lay there without a cry.

'What shall we call him among ourselves?' she said. 'Look! Art thou ever tired of looking? He carries thy very eyes. But the mouth——'

'Is thine, most dear. Who should know better than I?'

"Tis such a feeble mouth. Oh, so small! And yet it holds my heart between its lips. Give him to me now. He has been too long away.'

'Nay, let him lie; he has not yet begun to cry.'

'When he cries thou wilt give him back—eh? What a man of mankind thou art! If he cried he were only

the dearer to me. But, my life, what little name shall
we give him?'

The small body lay close to Holden's heart. It was
utterly helpless and very soft. He scarcely dared to
breathe for fear of crushing it. The caged green parrot
that is regarded as a sort of guardian-spirit in most
native households moved on its perch and fluttered a
drowsy wing.

'There is the answer,' said Holden. 'Mian Mittu has
spoken. He shall be The Parrot. When he is ready he will
talk mightily and run about. Mian Mittu is The Parrot in
thy—in the Mussulman tongue, is it not?'

'Why put me so far off?' said Ameera fretfully. 'Let
it be like unto some English name—but not wholly. For
he is mine.'

'Then call him Tota, for that is likest English.'

'Ay, Tota, and that is still the parrot. Forgive me,
my lord, for a minute ago, but in truth he is too little
to wear all the weight of Mian Mittu for name. He shall
be Tota—our Tota to us. Hearest thou, oh, small one?
Littlest, thou art Tota.' She touched the child's cheek,
and he waking wailed, and it was necessary to return
him to his mother, who soothed him with the wonderful
rhyme of *Aré koko, Jaré koko!*' which says—

'Oh, crow! Go, crow! Baby's sleeping sound,
And the wild plums grow in the jungle, only a penny a pound.
Only a penny a pound, *baba*, only a penny a pound.'

Reassured many times as to the price of those plums,
Tota cuddled himself down to sleep. The two sleek, white
well-bullocks in the courtyard were steadily chewing the
cud of their evening meal; old Pir Khan squatted at the
head of Holden's horse, his police sabre across his knees,
pulling drowsily at a big water-pipe that croaked like a

bull-frog in a pond. Ameera's mother sat spinning in
the lower verandah, and the wooden gate was shut
and barred. The music of a marriage-procession came
to the roof above the gentle hum of the city, and a string
of flying-foxes crossed the face of the low moon.

'I have prayed,' said Ameera after a long pause, 'I have
prayed for two things. First, that I may die in thy stead
if thy death is demanded, and in the second, that I may
die in the place of the child. I have prayed to the Prophet
and to Beebee Miriam [the Virgin Mary]. Thinkest thou
either will hear?'

'From thy lips who would not hear the lightest word?'

'I asked for straight talk, and thou hast given me
sweet talk. Will my prayers be heard?'

'How can I say? God is very good.'

'Of that I am not sure. Listen now. When I die, or
the child dies, what is thy fate? Living, thou wilt return
to the bold white *mem-log*, for kind calls to kind.'

'Not always.'

'With a woman, no; with a man it is otherwise. Thou
wilt in this life, later on, go back to thine own folk. That
I could almost endure, for I should be dead. But in thy
very death thou wilt be taken away to a strange place
and a paradise that I do not know.'

'Will it be paradise?'

'Surely, for who would harm thee? But we two—I
and the child—shall be elsewhere, and we cannot come
to thee, nor canst thou come to us. In the old days, before
the child was born, I did not think of these things; but
now I think of them always. It is very hard talk.'

'It will fall as it will fall. To-morrow we do not know,
but to-day and love we know well. Surely we are happy
now.'

'So happy that it were well to make our happiness
assured. And thy Beebee Miriam should listen to me;

for she is also a woman. But then she would envy me!
It is not seemly for men to worship a woman.'

Holden laughed aloud at Ameera's little spasm of
jealousy.

'Is it not seemly? Why didst thou not turn me from
worship of thee, then?'

'Thou a worshipper! And of me? My king, for all
thy sweet words, well I know that I am thy servant and
thy slave, and the dust under thy feet. And I would not
have it otherwise. See!'

Before Holden could prevent her she stooped forward
and touched his feet; recovering herself with a little
laugh she hugged Tota closer to her bosom. Then, almost
savagely—

'Is it true that the bold white *mem-log* live for three
times the length of my life? Is it true that they make
their marriages not before they are old women?'

'They marry as do others—when they are women.'

'That I know, but they wed when they are twenty-five.
Is that true?'

'That is true.'

'*Ya illah!* At twenty-five! Who would of his own will
take a wife even of eighteen? She is a woman—aging
every hour. Twenty-five! I shall be an old woman at that
age, and—— Those *mem-log* remain young for ever. How
I hate them!'

'What have they to do with us?'

'I cannot tell. I know only that there may now be
alive on this earth a woman ten years older than I who
may come to thee and take thy love ten years after I am
an old woman, gray-headed, and the nurse of Tota's son.
That is unjust and evil. They should die too.'

'Now, for all thy years thou art a child, and shalt
be picked up and carried down the staircase.'

'Tota! Have a care for Tota, my lord! Thou at least art

as foolish as any babe!' Ameera tucked Tota out of harm's way in the hollow of her neck, and was carried downstairs laughing in Holden's arms, while Tota opened his eyes and smiled after the manner of the lesser angels.

He was a silent infant, and, almost before Holden could realise that he was in the world, developed into a small gold-coloured little god and unquestioned despot of the house overlooking the city. Those were months of absolute happiness to Holden and Ameera—happiness withdrawn from the world, shut in behind the wooden gate that Pir Khan guarded. By day Holden did his work with an immense pity for such as were not so fortunate as himself, and a sympathy for small children that amazed and amused many mothers at the little station-gatherings. At nightfall he returned to Ameera,—Ameera, full of the wondrous doings of Tota; how he had been seen to clap his hands together and move his fingers with intention and purpose—which was manifestly a miracle—how later, he had of his own initiative crawled out of his low bedstead on to the floor and swayed on both feet for the space of three breaths.

'And they were long breaths, for my heart stood still with delight,' said Ameera.

Then Tota took the beasts into his councils—the well-bullocks, the little gray squirrels, the mongoose that lived in a hole near the well, and especially Mian Mittu, the parrot, whose tail he grievously pulled, and Mian Mittu screamed till Ameera and Holden arrived.

'Oh, villain! Child of strength! This to thy brother on the house-top! *Tobah, tobah!* Fie! Fie! But I know a charm to make him wise as Suleiman and Aflatoun [Solomon and Plato]. Now look,' said Ameera. She drew from an embroidered bag a handful of almonds. 'See! we count seven. In the name of God!'

She placed Mian Mittu, very angry and rumpled,

on the top of his cage, and seating herself between the babe and the bird she cracked and peeled an almond less white than her teeth. 'This is a true charm, my life, and do not laugh. See! I give the parrot one-half and Tota the other.' Mian Mittu with careful beak took his share from between Ameera's lips, and she kissed the other half into the mouth of the child, who ate it slowly with wondering eyes. 'This I will do each day of seven, and without doubt he who is ours will be a bold speaker and wise. Eh, Tota, what wilt thou be when thou art a man and I am gray-headed?' Tota tucked his fat legs into adorable creases. He could crawl, but he was not going to waste the spring of his youth in idle speech. He wanted Mian Mittu's tail to tweak.

When he was advanced to the dignity of a silver belt—which, with a magic square engraved on silver and hung round his neck, made up the greater part of his clothing—he staggered on a perilous journey down the garden to Pir Khan, and proffered him all his jewels in exchange for one little ride on Holden's horse, having seen his mother's mother chaffering with pedlars in the verandah. Pir Khan wept and set the untried feet on his own gray head in sign of fealty, and brought the bold adventurer to his mother's arms, vowing that Tota would be a leader of men ere his beard was grown.

One hot evening, while he sat on the roof between his father and mother watching the never-ending warfare of the kites that the city boys flew, he demanded a kite of his own with Pir Khan to fly it, because he had a fear of dealing with anything larger than himself, and when Holden called him a 'spark,' he rose to his feet and answered slowly in defence of his new-found individuality, '*Hum 'park nahin hai. Hum admi hai* [I am no spark, but a man.]'

The protest made Holden choke and devote himself

very seriously to a consideration of Tota's future. He
need hardly have taken the trouble. The delight of that
life was too perfect to endure. Therefore it was taken
away as many things are taken away in India—suddenly
and without warning. The little lord of the house, as Pir
Khan called him, grew sorrowful and complained of pains
who had never known the meaning of pain. Ameera, wild
with terror, watched him through the night, and in the
dawning of the second day the life was shaken out of
him by fever—the seasonal autumn fever. It seemed
altogether impossible that he could die, and neither
Ameera nor Holden at first believed the evidence of the
little body on the bedstead. Then Ameera beat her head
against the wall and would have flung herself down the
well in the garden had Holden not restrained her by
main force.

One mercy only was granted to Holden. He rode
to his office in broad daylight and found waiting him
an unusually heavy mail that demanded concentrated
attention and hard work. He was not, however, alive to
this kindness of the gods.

III

The first shock of a bullet is no more than a brisk
pinch. The wrecked body does not send in its protest to
the soul till ten or fifteen seconds later. Holden realised
his pain slowly, exactly as he had realised his happiness,
and with the same imperious necessity for hiding all trace
of it. In the beginning he only felt that there had been
a loss, and that Ameera needed comforting, where she
sat with her head on her knees shivering as Mian Mittu
from the house-top called, *Tota! Tota! Tota!* Later all his
world and the daily life of it rose up to hurt him. It was an

outrage that any one of the children at the band-stand in the evening should be alive and clamorous, when his own child lay dead. It was more than mere pain when one of them touched him, and stories told by over-fond fathers of their children's latest performances cut him to the quick. He could not declare his pain. He had neither help, comfort, nor sympathy; and Ameera at the end of each weary day would lead him through the hell of self-questioning reproach which is reserved for those who have lost a child, and believe that with a little—just a little more care—it might have been saved.

'Perhaps,' Ameera would say, 'I did not take sufficient heed. Did I, or did I not? The sun on the roof that day when he played so long alone and I was—*ahi!* braiding my hair—it may be that the sun then bred the fever. If I had warned him from the sun he might have lived. But, oh, my life, say that I am guiltless! Thou knowest that I loved him as I love thee. Say that there is no blame on me, or I shall die—I shall die!'

'There is no blame,—before God, none. It was written, and how could we do aught to save? What has been, has been. Let it go, beloved.'

'He was all my heart to me. How can I let the thought go when my arm tells me every night that he is not here? *Ahi! Ahi!* Oh, Tota, come back to me—come back again, and let us be all together as it was before!'

'Peace, peace! For thine own sake, and for mine also, if thou lovest me—rest.'

'By this I know thou dost not care; and how shouldst thou? The white men have hearts of stone and souls of iron. Oh, that I had married a man of mine own people—though he beat me—and had never eaten the bread of an alien!'

'Am I an alien—mother of my son?'

'What else—*Sahib?* . . . Oh, forgive me—forgive! The

death has driven me mad. Thou art the life of my heart, and the light of my eyes, and the breath of my life, and—and I have put thee from me, though it was but for a moment. If thou goest away, to whom shall I look for help? Do not be angry. Indeed, it was the pain that spoke and not thy slave.'

'I know, I know. We be two who were three. The greater need therefore that we should be one.'

They were sitting on the roof as of custom. The night was a warm one in early spring, and sheet-lightning was dancing on the horizon to a broken tune played by far-off thunder. Ameera settled herself in Holden's arms.

'The dry earth is lowing like a cow for the rain, and I—I am afraid. It was not like this when we counted the stars. But thou lovest me as much as before, though a bond is taken away? Answer!'

'I love more because a new bond has come out of the sorrow that we have eaten together, and that thou knowest.'

'Yea, I knew,' said Ameera in a very small whisper. 'But it is good to hear thee say so, my life, who art so strong to help. I will be a child no more, but a woman and an aid to thee. Listen! Give me my *sitar* and I will sing bravely.'

She took the light silver-studded *sitar* and began a song of the great hero Rajah Rasalu. The hand failed on the strings, the tune halted, checked, and at a low note turned off to the poor little nursery-rhyme about the wicked crow—

'And the wild plums grow in the jungle, only a penny a pound.
Only a penny a pound, *baba*—only . . .'

Then came the tears, and the piteous rebellion against fate till she slept, moaning a little in her sleep, with the

right arm thrown clear of the body as though it protected
something that was not there. It was after this night that
life became a little easier for Holden. The ever-present
pain of loss drove him into his work, and the work repaid
him by filling up his mind for nine or ten hours a day.
Ameera sat alone in the house and brooded, but grew
happier when she understood that Holden was more at
ease, according to the custom of women. They touched
happiness again, but this time with caution.

'It was because we loved Tota that he died. The
jealousy of God was upon us,' said Ameera. 'I have
hung up a large black jar before our window to turn the
evil eye from us, and we must make no protestations of
delight, but go softly underneath the stars, lest God find
us out. Is that not good talk, worthless one?'

She had shifted the accent on the word that means
'beloved,' in proof of the sincerity of her purpose. But
the kiss that followed the new christening was a thing
that any deity might have envied. They went about
henceforward saying, 'It is naught, it is naught;' and
hoping that all the Powers heard.

The Powers were busy on other things. They had
allowed thirty million people four years of plenty, wherein
men fed well and the crops were certain, and the birth-
rate rose year by year; the districts reported a purely
agricultural population varying from nine hundred to
two thousand to the square mile of the overburdened
earth; and the Member for Lower Tooting, wandering
about India in top-hat and frock-coat, talked largely
of the benefits of British rule, and suggested as the
one thing needful the establishment of a duly qualified
electoral system and a general bestowal of the franchise.
His long-suffering hosts smiled and made him welcome,
and when he paused to admire, with pretty picked words,
the blossom of the blood-red *dhak*-tree that had flowered

untimely for a sign of what was coming, they smiled more than ever.

It was the Deputy Commissioner of Kot-Kumharsen, staying at the club for a day, who lightly told a tale that made Holden's blood run cold as he overheard the end.

'He won't bother any one any more. Never saw a man so astonished in my life. By Jove, I thought he meant to ask a question in the House about it. Fellow-passenger in his ship—dined next him—bowled over by cholera and died in eighteen hours. You needn't laugh, you fellows. The Member for Lower Tooting is awfully angry about it; but he's more scared. I think he's going to take his enlightened self out of India.'

'I'd give a good deal if he were knocked over. It might keep a few vestrymen of his kidney to their own parish. But what's this about cholera? It's full early for anything of that kind,' said the warden of an unprofitable salt-lick.

'Don't know,' said the Deputy Commissioner reflectively. 'We've got locusts with us. There's sporadic cholera all along the north—at least we're calling it sporadic for decency's sake. The spring crops are short in five districts, and nobody seems to know where the rains are. It's nearly March now. I don't want to scare anybody, but it seems to me that Nature's going to audit her accounts with a big red pencil this summer.'

'Just when I wanted to take leave, too!' said a voice across the room.

'There won't be much leave this year, but there ought to be a great deal of promotion. I've come in to persuade the Government to put my pet canal on the list of famine-relief works. It's an ill-wind that blows no good. I shall get that canal finished at last.'

'Is it the old programme then,' said Holden; 'famine, fever, and cholera?'

'Oh no. Only local scarcity and an unusual prevalence
of seasonal sickness. You'll find it all in the reports if you
live till next year. You're a lucky chap. *You* haven't got a
wife to send out of harm's way. The hill-stations ought to
be full of women this year.'

'I think you're inclined to exaggerate the talk in the
bazars,' said a young civilian in the Secretariat. 'Now I
have observed——'

'I daresay you have,' said the Deputy Commissioner,
'but you've a great deal more to observe, my son. In the
meantime, I wish to observe to you——' and he drew him
aside to discuss the construction of the canal that was so
dear to his heart. Holden went to his bungalow and began
to understand that he was not alone in the world, and also
that he was afraid for the sake of another,—which is the
most soul-satisfying fear known to man.

Two months later, as the Deputy had foretold, Nature
began to audit her accounts with a red pencil. On the
heels of the spring-reapings came a cry for bread, and the
Government, which had decreed that no man should die
of want, sent wheat. Then came the cholera from all four
quarters of the compass. It struck a pilgrim-gathering of
half a million at a sacred shrine. Many died at the feet
of their god; the others broke and ran over the face
of the land carrying the pestilence with them. It smote a
walled city and killed two hundred a day. The people
crowded the trains, hanging on to the footboards and
squatting on the roofs of the carriages, and the cholera followed them, for at each station they dragged out the dead
and the dying. They died by the roadside, and the horses
of the Englishmen shied at the corpses in the grass.
The rains did not come, and the earth turned to iron
lest man should escape death by hiding in her. The
English sent their wives away to the hills and went
about their work, coming forward as they were bidden to

fill the gaps in the fighting-line. Holden, sick with fear of losing his chiefest treasure on earth, had done his best to persuade Ameera to go away with her mother to the Himalayas.

'Why should I go?' said she, one evening on the roof.

'There is sickness, and people are dying, and all the white *mem-log* have gone.'

'All of them?'

'All—unless perhaps there remain some old scald-head who vexes her husband's heart by running risk of death.'

'Nay; who stays is my sister, and thou must not abuse her, for I will be a scald-head too. I am glad all the bold *mem-log* are gone.'

'Do I speak to a woman or a babe? Go to the hills, and I will see to it that thou goest like a queen's daughter. Think, child. In a red-lacquered bullock cart, veiled and curtained, with brass peacocks upon the pole and red cloth hangings. I will send two orderlies for guard and——'

'Peace! Thou art the babe in speaking thus. What use are those toys to me? *He* would have patted the bullocks and played with the housings. For his sake, perhaps,—thou hast made me very English—I might have gone. Now, I will not. Let the *mem-log* run.'

'Their husbands are sending them, beloved.'

'Very good talk. Since when hast thou been my husband to tell me what to do? I have but borne thee a son. Thou art only all the desire of my soul to me. How shall I depart when I know that if evil befall thee by the breadth of so much as my littlest finger-nail—is that not small?—I should be aware of it though I were in paradise. And here, this summer thou mayest die—*ai, janee,* die! and in dying they might call to tend thee a white woman, and she would rob me in the last of thy love!'

'But love is not born in a moment or on a death-bed!'

'What dost thou know of love, stoneheart? She would take thy thanks at least and, by God and the Prophet and Beebee Miriam the mother of thy Prophet, that I will never endure. My lord and my love, let there be no more foolish talk of going away. Where thou art, I am. It is enough.' She put an arm round his neck and a hand on his mouth.

There are not many happinesses so complete as those that are snatched under the shadow of the sword. They sat together and laughed, calling each other openly by every pet name that could move the wrath of the gods. The city below them was locked up in its own torments. Sulphur fires blazed in the streets; the conches in the Hindu temples screamed and bellowed, for the gods were inattentive in those days. There was a service in the great Mahomedan shrine, and the call to prayer from the minarets was almost unceasing. They heard the wailing in the houses of the dead, and once the shriek of a mother who had lost a child and was calling for its return. In the gray dawn they saw the dead borne out through the city gates, each litter with its own little knot of mourners. Wherefore they kissed each other and shivered.

It was a red and heavy audit, for the land was very sick and needed a little breathing-space ere the torrent of cheap life should flood it anew. The children of immature fathers and undeveloped mothers made no resistance. They were cowed and sat still, waiting till the sword should be sheathed in November if it were so willed. There were gaps among the English, but the gaps were filled. The work of superintending famine-relief, cholera-sheds, medicine-distribution, and what little sanitation was possible, went forward because it was so ordered.

Holden had been told to keep himself in readiness to move to replace the next man who should fall. There were twelve hours in each day when he could not see Ameera, and she might die in three. He was considering what his pain would be if he could not see her for three months, or if she died out of his sight. He was absolutely certain that her death would be demanded—so certain, that when he looked up from the telegram and saw Pir Khan breathless in the doorway, he laughed aloud. 'And?' said he,——

'When there is a cry in the night and the spirit flutters into the throat, who has a charm that will restore? Come swiftly, Heaven-born! It is the black cholera.'

Holden galloped to his home. The sky was heavy with clouds, for the long-deferred rains were near and the heat was stifling. Ameera's mother met him in the courtyard, whimpering, 'She is dying. She is nursing herself into death. She is all but dead. What shall I do, *sahib*?'

Ameera was lying in the room in which Tota had been born. She made no sign when Holden entered, because the human soul is a very lonely thing and, when it is getting ready to go away, hides itself in a misty borderland where the living may not follow. The black cholera does its work quietly and without explanation. Ameera was being thrust out of life as though the Angel of Death had himself put his hand upon her. The quick breathing seemed to show that she was either afraid or in pain, but neither eyes nor mouth gave any answer to Holden's kisses. There was nothing to be said or done. Holden could only wait and suffer. The first drops of the rain began to fall on the roof and he could hear shouts of joy in the parched city.

The soul came back a little and the lips moved. Holden bent down to listen. 'Keep nothing of mine,' said Ameera. 'Take no hair from my head. *She* would make thee burn it later on. That flame I should feel. Lower! Stoop lower! Remember only that I was thine and bore thee a son. Though thou wed a white woman to-morrow, the pleasure of receiving in thy arms thy first son is taken from thee for ever. Remember me when thy son is born—the one that shall carry thy name before all men. His misfortunes be on my head. I bear witness—I bear witness'—the lips were forming the words on his ear—'that there is no God but—thee, beloved!'

Then she died. Holden sat still, and all thought was taken from him,—till he heard Ameera's mother lift the curtain.

'Is she dead, *sahib*?'

'She is dead.'

'Then I will mourn, and afterwards take an inventory of the furniture in this house. For that will be mine. The *sahib* does not mean to resume it? It is so little, so very little, *sahib*, and I am an old woman. I would like to lie softly.'

'For the mercy of God be silent a while. Go out and mourn where I cannot hear.'

'*Sahib*, she will be buried in four hours.'

'I know the custom. I shall go ere she is taken away. That matter is in thy hands. Look to it that the bed on which—on which she lies——'

'Aha! That beautifule red-lacquered bed. I have long desired——'

'That the bed is left here untouched for my disposal. All else in the house is thine. Hire a cart, take everything, go hence, and before sunrise let there be nothing in this house but that which I have ordered thee to respect.'

'I am an old woman. I would stay at least for the days of mourning, and the rains have just broken. Whither shall I go?'

'What is that to me? My order is that there is a going. The house-gear is worth a thousand rupees and my orderly shall bring thee a hundred rupees to-night.'

'That is very little. Think of the cart-hire.'

'It shall be nothing unless thou goest, and with speed. O woman, get hence and leave me with my dead!'

The mother shuffled down the staircase, and in her anxiety to take stock of the house-fittings forgot to mourn. Holden stayed by Ameera's side and the rain roared on the roof. He could not think connectedly by reason of the noise, though he made many attempts to do so. Then four sheeted ghosts glided dripping into the room and stared at him through their veils. They were the washers of the dead. Holden left the room and went out to his horse. He had come in a dead, stifling calm through ankle-deep dust. He found the courtyard a rain-lashed pond alive with frogs; a torrent of yellow water ran under the gate, and a roaring wind drove the bolts of the rain like buckshot against the mud-walls. Pir Khan was shivering in his little hut by the gate, and the horse was stamping uneasily in the water.

'I have been told the *sahib's* order,' said Pir Khan. 'It is well. This house is now desolate. I go also, for my monkey-face would be a reminder of that which has been. Concerning the bed, I will bring that to thy house yonder in the morning; but remember, *sahib*, it will be to thee a knife turning in a green wound. I go upon a pilgrimage, and I will take no money. I have grown fat in the protection of the Presence whose sorrow is my sorrow. For the last time I hold his stirrup.'

He touched Holden's foot with both hands and the horse sprang out into the road, where the creaking bamboos were whipping the sky and all the frogs were chuckling. Holden could not see for the rain in his face. He put his hands before his eyes and muttered—

'Oh, you brute! You utter brute!'

The news of his trouble was already in his bungalow.

He read the knowledge in his butler's eyes when Ahmed Khan brought in food, and for the first and last time in his life laid a hand upon his master's shoulder, saying, 'Eat, *sahib*, eat. Meat is good against sorrow. I also have known. Moreover the shadows come and go, *sahib*; the shadows come and go. These be curried eggs.'

Holden could neither eat nor sleep. The heavens sent down eight inches of rain in that night and washed the earth clean. The waters tore down walls, broke roads, and scoured open the shallow graves on the Mahomedan burying-ground. All next day it rained, and Holden sat still in his house considering his sorrow. On the morning of the third day he received a telegram which said only, 'Ricketts, Myndonie. Dying. Holden relieve. Immediate.' Then he thought that before he departed he would look at the house wherein he had been master and lord. There was a break in the weather, and the rank earth steamed with vapour.

He found that the rains had torn down the mud pillars of the gateway, and the heavy wooden gate that had guarded his life hung lazily from one hinge. There was grass three inches high in the courtyard; Pir Khan's lodge was empty, and the sodden thatch sagged between the beams. A gray squirrel was in possession of the verandah, as if the house had been untenanted for thirty years instead of three days. Ameera's mother had removed everything except some mildewed matting. The *tick-tick* of the little scorpions as they hurried across the floor was the only sound in the house. Ameera's room and the other one where Tota had lived were heavy with mildew; and the narrow staircase leading to the roof was streaked and stained with rain-borne mud. Holden saw all these things, and came out again to meet in the road Durga Dass, his landlord,—portly, affable, clothed in white muslin, and driving a Cee-spring buggy. He was overlooking his property to see how the roofs stood the stress of the first rains.

'I have heard,' said he, 'you will not take this place any more, *sahib*?'

'What are you going to do with it?'

'Perhaps I shall let it again.'

'Then I will keep it on while I am away.'

Durga Dass was silent for some time. 'You shall not take it on, *sahib*,' he said. 'When I was a young man I also——, but to-day I am a member of the Municipality. Ho! Ho! No. When the birds have gone what need to keep the nest? I will have it pulled down—the timber will sell for something always. It shall be pulled down, and the Municipality shall make a road across, as they desire, from the burning-ghaut to the city wall, so that no man may say where this house stood.'

The Return of Imray

The doors were wide, the story saith,
Out of the night came the patient wraith,
He might not speak, and he could not stir
A hair of the Baron's minniver—
Speechless and strengthless, a shadow thin,
He roved the castle to seek his kin.
And oh, 'twas a piteous thing to see
The dumb ghost follow his enemy!
                    The Baron.

IMRAY achieved the impossible. Without warning, for no conceivable motive, in his youth, at the threshold of his career he chose to disappear from the world—which is to say, the little Indian station where he lived.

Upon a day he was alive, well, happy, and in great evidence among the billiard-tables at his Club. Upon a morning he was not, and no manner of search could make sure where he might be. He had stepped out of his place; he had not appeared at his office at the proper time, and his dogcart was not upon the public roads. For these reasons, and because he was hampering, in a microscopical degree, the administration of the Indian Empire, that Empire paused for one microscopical moment to make inquiry into the fate of Imray. Ponds were dragged, wells were plumbed, telegrams were despatched down the lines of railways and to the nearest seaport town—twelve hundred miles away; but Imray was not at the end of the drag-ropes nor the telegraph wires. He was gone, and his place knew him no more. Then the work of the great Indian Empire swept forward, because it could not be delayed, and Imray from being a man became a mystery—such a thing as men talk over at their tables in the Club for a month, and then forget utterly. His guns, horses, and carts were sold to the highest bidder. His superior officer wrote an altogether absurd letter to his mother, saying that Imray had unaccountably disappeared, and his bungalow stood empty.

After three or four months of the scorching hot weather had gone by, my friend Strickland, of the Police, saw fit to rent the bungalow from the native landlord. This was before he was engaged to Miss Youghal—an affair which has been described in another place—and while he was pursuing his investigations into native life. His own life was sufficiently peculiar, and men complained of his manners and customs. There was always food in his house, but there were no regular times for meals. He ate, standing up and walking about, whatever he might find at the sideboard, and this is not good for human beings. His domestic equipment was limited to six rifles, three shot-guns, five saddles, and a collection of stiff-jointed mahseer-rods, bigger and stronger than the largest salmon-rods. These occupied one-half of his bungalow, and the other half was given up to Strickland and his dog Tietjens—an enormous Rampur slut who devoured daily the rations of two men. She spoke to Strickland in a language of her own; and whenever, walking abroad, she saw things calculated to destroy the peace of Her Majesty the Queen-Empress, she returned to her master and laid information. Strickland would take steps at once, and the end of his labours was trouble and fine and imprisonment for other people. The natives believed that Tietjens was a familiar spirit, and treated her with the great reverence that is born of hate and fear. One room in the bungalow was set apart for her special use. She owned a bedstead, a blanket, and a drinking-trough, and if any one came into Strickland's room at night her custom was to knock down the invader and give tongue till some one came with a light. Strickland owed his life to her when he was on the Frontier, in search of a local murderer, who came in the gray dawn to send Strickland much farther than the Andaman Islands. Tietjens caught the man as he was crawling into Strickland's tent with a dagger between his teeth; and after his record of iniquity was established in the eyes of the law he was hanged. From that date Tietjens wore a collar of rough silver, and employed a monogram on her night-blanket; and the blanket was of double woven Kashmir cloth, for she was a delicate dog.

Under no circumstances would she be separated from Strickland; and once, when he was ill with fever, made great trouble for the doctors, because she did not know how to help her master and would not allow another creature to attempt aid. Macarnaght, of the Indian Medical Service, beat her over her head with a gun-butt before she could understand that she must give room for those who could give quinine.

A short time after Strickland had taken Imray's bungalow, my business took me through that Station, and naturally, the Club quarters being full, I quartered myself upon Strickland. It was a desirable bungalow, eight-roomed and heavily thatched against any chance of leakage from rain. Under the pitch of the roof ran a ceiling-cloth which looked just as neat as a white-washed ceiling. The landlord had repainted it when Strickland took the bungalow. Unless you knew how Indian bungalows were built you would never have suspected that above the cloth lay the dark three-cornered cavern of the roof, where the beams and the underside of the thatch harboured all manner of rats, bats, ants, and foul things.

Tietjens met me in the verandah with a bay like the boom of the bell of St. Paul's, putting her paws on my shoulder to show she was glad to see me. Strickland had contrived to claw together a sort of meal which he called lunch, and immediately after it was finished went out about his business. I was left alone with Tietjens and my own affairs. The heat of the summer had broken up and turned to the warm damp of the rains. There was no motion in the heated air, but the rain fell like ramrods on the earth, and flung up a blue mist when it splashed back. The bamboos, and the custard-apples, the poinsettias, and the mango-trees in the garden stood still while the warm water lashed through them, and the frogs began to sing among the aloe hedges. A little before the light failed, and when the rain was at its worst, I sat in the back verandah and heard the water roar from the eaves, and scratched myself because I was covered with the thing called prickly-heat. Tietjens came out with me and put her head in my lap and was very sorrowful; so I gave her biscuits when tea was ready, and I took tea in the back verandah on account of the little coolness found there. The rooms of the house were dark behind me. I could smell Strickland's saddlery and the oil on his guns, and I had no desire to sit among these things. My own servant came to me in the twilight, the muslin of his clothes clinging tightly to his drenched body, and told me that a gentleman had called and wished to see some one. Very much against my will, but only because of the darkness of the rooms, I went into the naked drawing-room, telling my man to bring the lights. There might or might not have been a caller waiting—it seemed to me that I saw a figure by one of the windows—but when the lights came there was nothing save the spikes of the

rain without, and the smell of the drinking earth in my
nostrils. I explained to my servant that he was no wiser
than he ought to be, and went back to the verandah to
talk to Tietjens. She had gone out into the wet, and I
could hardly coax her back to me, even with biscuits
with sugar tops. Strickland came home, dripping wet,
just before dinner, and the first thing he said was,

'Has any one called?'

I explained, with apologies, that my servant had
summoned me into the drawing-room on a false alarm;
or that some loafer had tried to call on Strickland, and
thinking better of it had fled after giving his name.
Strickland ordered dinner, without comment, and since
it was a real dinner with a white tablecloth attached, we
sat down.

At nine o'clock Strickland wanted to go to bed,
and I was tired too. Tietjens, who had been lying
underneath the table, rose up, and swung into the least
exposed verandah as soon as her master moved to his
own room, which was next to the stately chamber set
apart for Tietjens. If a mere wife had wished to sleep out
of doors in that pelting rain it would not have mattered;
but Tietjens was a dog, and therefore the better animal.
I looked at Strickland, expecting to see him flay her with
a whip. He smiled queerly, as a man would smile after
telling some unpleasant domestic tragedy. 'She has done
this ever since I moved in here,' said he. 'Let her go.'

The dog was Strickland's dog, so I said nothing, but
I felt all that Strickland felt in being thus made light
of. Tietjens encamped outside my bedroom window, and
storm after storm came up, thundered on the thatch,
and died away. The lightning spattered the sky as a
thrown egg spatters a barn-door, but the light was pale
blue, not yellow; and, looking through my split-bamboo
blinds, I could see the great dog standing, not sleeping,

in the verandah, the hackles alift on her back, and her feet anchored as tensely as the drawn wire-rope of a suspension bridge. In the very short pauses of the thunder I tried to sleep, but it seemed that some one wanted me very urgently. He, whoever he was, was trying to call me by name, but his voice was no more than a husky whisper. The thunder ceased, and Tietjens went into the garden and howled at the low moon. Somebody tried to open my door, walked about and about through the house, and stood breathing heavily in the verandahs, and just when I was falling asleep I fancied that I heard a wild hammering and clamouring above my head or on the door.

I ran into Strickland's room and asked him whether he was ill, and had been calling for me. He was lying on his bed half dressed, a pipe in his mouth. 'I thought you'd come,' he said. 'Have I been walking round the house recently?'

I explained that he had been tramping in the dining-room and the smoking-room and two or three other places; and he laughed and told me to go back to bed. I went back to bed and slept till the morning, but through all my mixed dreams I was sure I was doing some one an injustice in not attending to his wants. What those wants were I could not tell; but a fluttering, whispering, bolt-fumbling, lurking, loitering Someone was reproaching me for my slackness, and, half awake, I heard the howling of Tietjens in the garden and the threshing of the rain.

I lived in that house for two days. Strickland went to his office daily, leaving me alone for eight or ten hours with Tietjens for my only companion. As long as the full light lasted I was comfortable, and so was Tietjens; but in the twilight she and I moved into the back verandah and cuddled each other for company. We were alone in the house, but none the less it was much too fully occupied by a tenant with whom I did not wish to interfere. I never saw him, but I could see the curtains between the rooms quivering where he had just passed through; I could hear the chairs creaking as the bamboos sprung under a weight that had just quitted them; and I could feel when I went to get a book from the dining-room that somebody was waiting in the shadows of the front verandah till I should have gone away. Tietjens made the twilight more interesting by glaring into the darkened rooms with every hair erect, and following the motions of something that I could not see. She never entered the rooms, but her eyes moved interestedly: that was quite sufficient. Only when my servant came to trim the lamps and make all light and habitable she would come in with me and spend her time sitting on her haunches, watching an invisible extra man as he moved about behind my shoulder. Dogs are cheerful companions.

I explained to Strickland, gently as might be, that I would go over to the Club and find for myself quarters there. I admired his hospitality, was pleased with his guns and rods, but I did not much care for his house and its atmosphere. He heard me out to the end, and then smiled very wearily, but without contempt, for he is a man who understands things. 'Stay on,' he said, 'and see what this thing means. All you have talked about I have known since I took the bungalow. Stay on and wait. Tietjens has left me. Are you going too?'

I had seen him through one little affair, connected with a heathen idol, that had brought me to the doors of a lunatic asylum, and I had no desire to help him through further experiences. He was a man to whom unpleasantnesses arrived as do dinners to ordinary people.

Therefore I explained more clearly than ever that I

liked him immensely, and would be happy to see him in the daytime; but that I did not care to sleep under his roof. This was after dinner, when Tietjens had gone out to lie in the verandah.

''Pon my soul, I don't wonder,' said Strickland, with his eyes on the ceiling-cloth. 'Look at that!'

The tails of two brown snakes were hanging between the cloth and the cornice of the wall. They threw long shadows in the lamplight.

'If you are afraid of snakes of course——' said Strickland.

I hate and fear snakes, because if you look into the eyes of any snake you will see that it knows all and more of the mystery of man's fall, and that it feels all the contempt that the Devil felt when Adam was evicted from Eden. Besides which its bite is generally fatal, and it twists up trouser legs.

'You ought to get your thatch overhauled,' I said. 'Give me a mahseer-rod, and we'll poke 'em down.'

'They'll hide among the roof-beams,' said Strickland. 'I can't stand snakes overhead. I'm going up into the roof. If I shake 'em down, stand by with a cleaning-rod and break their backs.'

I was not anxious to assist Strickland in his work, but I took the cleaning-rod and waited in the dining-room, while Strickland brought a gardener's ladder from the verandah, and set it against the side of the room. The snake-tails drew themselves up and disappeared. We could hear the dry rushing scuttle of long bodies running over the baggy ceiling cloth. Strickland took a lamp with him, while I tried to make clear to him the danger of hunting roof-snakes between a ceiling-cloth and a thatch, apart from the deterioration of property caused by ripping out ceiling-cloths.

'Nonsense!' said Strickland. 'They're sure to hide near

the walls by the cloth. The bricks are too cold for 'em, and the heat of the room is just what they like.' He put his hand to the corner of the stuff and ripped it from the cornice. It gave with a great sound of tearing, and Strickland put his head through the opening into the dark of the angle of the roof-beams. I set my teeth and lifted the rod, for I had not the least knowledge of what might descend.

'H'm!' said Strickland, and his voice rolled and rumbled in the roof. 'There's room for another set of rooms up here, and, by Jove, some one is occupying 'em!'

'Snakes?' I said from below.

'No. It's a buffalo. Hand me up the two last joints of a mahseer-rod, and I'll prod it. It's lying on the main roof-beam.'

I handed up the rod.

'What a nest for owls and serpents! No wonder the snakes live here,' said Strickland, climbing farther into the roof. I could see his elbow thrusting with the rod. 'Come out of that, whoever you are! Heads below there! It's falling.'

I saw the ceiling cloth nearly in the centre of the room bag with a shape that was pressing it downwards and downwards towards the lighted lamp on the table. I snatched the lamp out of danger and stood back. Then the cloth ripped out from the walls, tore, split, swayed, and shot down upon the table something that I dared not look at, till Strickland had slid down the ladder and was standing by my side.

He did not say much, being a man of few words; but he picked up the loose end of the tablecloth and threw it over the remnants on the table.

'It strikes me,' said he, putting down the lamp, 'our friend Imray has come back. Oh! you would, would you?'

There was a movement under the cloth, and a little snake wriggled out, to be back-broken by the butt of the mahseer-rod. I was sufficiently sick to make no remarks worth recording.

Strickland meditated, and helped himself to drinks. The arrangement under the cloth made no more signs of life.

'Is it Imray?' I said.

Strickland turned back the cloth for a moment, and looked.

'It is Imray,' he said; 'and his throat is cut from ear to ear.'

Then we spoke, both together and to ourselves: 'That's why he whispered about the house.'

Tietjens, in the garden, began to bay furiously. A little later her great nose heaved open the dining-room door.

She snuffed and was still. The tattered ceiling-cloth hung down almost to the level of the table, and there was hardly room to move away from the discovery.

Tietjens came in and sat down; her teeth bared under her lip and her forepaws planted. She looked at Strickland.

'It's a bad business, old lady,' said he. 'Men don't climb up into the roofs of their bungalows to die, and they don't fasten up the ceiling cloth behind 'em. Let's think it out.'

'Let's think it out somewhere else,' I said.

'Excellent idea! Turn the lamps out. We'll get into my room.'

I did not turn the lamps out. I went into Strickland's room first, and allowed him to make the darkness. Then he followed me, and we lit tobacco and thought. Strickland thought. I smoked furiously, because I was afraid.

'Imray is back,' said Strickland. 'The question is—who killed Imray? Don't talk, I've a notion of my own. When I took this bungalow I took over most of Imray's servants. Imray was guileless and inoffensive, wasn't he?'

I agreed; though the heap under the cloth had looked neither one thing nor the other.

'If I call in all the servants they will stand fast in a crowd and lie like Aryans. What do you suggest?'

'Call 'em in one by one,' I said.

'They'll run away and give the news to all their fellows,' said Strickland. 'We must segregate 'em. Do you suppose your servant knows anything about it?'

'He may, for aught I know; but I don't think it's likely. He has only been here two or three days,' I answered. 'What's your notion?'

'I can't quite tell. How the dickens did the man get the wrong side of the ceiling-cloth?'

There was a heavy coughing outside Strickland's bedroom door. This showed that Bahadur Khan, his body-servant, had waked from sleep and wished to put Strickland to bed.

'Come in,' said Strickland. 'It's a very warm night, isn't it?'

Bahadur Khan, a great, green-turbaned, six-foot Mahomedan, said that it was a very warm night; but that there was more rain pending, which, by his Honour's favour, would bring relief to the country.

'It will be so, if God pleases,' said Strickland, tugging off his boots. 'It is in my mind, Bahadur Khan, that I have worked thee remorselessly for many days—ever since that time when thou first camest into my service. What time was that?'

'Has the Heaven-born forgotten? It was when Imray Sahib went secretly to Europe without warning given;

and I—even I—came into the honoured service of the
protector of the poor.'

'And Imray Sahib went to Europe?'

'It is so said among those who were his servants.'

'And thou wilt take service with him when he returns?'

'Assuredly, Sahib. He was a good master, and cherished
his dependants.'

'That is true. I am very tired, but I go buck-shooting
to-morrow. Give me the little sharp rifle that I use for
black-buck; it is in the case yonder.'

The man stooped over the case; handed barrels,
stock, and fore-end to Strickland, who fitted all together,
yawning dolefully. Then he reached down to the gun-case,
took a solid-drawn cartridge, and slipped it into the breech
of the .360 Express.

'And Imray Sahib has gone to Europe secretly! That
is very strange, Bahadur Khan, is it not?'

'What do I know of the ways of the white man,
Heaven-born?'

'Very little, truly. But thou shalt know more anon.
It has reached me that Imray Sahib has returned from
his so long journeyings, and that even now he lies in the
next room, waiting his servant.'

'Sahib!'

The lamplight slid along the barrels of the rifle
as they levelled themselves at Bahadur Khan's broad
breast.

'Go and look!' said Strickland. 'Take a lamp. Thy
master is tired, and he waits thee. Go!'

The man picked up a lamp, and went into the
dining-room, Strickland following, and almost pushing
him with the muzzle of the rifle. He looked for a
moment at the black depths behind the ceiling-cloth;
at the writhing snake under foot; and last, a gray glaze
settling on his face, at the thing under the tablecloth.

'Hast thou seen?' said Strickland after a pause.

'I have seen. I am clay in the white man's hands. What does the Presence do?'

'Hang thee within the month. What else?'

'For killing him? Nay, Sahib, consider. Walking among us, his servants, he cast his eyes upon my child, who was four years old. Him he bewitched, and in ten days he died of the fever—my child!'

'What said Imray Sahib?'

'He said he was a handsome child, and patted him on the head; wherefore my child died. Wherefore I killed Imray Sahib in the twilight, when he had come back from office, and was sleeping. Wherefore I dragged him up into the roof-beams and made all fast behind him. The Heaven-born knows all things. I am the servant of the Heaven-born.'

Strickland looked at me above the rifle, and said, in the vernacular, 'Thou art witness to this saying? He has killed.'

Bahadur Khan stood ashen gray in the light of the one lamp. The need for justification came upon him very swiftly. 'I am trapped,' he said, 'but the offence was that man's. He cast an evil eye upon my child, and I killed and hid him. Only such as are served by devils,' he glared at Tietjens, couched stolidly before him, 'only such could know what I did.'

'It was clever. But thou shouldst have lashed him to the beam with a rope. Now, thou thyself wilt hang by a rope. Orderly!'

A drowsy policeman answered Strickland's call. He was followed by another, and Tietjens sat wondrous still.

'Take him to the police-station,' said Strickland. 'There is a case toward.'

'Do I hang, then?' said Bahadur Khan, making no attempt to escape, and keeping his eyes on the ground.

'If the sun shines or the water runs—yes!' said Strickland.

Bahadur Khan stepped back one long pace, quivered, and stood still. The two policemen waited further orders.

'Go!' said Strickland.

'Nay; but I go very swiftly,' said Bahadur Khan. 'Look! I am even now a dead man.'

He lifted his foot, and to the little toe there clung the head of the half-killed snake, firm fixed in the agony of death.

'I come of land-holding stock,' said Bahadur Khan, rocking where he stood. 'It were a disgrace to me to go to the public scaffold: therefore I take this way. Be it remembered that the Sahib's shirts are correctly enumerated, and that there is an extra piece of soap in his washbasin. My child was bewitched, and I slew the wizard. Why should you seek to slay me with the rope? My honour is saved, and—and—I die.'

At the end of an hour he died, as they die who are bitten by the little brown *karait*, and the policemen bore him and the thing under the tablecloth to their appointed places. All were needed to make clear the disappearance of Imray.

'This,' said Strickland, very calmly, as he climbed into bed, 'is called the nineteenth century. Did you hear what that man said?'

'I heard,' I answered. 'Imray made a mistake.'

'Simply and solely through not knowing the nature of the Oriental, and the coincidence of a little seasonal fever. Bahadur Khan had been with him for four years.'

I shuddered. My own servant had been with me for exactly that length of time. When I went over to my own room I found my man waiting, impassive as the copper head on a penny, to pull off my boots.

'What has befallen Bahadur Khan?' said I.

'He was bitten by a snake and died. The rest the Sahib knows,' was the answer.

'And how much of this matter hast thou known?'

'As much as might be gathered from One coming in in the twilight to seek satisfaction. Gently, Sahib. Let me pull off those boots.'

I had just settled to the sleep of exhaustion when I heard Strickland shouting from his side of the house—

'Tietjens has come back to her place!'

And so she had. The great deerhound was couched statelily on her own bedstead on her own blanket, while, in the next room, the idle, empty, ceiling-cloth waggled as it trailed on the table.

Moti Guj—Mutineer

ONCE upon a time there was a coffee-planter in India who wished to clear some forest land for coffee-planting. When he had cut down all the trees and burned the under-wood the stumps still remained. Dynamite is expensive and slow-fire slow. The happy medium for stump-clearing is the lord of all beasts, who is the elephant. He will either push the stump out of the ground with his tusks, if he has any, or drag it out with ropes. The planter, therefore, hired elephants by ones and twos and threes, and fell to work. The very best of all the elephants belonged to the very worst of all the drivers or mahouts; and the superior beast's name was Moti Guj. He was the absolute property of his mahout, which would never have been the case under native rule, for Moti Guj was a creature to be desired by kings; and his name, being translated, meant the Pearl Elephant. Because the British Government was in the land, Deesa, the mahout, enjoyed his property undisturbed. He was dissipated. When he had made much money through the strength of his elephant, he would get extremely drunk and give Moti Guj a beating with a tent-peg over the tender nails of the forefeet. Moti Guj never trampled the life out of Deesa on these occasions, for he knew that after the beating was over Deesa would embrace his trunk, and weep and call him his love and his life and the liver of his soul, and give him some liquor. Moti

Guj was very fond of liquor—arrack for choice, though he would drink palm-tree toddy if nothing better offered. Then Deesa would go to sleep between Moti Guj's forefeet, and as Deesa generally chose the middle of the public road, and as Moti Guj mounted guard over him and would not permit horse, foot, or cart to pass by, traffic was congested till Deesa saw fit to wake up.

There was no sleeping in the daytime on the planter's clearing: the wages were too high to risk. Deesa sat on Moti Guj's neck and gave him orders, while Moti Guj rooted up the stumps—for he owned a magnificent pair of tusks; or pulled at the end of a rope—for he had a magnificent pair of shoulders, while Deesa kicked him behind the ears and said he was the king of elephants. At evening time Moti Guj would wash down his three hundred pounds' weight of green food with a quart of arrack, and Deesa would take a share and sing songs between Moti Guj's legs till it was time to go to bed. Once a week Deesa led Moti Guj down to the river, and Moti Guj lay on his side luxuriously in the shallows, while Deesa went over him with a coir-swab and a brick. Moti Guj never mistook the pounding blow of the latter for the smack of the former that warned him to get up and turn over on the other side. Then Deesa would look at his feet, and examine his eyes, and turn up the fringes of his mighty ears in case of sores or budding ophthalmia. After inspection, the two would 'come up with a song from the sea,' Moti Guj all black and shining, waving a torn tree branch twelve feet long in his trunk, and Deesa knotting up his own long wet hair.

It was a peaceful, well-paid life till Deesa felt the return of the desire to drink deep. He wished for an orgy. The little draughts that led nowhere were taking the manhood out of him.

He went to the planter, and 'My mother's dead,' said he, weeping.

'She died on the last plantation two months ago; and she died once before that when you were working for me last year,' said the planter, who knew something of the ways of nativedom.

'Then it's my aunt, and she was just the same as a mother to me,' said Deesa, weeping more than ever. 'She has left eighteen small children entirely without bread, and it is I who must fill their little stomachs,' said Deesa, beating his head on the floor.

'Who brought you the news?' said the planter.

'The post,' said Deesa.

'There hasn't been a post here for the past week. Get back to your lines!'

'A devastating sickness has fallen on my village, and all my wives are dying,' yelled Deesa, really in tears this time.

'Call Chihun, who comes from Deesa's village,' said the planter. 'Chihun, has this man a wife?'

'He!' said Chihun. 'No. Not a woman of our village would look at him. They'd sooner marry the elephant.' Chihun snorted. Deesa wept and bellowed.

'You will get into a difficulty in a minute,' said the planter. 'Go back to your work!'

'Now I will speak Heaven's truth,' gulped Deesa, with an inspiration. 'I haven't been drunk for two months. I desire to depart in order to get properly drunk afar off and distant from this heavenly plantation. Thus I shall cause no trouble.'

A flickering smile crossed the planter's face. 'Deesa,' said he, 'you've spoken the truth, and I'd give you leave on the spot if anything could be done with Moti Guj while you're away. You know that he will only obey your orders.'

'May the Light of the Heavens live forty thousand years. I shall be absent but ten little days. After that, upon my faith and honour and soul, I return. As to the inconsiderable interval, have I the gracious permission of the Heaven-born to call up Moti Guj?'

Permission was granted, and, in answer to Deesa's shrill yell, the lordly tusker swung out of the shade of a clump of trees where he had been squirting dust over himself till his master should return.

'Light of my heart, Protector of the Drunken, Mountain of Might, give ear,' said Deesa, standing in front of him.

Moti Guj gave ear, and saluted with his trunk. 'I am going away,' said Deesa.

Moti Guj's eyes twinkled. He liked jaunts as well as his master. One could snatch all manner of nice things from the roadside then.

'But you, you fubsy old pig, must stay behind and work.' The twinkle died out as Moti Guj tried to look delighted. He hated stump-hauling on the plantation. It hurt his teeth.

'I shall be gone for ten days, oh Delectable One. Hold up your near forefoot and I'll impress the fact upon it, warty toad of a dried mud-puddle.' Deesa took a tent-peg and banged Moti Guj ten times on the nails. Moti Guj grunted and shuffled from foot to foot.

'Ten days,' said Deesa, 'you must work and haul and root trees as Chihun here shall order you. Take up Chihun and set him on your neck!' Moti Guj curled the tip of his trunk, Chihun put his foot there and was swung on to the neck. Deesa handed Chihun the heavy *ankus*, the iron elephant-goad.

Chihun thumped Moti Guj's bald head as a paviour thumps a kerbstone.

Moti Guj trumpeted.

'Be still, hog of the backwoods. Chihun's your mahout for ten days. And now bid me good-bye, beast after mine own heart. Oh, my lord, my king! Jewel of all created elephants, lily of the herd, preserve your honoured health; be virtuous. Adieu!'

Moti Guj lapped his trunk round Deesa and swung him into the air twice. That was his way of bidding the man good-bye.

'He'll work now,' said Deesa to the planter. 'Have I leave to go?'

The planter nodded, and Deesa dived into the woods. Moti Guj went back to haul stumps.

Chihun was very kind to him, but he felt unhappy and forlorn notwithstanding. Chihun gave him balls of spices, and tickled him under the chin, and Chihun's little baby cooed to him after work was over, and Chihun's wife called him a darling; but Moti Guj was a bachelor by instinct, as Deesa was. He did not understand the domestic emotions. He wanted the light of his universe back again—the drink and the drunken slumber, the savage beatings and the savage caresses.

None the less he worked well, and the planter wondered. Deesa had vagabonded along the roads till he met a marriage procession of his own caste and, drinking, dancing, and tippling, had drifted past all knowledge of the lapse of time.

The morning of the eleventh day dawned, and there returned no Deesa. Moti Guj was loosed from his ropes for the daily stint. He swung clear, looked round, shrugged his shoulders, and began to walk away, as one having business elsewhere.

'Hi! ho! Come back you,' shouted Chihun. 'Come back, and put me on your neck, Misborn Mountain. Return, Splendour of the Hillsides. Adornment of all India, heave to, or I'll bang every toe off your fat forefoot!'

Moti Guj gurgled gently, but did not obey. Chihun ran after him with a rope and caught him up. Moti Guj put his ears forward, and Chihun knew what that meant, though he tried to carry it off with high words.

'None of your nonsense with me,' said he. 'To your pickets, Devil-son.'

'Hrrump!' said Moti Guj, and that was all—that and the forebent ears.

Moti Guj put his hands in his pockets, chewed a branch for a toothpick, and strolled about the clearing, making jest of the other elephants, who had just set to work.

Chihun reported the state of affairs to the planter, who came out with a dog-whip and cracked it furiously. Moti Guj paid the white man the compliment of charging him nearly a quarter of a mile across the clearing and 'Hrrumphing' him into the verandah. Then he stood outside the house chuckling to himself, and shaking all over with the fun of it, as an elephant will.

'We'll thrash him,' said the planter. 'He shall have the finest thrashing that ever elephant received. Give Kala Nag and Nazim twelve foot of chain apiece, and tell them to lay on twenty blows.'

Kala Nag—which means Black Snake—and Nazim were two of the biggest elephants in the lines, and one of their duties was to administer the graver punishments, since no man can beat an elephant properly.

They took the whipping-chains and rattled them in their trunks as they sidled up to Moti Guj, meaning to hustle him between them. Moti Guj had never, in all his life of thirty-nine years, been whipped, and he did not intend to open new experiences. So he waited, weaving his head from right to left, and measuring the precise spot in Kala Nag's fat side where a blunt tusk would sink deepest. Kala Nag had no tusks; the chain was his

badge of authority; but he judged it good to swing wide of
Moti Guj at the last minute, and seem to appear as if he
had brought out the chain for amusement. Nazim turned
round and went home early. He did not feel fighting-fit
that morning, and so Moti Guj was left standing alone
with his ears cocked.

That decided the planter to argue no more, and
Moti Guj rolled back to his inspection of the clearing.
An elephant who will not work, and is not tied up, is
not quite so manageable as an eighty-one ton gun loose
in a heavy sea-way. He slapped old friends on the back
and asked them if the stumps were coming away easily;
he talked nonsense concerning labour and the inalienable
rights of elephants to a long 'nooning'; and, wandering to
and fro, thoroughly demoralised the garden till sundown,
when he returned to his pickets for food.

'If you won't work you shan't eat,' said Chihun angrily.
'You're a wild elephant, and no educated animal at all.
Go back to your jungle.'

Chihun's little brown baby, rolling on the floor of
the hut, stretched its fat arms to the huge shadow in
the doorway. Moti Guj knew well that it was the dearest
thing on earth to Chihun. He swung out his trunk with a
fascinating crook at the end, and the brown baby threw
itself shouting upon it. Moti Guj made fast and pulled up
till the brown baby was crowing in the air twelve feet
above his father's head.

'Great Chief!' said Chihun. 'Flour cakes of the best,
twelve in number, two feet across, and soaked in rum
shall be yours on the instant, and two hundred pounds'
weight of fresh-cut young sugar-cane therewith. Deign
only to put down safely that insignificant brat who is
my heart and my life to me.'

Moti Guj tucked the brown baby comfortably between
his forefeet, that could have knocked into toothpicks all

Chihun's hut, and waited for his food. He ate it, and the brown baby crawled away. Moti Guj dozed, and thought of Deesa. One of many mysteries connected with the elephant is that his huge body needs less sleep than anything else that lives. Four or five hours in the night suffice—two just before midnight, lying down on one side; two just after one o'clock, lying down on the other. The rest of the silent hours are filled with eating and fidgeting and long grumbling soliloquies.

At midnight, therefore, Moti Guj strode out of his pickets, for a thought had come to him that Deesa might be lying drunk somewhere in the dark forest with none to look after him. So all that night he chased through the undergrowth, blowing and trumpeting and shaking his ears. He went down to the river and blared across the shallows where Deesa used to wash him, but there was no answer. He could not find Deesa, but he disturbed all the elephants in the lines, and nearly frightened to death some gipsies in the woods.

At dawn Deesa returned to the plantation. He had been very drunk indeed, and he expected to fall into trouble for outstaying his leave. He drew a long breath when he saw that the bungalow and the plantation were still uninjured; for he knew something of Moti Guj's temper; and reported himself with many lies and salaams. Moti Guj had gone to his pickets for breakfast. His night exercise had made him hungry.

'Call up your beast,' said the planter, and Deesa shouted in the mysterious elephant-language, that some mahouts believe came from China at the birth of the world, when elephants and not men were masters. Moti Guj heard and came. Elephants do not gallop. They move from spots at varying rates of speed. If an elephant wished to catch an express train he could not gallop, but he could catch the train. Thus Moti Guj was at the planter's door almost before Chihun noticed that he had left his pickets. He fell into Deesa's arms trumpeting with joy, and the man and beast wept and slobbered over each other, and handled each other from head to heel to see that no harm had befallen.

'Now we will get to work,' said Deesa. 'Lift me up, my son and my joy.'

Moti Guj swung him up and the two went to the coffee-clearing to look for irksome stumps.

The planter was too astonished to be very angry.

By Word of Mouth

Not though you die to-night, O Sweet, and wail,
*   A spectre at my door,*
Shall mortal Fear make Love immortal fail—
*   I shall but love you more,*
Who, from Death's house returning, give me still
One moment's comfort in my matchless ill.
                                        Shadow Houses.

THIS tale may be explained by those who know how souls are made, and where the bounds of the Possible are put down. I have lived long enough in this India to know that it is best to know nothing, and can only write the story as it happened.

Dumoise was our Civil Surgeon at Meridki, and we called him 'Dormouse,' because he was a round little, sleepy little man. He was a good Doctor and never quarrelled with any one, not even with our Deputy Commissioner who had the manners of a bargee and the tact of a horse. He married a girl as round and as sleepy-looking as himself. She was a Miss Hillardyce, daughter of 'Squash' Hillardyce of the Berars, who married his Chief's daughter by mistake. But that is another story.

A honeymoon in India is seldom more than a week long; but there is nothing to hinder a couple from extending it over two or three years. India is a delightful country for married folk who are wrapped up in one another. They can live absolutely alone and without interruption—just

as the Dormice did. Those two little people retired from
the world after their marriage, and were very happy.
They were forced, of course, to give occasional dinners,
but they made no friends thereby, and the Station went
its own way and forgot them; only saying, occasionally,
that Dormouse was the best of good fellows though dull. A
Civil Surgeon who never quarrels is a rarity, appreciated
as such.

Few people can afford to play Robinson Crusoe anywhere—least of all in India, where we are few in the
land and very much dependent on each other's kind
offices. Dumoise was wrong in shutting himself from the
world for a year, and he discovered his mistake when an
epidemic of typhoid broke out in the Station in the heart
of the cold weather, and his wife went down. He was a shy
little man, and five days were wasted before he realised
that Mrs. Dumoise was burning with something worse
than simple fever, and three days more passed before he
ventured to call on Mrs. Shute, the Engineer's wife, and
timidly speak about his trouble. Nearly every household
in India knows that Doctors are very helpless in typhoid.
The battle must be fought out between Death and the
Nurses minute by minute and degree by degree. Mrs.
Shute almost boxed Dumoise's ears for what she called
his 'criminal delay,' and went off at once to look after the
poor girl. We had seven cases of typhoid in the Station
that winter and, as the average of death is about one in
every five cases, we felt certain that we should have to
lose somebody. But all did their best. The women sat up
nursing the women, and the men turned to and tended
the bachelors who were down, and we wrestled with
those typhoid cases for fifty-six days, and brought them
through the Valley of the Shadow in triumph. But, just
when we thought all was over, and were going to give a
dance to celebrate the victory, little Mrs. Dumoise got a

relapse and died in a week, and the Station went to the funeral. Dumoise broke down utterly at the brink of the grave, and had to be taken away.

After the death Dumoise crept into his own house and refused to be comforted. He did his duties perfectly, but we all felt that he should go on leave, and the other men of his own Service told him so. Dumoise was very thankful for the suggestion—he was thankful for anything in those days—and went to Chini on a walking-tour. Chini is some twenty marches from Simla, in the heart of the Hills, and the scenery is good if you are in trouble. You pass through big, still deodar forests, and under big, still cliffs, and over big, still grass-downs swelling like a woman's breasts; and the wind across the grass, and the rain among the deodars say—'Hush—hush—hush.' So little Dumoise was packed off to Chini, to wear down his grief with a full-plate camera and a rifle. He took also a useless bearer, because the man had been his wife's favourite servant. He was idle and a thief, but Dumoise trusted everything to him.

On his way back from Chini, Dumoise turned aside to Bagi, through the Forest Reserve which is on the spur of Mount Huttoo. Some men who have travelled more than a little say that the march from Kotegarh to Bagi is one of the finest in creation. It runs through dark wet forest, and ends suddenly in bleak, nipped hillside and black rocks. Bagi dâk-bungalow is open to all the winds and is bitterly cold. Few people go to Bagi. Perhaps that was the reason why Dumoise went there. He halted at seven in the evening, and his bearer went down the hillside to the village to engage coolies for the next day's march. The sun had set, and the night-winds were beginning to croon among the rocks. Dumoise leaned on the railing of the verandah, waiting for his bearer to return. The man came back almost immediately after he had disappeared, and at such a rate that Dumoise fancied he must have crossed a bear. He was running as hard as he could up the face of the hill.

But there was no bear to account for his terror. He raced to the verandah and fell down, the blood spurting from his nose and his face iron-gray. Then he gurgled— 'I have seen the *Memsahib*! I have seen the *Memsahib*!'

'Where?' said Dumoise.

'Down there, walking on the road to the village. She was in a blue dress, and she lifted the veil of her bonnet and said— "Ram Dass, give my *salaams* to the *Sahib*, and tell him that I shall meet him next month at Nuddea." Then I ran away, because I was afraid.'

What Dumoise said or did I do not know. Ram Dass declares that he said nothing, but walked up and down the verandah all the cold night, waiting for the *Memsahib* to come up the hill, and stretching out his arms into the dark like a madman. But no *Memsahib* came, and, next day, he went on to Simla cross-questioning the bearer every hour.

Ram Dass could only say that he had met Mrs. Dumoise, and that she had lifted up her veil and given him the message which he had faithfully repeated to Dumoise. To this statement Ram Dass adhered. He did not know where Nuddea was, had no friends at Nuddea, and would most certainly never go to Nuddea, even though his pay were doubled.

Nuddea is in Bengal, and has nothing whatever to do with a Doctor serving in the Punjab. It must be more than twelve hundred miles south of Meridki.

Dumoise went through Simla without halting, and returned to Meridki, there to take over charge from the man who had been officiating for him during his tour. There were some Dispensary accounts to be explained, and some recent orders of the Surgeon-General to be noted, and, altogether, the taking-over was a full day's work. In the evening Dumoise told his *locum tenens*, who was an old friend of his bachelor days, what had happened at Bagi; and the man said that Ram Dass might as well have chosen Tuticorin while he was about it.

At that moment a telegraph-peon came in with a telegram from Simla, ordering Dumoise not to take over charge at Meridki, but to go at once to Nuddea on special duty. There was a nasty outbreak of cholera at Nuddea, and the Bengal Government being short-handed, as usual, had borrowed a Surgeon from the Punjab.

Dumoise threw the telegram across the table and said—'Well?'

The other Doctor said nothing. It was all that he could say.

Then he remembered that Dumoise had passed through Simla on his way from Bagi; and thus might, possibly, have heard first news of the impending transfer.

He tried to put the question and the implied suspicion into words, but Dumoise stopped him with—'If I had desired *that*, I should never have come back from Chini. I was shooting there. I wish to live, for I have things to do . . . but I shall not be sorry.'

The other man bowed his head, and helped, in the twilight, to pack up Dumoise's just opened trunks. Ram Dass entered with the lamps.

'Where is the *Sahib* going?' he asked.

'To Nuddea,' said Dumoise softly.

Ram Dass clawed Dumoise's knees and boots and begged him not to go. Ram Dass wept and howled till he was turned out of the room. Then he wrapped up all his belongings and came back to ask for a character. He was not going to Nuddea to see his *Sahib* die and, perhaps, to die himself.

So Dumoise gave the man his wages and went down

to Nuddea alone, the other Doctor bidding him good-bye as one under sentence of death.

Eleven days later he had joined his *Memsahib*; and the Bengal Government had to borrow a fresh Doctor to cope with that epidemic at Nuddea. The first importation lay dead in Chooadanga Dâk-Bungalow.

Toomai of the Elephants

I will remember what I was. I am sick of rope and chain.
  I will remember my old strength and all my forest affairs.
I will not sell my back to man for a bundle of sugar-cane,
  I will go out to my own kind, and the wood-folk in their lairs.

I will go out until the day, until the morning break,
  Out to the winds' untainted kiss, the waters' clean caress:
I will forget my ankle-ring and snap my picket-stake.
  I will revisit my lost loves, and playmates masterless!

KALA NAG, which means Black Snake, had served the Indian Government in every way that an elephant could serve it for forty-seven years, and as he was fully twenty years old when he was caught, that makes him nearly seventy—a ripe age for an elephant. He remembered pushing, with a big leather pad on his forehead, at a gun stuck in deep mud, and that was before the Afghan War of 1842, and he had not then come to his full strength. His mother, Radha Pyari,—Radha the darling,—who had been caught in the same drive with Kala Nag, told him, before his little milk-tusks had dropped out, that elephants who were afraid always got hurt; and Kala Nag knew that that advice was good, for the first time that he saw a shell burst he backed, screaming, into a stand of piled rifles, and the bayonets pricked him in all his softest places. So before he was twenty-five he gave up being afraid, and so he was the best-loved and the best-looked-after elephant in the service of the Government of India. He had carried tents, twelve hundred pounds' weight of tents, on the march in Upper India; he had been hoisted into a ship at the end of a steam-crane and taken for days across the water, and made to carry a mortar on his back in a strange and rocky country very far from India, and had seen the Emperor Theodore lying dead in Magdala, and had come back again in the steamer, entitled, so the soldiers said, to the Abyssinian War medal. He had seen his fellow-elephants die of cold and epilepsy and starvation and sunstroke up at a place called Ali Musjid, ten years later; and afterwards he had been sent down thousands of miles south to haul and pile big baulks of teak in the timber-yards at Moulmein. There he had half killed an insubordinate young elephant who was shirking his fair share of the work.

After that he was taken off timber-hauling, and employed, with a few score other elephants who were trained to the business, in helping to catch wild elephants among the Garo hills. Elephants are very strictly pre-served by the Indian Government. There is one whole department which does nothing else but hunt them, and catch them, and break them in, and send them up and down the country as they are needed for work.

Kala Nag stood ten fair feet at the shoulders, and his tusks had been cut off short at five feet, and bound round the ends, to prevent them splitting, with bands of copper; but he could do more with those stumps than any untrained elephant could do with the real sharpened ones.

When, after weeks and weeks of cautious driving of scattered elephants across the hills, the forty or fifty wild monsters were driven into the last stockade, and the big drop-gate, made of tree-trunks lashed together, jarred down behind them, Kala Nag, at the word of command, would go into that flaring, trumpeting pandemonium (generally at night, when the flicker of the torches made it difficult to judge distances), and, picking out the biggest and wildest tusker of the mob, would hammer him and hustle him into quiet while the men on the backs of the other elephants roped and tied the smaller ones.

There was nothing in the way of fighting that Kala Nag, the old wise Black Snake, did not know, for he had stood up more than once in his time to the charge of the wounded tiger, and, curling up his soft trunk to be out of harm's way, had knocked the springing brute sideways in mid-air with a quick sickle-cut of his head, that he had invented all by himself; had knocked him over, and kneeled upon him with his huge knees till the life went out with a gasp and a howl, and there was only a fluffy striped thing on the ground for Kala Nag to pull by the tail.

'Yes,' said Big Toomai, his driver, the son of Black Toomai who had taken him to Abyssinia, and grandson of Toomai of the Elephants who had seen him caught, 'there is nothing that the Black Snake fears except me. He has seen three generations of us feed him and groom him, and he will live to see four.'

'He is afraid of *me* also,' said Little Toomai, standing up to his full height of four feet, with only one rag upon him. He was ten years old, the eldest son of Big Toomai, and, according to custom, he would take his father's place on Kala Nag's neck when he grew up, and would handle the heavy iron ankus, the elephant-goad that had been worn smooth by his father, and his grandfather, and his great-grandfather. He knew what he was talking of; for he had been born under Kala Nag's shadow, had played with the end of his trunk before he could walk, had taken him down to water as soon as he could walk, and Kala Nag would no more have dreamed of disobeying his shrill little orders than he would have dreamed of killing him on that day when Big Toomai carried the little brown baby under Kala Nag's tusks, and told him to salute his master that was to be.

'Yes,' said Little Toomai, 'he is afraid of *me*,' and he took long strides up to Kala Nag, called him a fat old pig, and made him lift up his feet one after the other.

'Wah!' said Little Toomai, 'thou art a big elephant,' and he wagged his fluffy head, quoting his father. 'The Government may pay for elephants, but they belong to us mahouts. When thou art old, Kala Nag, there will come some rich Rajah, and he will buy thee from the Government, on account of thy size and thy manners, and then thou wilt having nothing to do but to carry gold earrings in thy ears, and a gold howdah on thy back, and a red cloth covered with gold on thy sides, and walk at the head of the processions of the King. Then I shall sit on thy neck, O Kala Nag, with a silver ankus, and men will run before us with golden sticks, crying, "Room for the King's elephant!" That will be good, Kala Nag, but not so good as this hunting in the jungles.'

'Umph!' said Big Toomai. 'Thou art a boy, and as wild as a buffalo-calf. This running up and down among the hills is not the best Government service. I am getting old, and I do not love wild elephants. Give me brick elephant-lines, one stall to each elephant, and big stumps to tie them to safely, and flat, broad roads to exercise upon, instead of this come-and-go camping. Aha, the Cawnpore barracks were good. There was a bazar close by, and only three hours' work a day.'

Little Toomai remembered the Cawnpore elephant-lines and said nothing. He very much preferred the camp life, and hated those broad, flat roads, with the daily grubbing for grass in the forage-reserve, and the long hours when there was nothing to do except to watch Kala Nag fidgeting in his pickets.

What Little Toomai liked was the scramble up bridle-
paths that only an elephant could take; the dip into
the valley below; the glimpses of the wild elephants
browsing miles away; the rush of the frightened pig
and peacock under Kala Nag's feet; the blinding warm
rains, when all the hills and valleys smoked; the beautiful
misty mornings when nobody knew where they would
camp that night; the steady, cautious drive of the wild
elephants, and the mad rush and blaze and hullabaloo
of the last night's drive, when the elephants poured into
the stockade like boulders in a landslide, found that they
could not get out, and flung themselves at the heavy posts
only to be driven back by yells and flaring torches and
volleys of blank cartridge.

Even a little boy could be of use there, and Toomai
was as useful as three boys. He would get his torch
and wave it, and yell with the best. But the really
good time came when the driving out began, and the
Keddah—that is, the stockade—looked like a picture of
the end of the world, and men had to make signs to one
another, because they could not hear themselves speak.
Then Little Toomai would climb up to the top of one
of the quivering stockade-posts, his sun-bleached brown
hair flying loose all over his shoulders, and he looking like
a goblin in the torch-light; and as soon as there was a lull
you could hear his high-pitched yells of encouragement to
Kala Nag, above the trumpeting and crashing, and snapping of ropes, and groans of the tethered elephants. '*Maîl,
maîl, Kala Nag!* [Go on, go on, Black Snake!] *Dant do!*
[Give him the tusk!] *Somalo! Somalo!* [Careful, careful!]
Maro! Mar! [Hit him, hit him!] Mind the post! *Arré! Arré!
Hai! Yai! Kya-a-ah!*' he would shout, and the big fight
between Kala Nag and the wild elephant would sway to
and fro across the Keddah, and the old elephant-catchers
would wipe the sweat out of their eyes, and find time to

nod to Little Toomai wriggling with joy on the top of the posts.

He did more than wriggle. One night he slid down from the post and slipped in between the elephants, and threw up the loose end of a rope, which had dropped, to a driver who was trying to get a purchase on the leg of a kicking young calf (calves always give more trouble than full-grown animals). Kala Nag saw him, caught him in his trunk, and handed him up to Big Toomai, who slapped him then and there, and put him back on the post.

Next morning he gave him a scolding, and said: 'Are not good brick elephant-lines and a little tent-carrying enough, that thou must needs go elephant-catching on thy own account, little worthless? Now those foolish hunters, whose pay is less than my pay, have spoken to Petersen Sahib of the matter.' Little Toomai was frightened. He did not know much of white men, but Petersen Sahib was the greatest white man in the world to him. He was the head of all the Keddah operations—the man who caught all the elephants for the Government of India, and who knew more about the ways of elephants than any living man.

'What—what will happen?' said Little Toomai.

'Happen! the worst that can happen. Petersen Sahib is a madman. Else why should he go hunting these wild devils? He may even require thee to be an elephant-catcher, to sleep anywhere in these fever-filled jungles, and at last to be trampled to death in the Keddah. It is well that this nonsense ends safely. Next week the catching is over, and we of the plains are sent back to our stations. Then we will march on smooth roads, and forget all this hunting. But, son, I am angry that thou shouldst meddle in the business that belongs to these dirty Assamese jungle-folk. Kala Nag will obey none but me, so I must go with him into the Keddah; but he is only a fighting elephant, and he does not help to rope them. So I sit at my ease, as befits a mahout,—not a mere hunter,—a mahout, I say, and a man who gets a pension at the end of his service. Is the family of Toomai of the Elephants to be trodden underfoot in the dirt of a Keddah? Bad one! Wicked one! Worthless son! Go and wash Kala Nag and attend to his ears, and see that there are no thorns in his feet; or else Petersen Sahib will surely catch thee and make thee a wild hunter—a follower of elephants' foot-tracks, a jungle-bear. Bah! Shame! Go!'

Little Toomai went off without saying a word, but he told Kala Nag all his grievances while he was examining his feet. 'No matter,' said Little Toomai, turning up the fringe of Kala Nag's huge right ear. 'They have said my name to Petersen Sahib, and perhaps—and perhaps—and perhaps—who knows? Hai! That is a big thorn that I have pulled out!'

The next few days were spent in getting the elephants together, in walking the newly caught wild elephants up and down between a couple of tame ones, to prevent them from giving too much trouble on the downward march to the plains, and in taking stock of the blankets and ropes and things that had been worn out or lost in the forest.

Petersen Sahib came in on his clever she-elephant Pudmini. He had been paying off other camps among the hills, for the season was coming to an end, and there was a native clerk sitting at a table under a tree to pay the drivers their wages. As each man was paid he went back to his elephant, and joined the line that stood ready to start. The catchers, and hunters, and beaters, the men of the regular Keddah, who stayed in the jungle year in and year out, sat on the backs of the elephants that belonged to Petersen Sahib's permanent force, or leaned against the trees with their guns across their arms, and made fun of the drivers who were going away, and laughed

when the newly caught elephants broke the line and
ran about.

Big Toomai went up to the clerk with Little Toomai
behind him, and Machua Appa, the head-tracker, said
in an undertone to a friend of his, 'There goes one piece
of good elephant-stuff at least. 'Tis a pity to send that
young jungle-cock to moult in the plains.'

Now Petersen Sahib had ears all over him, as a
man must have who listens to the most silent of all
living things—the wild elephant. He turned where he
was lying all along on Pudmini's back, and said, 'What
is that? I did not know of a man among the plains-drivers
who had wit enough to rope even a dead elephant.'

'This is not a man, but a boy. He went into the Keddah
at the last drive, and threw Barmao there the rope when
we were trying to get that young calf with the blotch on
his shoulder away from his mother.'

Machua Appa pointed at Little Toomai, and Petersen
Sahib looked, and Little Toomai bowed to the earth.

'He throw a rope? He is smaller than a picket-pin.
Little one, what is thy name?' said Petersen Sahib.

Little Toomai was too frightened to speak, but Kala
Nag was behind him, and Toomai made a sign with his
hand, and the elephant caught him up in his trunk and
held him level with Pudmini's forehead, in front of the
great Petersen Sahib. Then Little Toomai covered his
face with his hands, for he was only a child, and except
where elephants were concerned, he was just as bashful
as a child could be.

'Oho!' said Petersen Sahib, smiling underneath his
moustache, 'and why didst thou teach thy elephant *that*
trick? Was it to help thee steal green corn from the roofs
of the houses when the ears are put out to dry?'

'Not green corn, Protector of the Poor,—melons,'
said Little Toomai, and all the men sitting about broke

into a roar of laughter. Most of them had taught their elephants that trick when they were boys. Little Toomai was hanging eight feet up in the air, and he wished very much that he were eight feet under ground.

'He is Toomai, my son, Sahib,' said Big Toomai, scowling. 'He is a very bad boy, and he will end in a jail, Sahib.'

'Of that I have my doubts,' said Petersen Sahib. 'A boy who can face a full Keddah at his age does not end in jails. See, little one, here are four annas to spend in sweetmeats because thou hast a little head under that great thatch of hair. In time thou mayest become a hunter too.' Big Toomai scowled more than ever. 'Remember, though, that Keddahs are not good for children to play in,' Petersen Sahib went on.

'Must I never go there, Sahib?' asked Little Toomai, with a big gasp.

'Yes.' Peter Sahib smiled again. 'When thou hast seen the elephants dance. That is the proper time. Come to me when thou hast seen the elephants dance, and then I will let thee go into all the Keddahs.'

There was another roar of laughter, for that is an old joke among elephant-catchers, and it means just never. There are great cleared flat places hidden away in the forests that are called elephants' ball-rooms, but even these are only found by accident, and no man has ever seen the elephants dance. When a driver boasts of his skill and bravery the other drivers say, 'And when didst *thou* see the elephants dance?'

Kala Nag put Little Toomai down, and he bowed to the earth again and went away with his father, and gave the silver four-anna piece to his mother, who was nursing his baby brother, and they all were put up on Kala Nag's back, and the line of grunting, squealing elephants rolled down the hill-path to the plains. It was a very lively march on account of the new elephants, who gave trouble at every ford, and who needed coaxing or beating every other minute.

Big Toomai prodded Kala Nag spitefully, for he was very angry, but Little Toomai was too happy to speak. Petersen Sahib had noticed him, and given him money, so he felt as a private soldier would feel if he had been called out of the ranks and praised by his commander-in-chief.

'What did Petersen Sahib mean by the elephant-dance?' he said, at last, softly to his mother.

Big Toomai heard him and grunted. 'That thou shouldst never be one of these hill-buffaloes of trackers. *That* was what he meant. Oh, you in front, what is blocking the way?'

An Assamese driver, two or three elephants ahead, turned round angrily, crying: 'Bring up Kala Nag, and knock this youngster of mine into good behaviour. Why should Petersen Sahib have chosen *me* to go down with you donkeys of the rice-fields? Lay your beast alongside, Toomai, and let him prod with his tusks. By all the gods of the Hills, these new elephants are possessed, or else they can smell their companions in the jungle.'

Kala Nag hit the new elephant in the ribs and knocked the wind out of him, as Big Toomai said, 'We have swept the hills of wild elephants at the last catch. It is only your carelessness in driving. Must I keep order along the whole line?'

'Hear him!' said the other driver. '*We* have swept the hills! Ho! ho! You are very wise, you plains-people. Anyone but a mud-head who never saw the jungle would know that *they* know that the drives are ended for the season. Therefore all the wild elephants to-night will——but why should I waste wisdom on a river-turtle?'

'What will they do?' Little Toomai called out.

'*Ohé*, little one. Art thou there? Well, I will tell thee, for thou hast a cool head. They will dance, and it behoves thy father, who has swept *all* the hills of *all* the elephants, to double-chain his pickets to-night.'

'What talk is this?' said Big Toomai. 'For forty years, father and son, we have tended elephants, and we have never heard such moonshine about dances.'

'Yes; but a plains-man who lives in a hut knows only the four walls of his hut. Well, leave thy elephants unshackled to-night and see what comes; as for their dancing, I have seen the place where——*Bapree-Bap!* how many windings has the Dihang River? Here is another ford, and we must swim the calves. Stop still, you behind there.'

And in this way, talking and wrangling and splashing through the rivers, they made their first march to a sort of receiving-camp for the new elephants; but they lost their tempers long before they got there.

Then the elephants were chained by their hind legs to their big stumps of pickets, and extra ropes were fitted to the new elephants, and the fodder was piled before them, and the hill-drivers went back to Petersen Sahib through the afternoon light, telling the plains-drivers to be extra careful that night, and laughing when the plains-drivers asked the reason.

Little Toomai attended to Kala Nag's supper, and as evening fell wandered through the camp, unspeakably happy, in search of a tom-tom. When an Indian child's heart is full, he does not run about and make a noise in an irregular fashion. He sits down to a sort of revel all by himself. And Little Toomai had been spoken to by Petersen Sahib! If he had not found what he wanted, I believe he would have burst. But the sweetmeat-seller in the camp lent him a little tom-tom—a drum beaten with the flat of the hand—and he sat down, cross-legged, before Kala Nag as the stars began to come out, the tom-tom in his lap, and he thumped and he thumped and he thumped, and the more he thought of the great honour that had been done to him, the more he thumped, all alone among the elephant-fodder. There was no tune and no words, but the thumping made him happy.

The new elephants strained at their ropes, and squealed and trumpeted from time to time, and he could hear his mother in the camp hut putting his small brother to sleep with an old, old song about the great God Shiv, who once told all the animals what they should eat. It is a very soothing lullaby, and the first verse says:

> Shiv, who poured the harvest and made the winds to blow,
> Sitting at the doorways of a day of long ago,
> Gave to each his portion, food and toil and fate,
> From the King upon the *guddee* to the Beggar at the gate.
>> All things made he—Shiva the Preserver.
>> Mahadeo! Mahadeo! He made all,—
>> Thorn for the camel, fodder for the kine,
>> And mother's heart for sleepy head, O little son of mine!

Little Toomai came in with a joyous *tunk-a-tunk* at the end of each verse, till he felt sleepy and stretched himself on the fodder at Kala Nag's side.

At last the elephants began to lie down one after another, as is their custom, till only Kala Nag at the right of the line was left standing up; and he rocked slowly from side to side, his ears put forward to listen to the night wind as it blew very slowly across the hills. The air was full of all the night noises that, taken together, make one big silence—the click of one bamboo-stem against the other, the rustle of something alive in the undergrowth, the scratch and squawk of a half-waked bird (birds are awake in the night much more often than we imagine), and the fall of water ever so far away. Little Toomai

slept for some time, and when he waked it was brilliant
moonlight, and Kala Nag was still standing up with his
ears cocked. Little Toomai turned, rustling in the fodder,
and watched the curve of his big back against half the
stars in heaven; and while he watched he heard, so far
away that it sounded no more than a pinhole of noise
pricked through the stillness, the 'hoot-toot' of a wild
elephant.

All the elephants in the lines jumped up as if they had
been shot, and their grunts at last waked the sleeping
mahouts, and they came out and drove in the picket-pegs
with big mallets, and tightened this rope and knotted
that till all was quiet. One new elephant had nearly
grubbed up his picket, and Big Toomai took off Kala
Nag's leg-chain and shackled that elephant fore-foot to
hind-foot, but slipped a loop of grass-string round Kala
Nag's leg, and told him to remember that he was tied fast.
He knew that he and his father and his grandfather had
done the very same thing hundreds of times before. Kala
Nag did not answer to the order by gurgling, as he usually
did. He stood still, looking out across the moonlight, his
head a little raised, and his ears spread like fans, up to
the great folds of the Garo hills.

'Look to him if he grows restless in the night,'
said Big Toomai to Little Toomai, and he went into
the hut and slept. Little Toomai was just going to
sleep, too, when he heard the coir string snap with
a little 'tang,' and Kala Nag rolled out of his pickets
as slowly and as silently as a cloud rolls out of the
mouth of a valley. Little Toomai pattered after him,
barefooted, down the road in the moonlight, calling
under his breath, 'Kala Nag! Kala Nag! Take me with
you, O Kala Nag!' The elephant turned without a sound,
took three strides back to the boy in the moonlight, put
down his trunk, swung him up to his neck, and almost

before Little Toomai had settled his knees slipped into the forest.

There was one blast of furious trumpeting from the lines, and then the silence shut down on everything, and Kala Nag began to move. Sometimes a tuft of high grass washed along his sides as a wave washes along the sides of a ship, and sometimes a cluster of wild-pepper vines would scrape along his back, or a bamboo would creak where his shoulder touched it; but between those times he moved absolutely without any sound, drifting through the thick Garo forest as though it had been smoke. He was going uphill, but though Little Toomai watched the stars in the rifts of the trees, he could not tell in what direction.

Then Kala Nag reached the crest of the ascent and stopped for a minute, and Little Toomai could see the tops of the trees lying all speckled and furry under the moonlight for miles and miles, and the blue-white mist over the river in the hollow. Toomai leaned forward and looked, and he felt that the forest was awake below him—awake and alive and crowded. A big brown fruit-eating bat brushed past his ear; a porcupine's quills rattled in the thicket; and in the darkness between the tree-stems he heard a hog-bear digging hard in the moist, warm earth, and snuffing as it digged.

Then the branches closed over his head again, and Kala Nag began to go slowly down into the valley—not quietly this time, but as a runaway gun goes down a steep bank—in one rush. The huge limbs moved as steadily as pistons, eight feet to each stride, and the wrinkled skin of the elbow-points rustled. The undergrowth on either side of him ripped with a noise like torn canvas, and the saplings that he heaved away right and left with his shoulders sprang back again, and banged him on the flank, and great trails of creepers, all matted together, hung from his tusks as he threw his head from side to side and ploughed out his pathway. Then Little Toomai laid himself down close to the great neck, lest a swinging bough should sweep him to the ground, and he wished that he were back in the lines again.

The grass began to get squashy, and Kala Nag's feet sucked and squelched as he put them down, and the night mist at the bottom of the valley chilled Little Toomai. There was a splash and a trample, and the rush of running water, and Kala Nag strode through the bed of a river, feeling his way at each step. Above the noise of the water, as it swirled round the elephant's legs, Little Toomai could hear more splashing and some trumpeting both up stream and down—great grunts and angry snortings, and all the mist about him seemed to be full of rolling, wavy shadows.

'Ai!' he said, half aloud, his teeth chattering. 'The elephant-folk are out to-night. It is the dance, then.'

Kala Nag swashed out of the water, blew his trunk clear, and began another climb; but this time he was not alone, and he had not to make his path. That was made already, six feet wide, in front of him, where the bent jungle-grass was trying to recover itself and stand up. Many elephants must have gone that way only a few minutes before. Little Toomai looked back, and behind him a great wild tusker, with his little pig's eyes glowing like hot coals, was just lifting himself out of the misty river. Then the trees closed up again, and they went on and up, with trumpetings and crashings, and the sound of breaking branches on every side of them.

At last Kala Nag stood still between two tree-trunks at the very top of the hill. They were part of a circle of trees that grew round an irregular space of some three or four acres, and in all that space, as Little Toomai could see, the ground had been trampled down as hard as a brick floor. Some trees grew in the centre of the clearing, but their bark was rubbed away, and the white wood beneath showed all shiny and polished in the patches of moonlight. There were creepers hanging from the upper branches, and the bells of the flowers of the creepers, great waxy white things like convolvuluses, hung down fast asleep; but within the limits of the clearing there was not a single blade of green—nothing but the trampled earth.

The moonlight showed it all iron-grey, except where some elephants stood upon it, and their shadows were inky black. Little Toomai looked, holding his breath, with his eyes starting out of his head, and as he looked, more and more and more elephants swung out into the open from between the tree-trunks. Little Toomai could count only up to ten, and he counted again and again on his fingers till he lost count of the tens, and his head began to swim. Outside the clearing he could hear them crashing in the undergrowth as they worked their way up the hillside; but as soon as they were within the circle of the tree-trunks they moved like ghosts.

There were white-tusked wild males, with fallen leaves and nuts and twigs lying in the wrinkles of their necks and the folds of their ears; fat, slow-footed she-elephants, with restless little pinky-black calves only three or four feet high running under their stomachs; young elephants with their tusks just beginning to show, and very proud of them; lanky, scraggy old-maid elephants, with their hollow, anxious faces, and trunks like rough bark; savage old bull-elephants, scarred from shoulder to flank with great weals and cuts of bygone fights, and the caked dirt of their solitary mud-baths dropping from their shoulders; and there was one with a broken tusk and the marks of the full-stroke, the terrible drawing scrape, of a tiger's claws on his side.

They were standing head to head, or walking to and

fro across the ground in couples, or rocking and swaying all by themselves—scores and scores of elephants.

Toomai knew that so long as he lay still on Kala Nag's neck nothing would happen to him; for even in the rush and scramble of a Keddah-drive a wild elephant does not reach up with his trunk and drag a man off the neck of a tame elephant; and these elephants were not thinking of men that night. Once they started and put their ears forward when they heard the chinking of a leg-iron in the forest, but it was Pudmini, Petersen Sahib's pet elephant, her chain snapped short off, grunting, snuffling up the hillside. She must have broken her pickets, and come straight from Petersen Sahib's camp; and Little Toomai saw another elephant, one that he did not know, with deep rope-galls on his back and breast. He, too, must have run away from some camp in the hills about.

At last there was no sound of any more elephants moving in the forest, and Kala Nag rolled out from his station between the trees and went into the middle of the crowd, clucking and gurgling, and all the elephants began to talk in their own tongue, and to move about.

Still lying down, Little Toomai looked down upon scores and scores of broad backs, and wagging ears, and tossing trunks, and little rolling eyes. He heard the click of tusks as they crossed other tusks by accident, and the dry rustle of trunks twined together, and the chafing of enormous sides and shoulders in the crowd, and the incessant flick and *hissh* of the great tails. Then a cloud came over the moon, and he sat in black darkness; but the quiet, steady hustling and pushing and gurgling went on just the same. He knew that there were elephants all round Kala Nag, and that there was no chance of backing him out of the assembly; so he set his teeth and shivered. In a Keddah at least there was torch-light and shouting, but here he was all alone in the dark, and once a trunk came up and touched him on the knee.

Then an elephant trumpeted, and they all took it up for five or ten terrible seconds. The dew from the trees above spattered down like rain on the unseen backs, and a dull booming noise began, not very loud at first, and Little Toomai could not tell what it was; but it grew and grew, and Kala Nag lifted up one fore-foot and then the other, and brought them down on the ground—one-two, one-two, as steadily as trip-hammers. The elephants were stamping all together now, and it sounded like a war-drum beaten at the mouth of a cave. The dew fell from the trees till there was no more left to fall, and the booming went on, and the ground rocked and shivered, and Little Toomai put his hands up to his ears to shut out the sound. But it was all one gigantic jar that ran through him—this stamp of hundreds of heavy feet on the raw earth. Once or twice he could feel Kala Nag and all the others surge forward a few strides, and the thumping would change to the crushing sound of juicy green things being bruised, but in a minute or two the boom of feet on hard earth began again. A tree was creaking and groaning somewhere near him. He put out his arm and felt the bark, but Kala Nag moved forward, still tramping, and he could not tell where he was in the clearing. There was no sound from the elephants, except once, when two or three little calves squeaked together. Then he heard a thump and a shuffle, and the booming went on. It must have lasted fully two hours, and Little Toomai ached in every nerve; but he knew by the smell of the night air that the dawn was coming.

The morning broke in one sheet of pale yellow behind the green hills, and the booming stopped with the first ray, as though the light had been an order. Before Little Toomai had got the ringing out of his head, before even he had shifted his position, there was not an elephant in sight except Kala Nag, Pudmini, and the elephant with the rope-galls, and there was neither sign nor rustle nor whisper down the hillsides to show where the others had gone.

Little Toomai stared again and again. The clearing, as he remembered it, had grown in the night. More trees stood in the middle of it, but the undergrowth and the jungle-grass at the sides had been rolled back. Little Toomai stared once more. Now he understood the trampling. The elephants had stamped out more room—had stamped the thick grass and juicy cane to trash, the trash into slivers, the slivers into tiny fibres, and the fibres into hard earth.

'Wah!' said Little Toomai, and his eyes were very heavy. 'Kala Nag, my lord, let us keep by Pudmini and go to Petersen Sahib's camp, or I shall drop from thy neck.'

The third elephant watched the two go away, snorted, wheeled round, and took his own path. He may have belonged to some little native king's establishment, fifty or sixty or a hundred miles away.

Two hours later, as Petersen Sahib was eating early breakfast, the elephants, who had been double-chained that night, began to trumpet, and Pudmini, mired to the shoulders, with Kala Nag, very foot-sore, shambled into the camp.

Little Toomai's face was grey and pinched, and his hair was full of leaves and drenched with dew; but he tried to salute Petersen Sahib, and cried faintly: 'The dance—the elephant-dance! I have seen it, and—I die!' As Kala Nag sat down, he slid off his neck in a dead faint.

But, since native children have no nerves worth speaking of, in two hours he was lying very contentedly in Petersen Sahib's hammock with Petersen Sahib's shooting-coat under his head, and a glass of warm milk, a little brandy, with a dash of quinine inside of him; and while the old hairy, scarred hunters of the jungles sat three-deep before him, looking at him as though he were a spirit, he told his tale in short words, as a child will, and wound up with:

'Now, if I lie in one word, send men to see, and they will find that the elephant-folk have trampled down more room in their dance-room, and they will find ten and ten, and many times ten, tracks leading to that dance-room. They made more room with their feet. I have seen it. Kala Nag took me, and I saw. Also Kala Nag is very leg-weary!'

Little Toomai lay back and slept all through the long afternoon and into the twilight, and while he slept Petersen Sahib and Machua Appa followed the track of the two elephants for fifteen miles across the hills. Petersen Sahib had spent eighteen years in catching elephants, and he had only once before found such a dance-place. Machua Appa had no need to look twice at the clearing to see what had been done there, or to scratch with his toe in the packed, rammed earth.

'The child speaks truth,' said he. 'All this was done last night, and I have counted seventy tracks crossing the river. See, Sahib, where Pudmini's leg-iron cut the bark off that tree! Yes; she was there too.'

They looked at each other, and up and down, and they wondered; for the ways of elephants are beyond the wit of any man, black or white, to fathom.

'Forty years and five,' said Machua Appa, 'have I followed my lord the elephant, but never have I heard that any child of man had seen what this child has seen. By all the Gods of the Hills, it is—what can we say?' and he shook his head.

When they got back to camp it was time for the

evening meal. Petersen Sahib ate alone in his tent, but
he gave orders that the camp should have two sheep and
some fowls, as well as a double ration of flour and rice
and salt, for he knew that there would be a feast.

Big Toomai had come up hot-foot from the camp
in the plains to search for his son and his elephant,
and now that he had found them he looked at them
as though he were afraid of them both. And there was
a feast by the blazing camp-fires in front of the lines of
picketed elephants, and Little Toomai was the hero of it
all; and the big brown elephant-catchers, the trackers and
drivers and ropers, and the men who know all the secrets
of breaking the wildest elephants, passed him from one to
the other, and they marked his forehead with blood from
the breast of a newly killed jungle-cock, to show that he
was a forester, initiated and free of all the jungles.

And at last, when the flames died down, and the red
light of the logs made the elephants look as though they
had been dipped in blood too, Machua Appa, the head
of all the drivers of all the Keddahs,—Machua Appa,
Petersen Sahib's other self, who had never seen a made
road in forty years: Machua Appa, who was so great that
he had no other name than Machua Appa,—leaped to
his feet, with Little Toomai held high in the air above
his head, and shouted: 'Listen, my brothers. Listen, too,
you my lords in the lines there, for I, Machua Appa,
am speaking! This little one shall no more be called
Little Toomai, but Toomai of the Elephants, as his
great-grandfather was called before him. What never
man has seen he has seen through the long night, and
the favour of the elephant-folk and of the Gods of the
Jungles is with him. He shall become a great tracker;
he shall become greater than I, even I—Machua Appa!
He shall follow the new trail, and the stale trail, and
the mixed trail, with a clear eye! He shall take no harm

in the Keddah when he runs under their bellies to rope the wild tuskers; and if he slips before the feet of the charging bull-elephant, that bull-elephant shall know who he is and shall not crush him. *Aihai!* my lords in the chains,' —he whirled up the line of pickets,— 'here is the little one that has seen your dances in your hidden places—the sight that never man saw! Give him honour, my lords! *Salaam karo*, my children! Make your salute to Toomai of the Elephants! Gunga Pershad, ahaa! Hira Guj, Birchi Guj, Kuttar Guj, ahaa! Pudmini,—thou hast seen him at the dance, and thou too, Kala Nag, my pearl among elephants!—ahaa! Together! To Toomai of the Elephants. *Barrao!*'

And at that last wild yell the whole line flung up their trunks till the tips touched their foreheads, and broke out into the full salute, the crashing trumpet-peal that only the Viceroy of India hears—the Salaam-ut of the Keddah.

But it was all for the sake of Little Toomai, who had seen what never man had seen before—the dance of the elephants at night and alone in the heart of the Garo hills!

Red Dog

For our white and our excellent nights—for the nights of swift running,
Fair ranging, far seeing, good hunting, sure cunning!
For the smells of the dawning, untainted, ere dew has departed!
For the rush through the mist, and the quarry blind-started!
For the cry of our mates when the sambhur has wheeled and is standing
at bay,
For the risk and the riot of night!
For the sleep at the lair-mouth by day,
It is met, and we go to the fight.
Bay! O Bay!

IT was after the letting in of the Jungle that the pleasantest part of Mowgli's life began. He had the good conscience that comes from paying debts; all the Jungle was his friend, and just a little afraid of him. The things that he did and saw and heard when he was wandering from one people to another, with or without his four companions, would make many many stories, each as long as this one. So you will never be told how he met the Mad Elephant of Mandla, who killed two-and-twenty bullocks drawing eleven carts of coined silver to the Government Treasury, and scattered the shiny rupees in the dust; how he fought Jacala, the Crocodile, all one long night in the Marshes of the North, and broke his skinning-knife on the brute's backplates; how he found a new and longer knife round the neck of a man who had been killed by a wild boar, and how he tracked that boar and killed him as a fair price for the knife; how he was caught up once in the Great Famine, by the moving of the deer, and

nearly crushed to death in the swaying hot herds; how
he saved Hathi the Silent from being once more trapped
in a pit with a stake at the bottom, and how, next day,
he himself fell into a very cunning leopard-trap, and how
Hathi broke the thick wooden bars to pieces above him;
how he milked the wild buffaloes in the swamp, and
how——

But we must tell one tale at a time. Father and
Mother Wolf died, and Mowgli rolled a big boulder against
the mouth of their cave, and cried the Death Song over
them; Baloo grew very old and stiff, and even Bagheera,
whose nerves were steel and whose muscles were iron,
was a shade slower on the kill than he had been. Akela
turned from gray to milky white with pure age; his ribs
stuck out, and he walked as though he had been made of
wood, and Mowgli killed for him. But the young wolves,
the children of the disbanded Seeonee Pack, throve and
increased, and when there were about forty of them,
masterless, full-voiced, clean-footed five-year-olds, Akela
told them that they ought to gather themselves together
and follow the Law, and run under one head, as befitted
the Free People.

This was not a question in which Mowgli concerned
himself, for, as he said, he had eaten sour fruit, and he
knew the tree it hung from; but when Phao, son of Phaona
(his father was the Gray Tracker in the days of Akela's
headship), fought his way to the leadership of the Pack,
according to the Jungle Law, and the old calls and songs
began to ring under the stars once more, Mowgli came
to the Council Rock for memory's sake. When he chose
to speak the Pack waited till he had finished, and he sat
at Akela's side on the rock above Phao. Those were days
of good hunting and good sleeping. No stranger cared to
break into the jungles that belonged to Mowgli's people,
as they called the Pack, and the young wolves grew fat

and strong, and there were many cubs to bring to the Looking-over. Mowgli always attended a Looking-over, remembering the night when a black panther bought a naked brown baby into the pack, and the long call, 'Look, look well, O Wolves,' made his heart flutter. Otherwise, he would be far away in the Jungle with his four brothers, tasting, touching, seeing, and feeling new things.

One twilight when he was trotting leisurely across the ranges to give Akela the half of a buck that he had killed, while the Four jogged behind him, sparring a little, and tumbling one another over for joy of being alive, he heard a cry that had never been heard since the bad days of Shere Khan. It was what they call in the Jungle the *pheeal*, a hideous kind of shriek that the jackal gives when he is hunting behind a tiger, or when there is a big killing afoot. If you can imagine a mixture of hate, triumph, fear, and despair, with a kind of leer running through it, you will get some notion of the *pheeal* that rose and sank and wavered and quavered far away across the Waingunga. The Four stopped at once, bristling and growling. Mowgli's hand went to his knife, and he checked, the blood in his face, his eyebrows knotted.

'There is no Striped One dare kill here,' he said.

'That is not the cry of the Forerunner,' answered Gray Brother. 'It is some great killing. Listen!'

It broke out again, half sobbing and half chuckling, just as though the jackal had soft human lips. Then Mowgli drew deep breath, and ran to the Council Rock, overtaking on his way hurrying wolves of the Pack. Phao and Akela were on the Rock together, and below them, every nerve strained, sat the others. The mothers and the cubs were cantering off to their lairs; for when the *pheeal* cries it is no time for weak things to be abroad.

They could hear nothing except the Waingunga rushing and gurgling in the dark, and the light evening winds among the tree-tops, till suddenly across the river a wolf called. It was no wolf of the Pack, for they were all at the Rock. The note changed to a long, despairing bay; and 'Dhole!' it said, 'Dhole! dhole! dhole!' They heard tired feet on the rocks, and a gaunt wolf, streaked with red on his flanks, his right fore-paw useless, and his jaws white with foam, flung himself into the circle and lay gasping at Mowgli's feet.

'Good hunting! Under whose Headship?' said Phao gravely.

'Good hunting! Won-tolla am I,' was the answer. He meant that he was a solitary wolf, fending for himself, his mate, and his cubs in some lonely lair, as do many wolves in the south. Won-tolla means an Outlier—one who lies out from any Pack. Then he panted, and they could see his heart-beats shake him backward and forward.

'What moves?' said Phao, for that is the question all the Jungle asks after the *pheeal* cries.

'The dhole, the dhole of the Dekkan—Red Dog, the Killer! They came north from the south saying the Dekkan was empty and killing out by the way. When this moon was new there were four to me—my mate and three cubs. She would teach them to kill on the grass plains, hiding to drive the buck, as we do who are of the open. At midnight I heard them together, full tongue on the trail. At the dawn-wind I found them stiff in the grass—four, Free People, four when this moon was new. Then sought I my Blood-Right and found the dhole.'

'How many?' said Mowgli quickly; the Pack growled deep in their throats.

'I do not know. Three of them will kill no more, but at the last they drove me like the buck; on my three legs they drove me. Look, Free People!'

He thrust out his mangled fore-foot, all dark with dried blood. There were cruel bites low down on his side, and his throat was torn and worried.

'Eat,' said Akela, rising up from the meat Mowgli had brought him, and the Outlier flung himself on it.

'This shall be no loss,' he said humbly, when he had taken off the first edge of his hunger. 'Give me a little strength, Free People, and I also will kill. My lair is empty that was full when this moon was new, and the Blood Debt is not all paid.'

Phao heard his teeth crack on a haunch-bone and grunted approvingly.

'We shall need those jaws,' said he. 'Were there cubs with the dhole?'

'Nay, nay. Red Hunters all: grown dogs of their Pack, heavy and strong for all that they eat lizards in the Dekkan.'

What Won-tolla had said meant that the dhole, the red hunting-dog of the Dekkan, was moving to kill, and the Pack knew well that even the tiger will surrender a new kill to the dhole. They drive straight through the Jungle, and what they meet they pull down and tear to pieces. Though they are not as big nor half as cunning as the wolf, they are very strong and very numerous. The dhole, for instance, do not begin to call themselves a pack till they are a hundred strong; whereas forty wolves make a very fair pack indeed. Mowgli's wanderings had taken him to the edge of the high grassy downs of the Dekkan, and he had seen the fearless dholes sleeping and playing and scratching themselves in the little hollows and tussocks that they use for lairs. He despised and hated them because they did not smell like the Free People, because they did not live in caves, and, above all, because they had hair between their toes while he and his friends were clean-footed. But he knew, for Hathi had told him, what a terrible thing a dhole hunting-pack was. Even Hathi moves aside from their line, and until they are killed, or till game is scarce, they will go forward.

Akela knew something of the dholes, too, for he said to Mowgli quietly, 'It is better to die in a Full Pack than leaderless and alone. This is good hunting, and—my last. But, as men live, thou hast very many more nights and days, Little Brother. Go north and lie down, and if any live after the dhole has gone by he shall bring thee word of the fight.'

'Ah,' said Mowgli, quite gravely, 'must I go to the marshes and catch little fish and sleep in a tree, or must I ask help of the *Bandar-log* and crack nuts, while the Pack fight below?'

'It is to the death,' said Akela. 'Thou hast never met the dhole—the Red Killer. Even the Striped One——'

'*Aowa! Aowa!*' said Mowgli pettingly. 'I have killed one striped ape, and sure am I in my stomach that Shere Khan would have left his own mate for meat to the dhole if he had winded a pack across three ranges. Listen now: There was a wolf, my father, and there was a wolf, my mother, and there was an old gray wolf (not too wise: he is white now) was my father and my mother. Therefore I—' he raised his voice, 'I say that when the dhole come, and if the dhole come, Mowgli and the Free People are of one skin for that hunting; and I say, by the Bull that bought me—by the Bull Bagheera paid for me in the old days which ye of the Pack do not remember—*I* say, that the Trees and the River may hear and hold fast if I forget; *I* say that this my knife shall be as a tooth to the Pack—and I do not think it is so blunt. This is my Word which has gone from me.'

'Thou dost not know the dhole, man with a wolf's tongue,' said Won-tolla. 'I look only to clear the Blood Debt against them ere they have me in many pieces.

They move slowly, killing out as they go, but in two days a little strength will come back to me and I turn again for the Blood Debt. But for *ye*, Free People, my word is that ye go north and eat but little for a while till the dhole are gone. There is no meat in this hunting.'

'Hear the Outlier!' said Mowgli with a laugh. 'Free People, we must go north and dig lizards and rats from the bank, lest by any chance we meet the dhole. He must kill out our hunting-grounds, while we lie hid in the north till it please him to give us our own again. He is a dog—and the pup of a dog—red, yellow-bellied, lairless, and haired between every toe! He counts his cubs six and eight at the litter, as though he were Chikai, the little leaping rat. Surely we must run away, Free People, and beg leave of the peoples of the north for the offal of dead cattle! Ye know the saying: "North are the vermin; south are the lice. *We* are the Jungle." Choose ye, O choose. It is good hunting! For the Pack—for the Full Pack—for the lair and the litter; for the in-kill and the out-kill; for the mate that drives the doe and the little, little cub within the cave; it is met!—it is met!—it is met!'

The Pack answered with one deep, crashing bark that sounded in the night like a big tree falling. 'It is met!' they cried.

'Stay with these,' said Mowgli to the Four. 'We shall need every tooth. Phao and Akela must make ready the battle. I go to count the dogs.'

'It is death!' Won-tolla cried, half rising. 'What can such a hairless one do against the Red Dog? Even the Striped One, remember——'

'Thou art indeed an Outlier,' Mowgli called back; 'but we will speak when the dholes are dead. Good hunting all!'

He hurried off into the darkness, wild with excitement, hardly looking where he set foot, and the natural consequence was that he tripped full length over Kaa's great coils where the python lay watching a deer-path near the river.

'*Kssha!*' said Kaa angrily. 'Is this jungle-work, to stamp and tramp and undo a night's hunting—when the game are moving so well, too?'

'The fault was mine,' said Mowgli, picking himself up. 'Indeed I was seeking thee, Flathead, but each time we meet thou art longer and broader by the length of my arm. There is none like thee in the Jungle, wise, old, strong, and most beautiful Kaa.'

'Now whither does *this* trail lead?' Kaa's voice was gentler. 'Not a moon since there was a Manling with a knife threw stones at my head and called me bad little tree-cat names, because I lay asleep in the open.'

'Ay, and turned every driven deer to all the winds, and Mowgli was hunting, and this same Flathead was too deaf to hear his whistle, and leave the deer-roads free,' Mowgli answered composedly, sitting down among the painted coils.

'Now this same Manling comes with soft, tickling words to this same Flathead, telling him that he is wise and strong and beautiful, and this same old Flathead believes and makes a place, thus, for this same stone-throwing Manling, and——Art thou at ease now? Could Bagheera give thee so good a resting-place?'

Kaa had, as usual, made a sort of soft half-hammock of himself under Mowgli's weight. The boy reached out in the darkness, and gathered in the supple cable-like neck till Kaa's head rested on his shoulder, and then he told him all that had happened in the Jungle that night.

'Wise I may be,' said Kaa at the end; 'but deaf I surely am. Else I should have heard the *pheeal*. Small wonder the Eaters of Grass are uneasy. How many be the dhole?'

'I have not yet seen. I came hot-foot to thee. Thou art older than Hathi. But oh, Kaa,'—here Mowgli wriggled with sheer joy,—'it will be good hunting. Few of us will see another moon.'

'Dost *thou* strike in this? Remember thou art a Man; and remember what Pack cast thee out. Let the Wolf look to the Dog. *Thou* art a Man.'

'Last year's nuts are this year's black earth,' said Mowgli. 'It is true that I am a Man, but it is in my stomach that this night I have said that I am a Wolf. I called the River and the Trees to remember. I am of the Free People, Kaa, till the dhole has gone by.'

'Free People,' Kaa grunted. 'Free thieves! And thou hast tied thyself into the death-knot for the sake of the memory of the dead wolves? This is no good hunting.'

'It is my Word which I have spoken. The Trees know, the River knows. Till the dhole have gone by my Word comes not back to me.'

'*Ngssh!* This changes all trails. I had thought to take thee away with me to the northern marshes, but the Word—even the Word of a little, naked, hairless Manling—is the Word. Now I, Kaa, say——'

'Think well, Flathead, lest thou tie thyself into the death-knot also. I need no Word from thee, for well I know——'

'Be it so, then,' said Kaa. 'I will give no Word; but what is in thy stomach to do when the dhole come?'

'They must swim the Waingunga. I thought to meet them with my knife in the shallows, the Pack behind me; and so stabbing and thrusting, we a little might turn them down-stream, or cool their throats.'

'The dhole do not turn and their throats are hot,' said Kaa. 'There will be neither Manling nor Wolf-cub when that hunting is done, but only dry bones.'

'*Alala!* If we die, we die. It will be most good hunting.

But my stomach is young, and I have not seen many Rains. I am not wise nor strong. Hast thou a better plan, Kaa?'

'I have seen a hundred and a hundred Rains. Ere Hathi cast his milk-tushes my trail was big in the dust. By the First Egg, I am older than many trees, and I have seen all that the Jungle has done.'

'But *this* is new hunting,' said Mowgli. 'Never before have the dhole crossed our trail.'

'What is has been. What will be is no more than a forgotten year striking backward. Be still while I count those my years.'

For a long hour Mowgli lay back among the coils, while Kaa, his head motionless on the ground, thought of all that he had seen and known since the day he came from the egg. The light seemed to go out of his eyes and leave them like stale opals, and now and again he made little stiff passes with his head, right and left, as though he were hunting in his sleep. Mowgli dozed quietly, for he knew that there is nothing like sleep before hunting, and he was trained to take it at any hour of the day or night.

Then he felt Kaa's back grow bigger and broader below him as the huge python puffed himself out, hissing with the noise of a sword drawn from a steel scabbard.

'I have seen all the dead seasons,' Kaa said at last, 'and the great trees and the old elephants, and the rocks that were bare and sharp-pointed ere the moss grew. Art *thou* still alive, Manling?'

'It is only a little after moonset,' said Mowgli. 'I do not understand——'

'*Hssh!* I am again Kaa. I knew it was but a little time. Now we will go to the river, and I will show thee what is to be done against the dhole.'

He turned, straight as an arrow, for the main stream

of the Waingunga, plunging in a little above the pool that hid the Peace Rock, Mowgli at his side.

'Nay, do not swim. I go swiftly. My back, Little Brother.'

Mowgli tucked his left arm round Kaa's neck, dropped his right close to his body, and straightened his feet. Then Kaa breasted the current as he alone could, and the ripple of the checked water stood up in a frill round Mowgli's neck, and his feet were waved to and fro in the eddy under the python's lashing sides. A mile or two above the Peace Rock the Waingunga narrows between a gorge of marble rocks from eighty to a hundred feet high, and the current runs like a mill-race between and over all manner of ugly stones. But Mowgli did not trouble his head about the water; little water in the world could have given him a moment's fear. He was looking at the gorge on either side and sniffing uneasily, for there was a sweetish-sourish smell in the air, very like the smell of a big ant-hill on a hot day. Instinctively he lowered himself in the water, only raising his head to breathe from time to time, and Kaa came to anchor with a double twist of his tail round a sunken rock, holding Mowgli in the hollow of a coil, while the water raced on.

'This is the Place of Death,' said the boy. 'Why do we come here?'

'They sleep,' said Kaa. 'Hathi will not turn aside for the Striped One. Yet Hathi and the Striped One together turn aside for the dhole, and the dhole they say turn aside for nothing. And yet for whom do the Little People of the Rocks turn aside? Tell me, Master of the Jungle, who is the Master of the Jungle?'

'These,' Mowgli whispered. 'It is the Place of Death. Let us go.'

'Nay, look well, for they are asleep. It is as it was when I was not the length of thy arm.'

The split and weatherworn rocks of the gorge of

the Waingunga had been used since the beginning of
the Jungle by the Little People of the Rocks—the busy,
furious, black wild bees of India; and, as Mowgli knew
well, all trails turned off half a mile before they reached
the gorge. For centuries the Little People had hived and
swarmed from cleft to cleft, and swarmed again, staining
the white marble with stale honey, and made their combs
tall and deep in the dark of the inner caves, where neither
man nor beast nor fire nor water had ever touched them.
The length of the gorge on both sides was hung as it were
with black shimmery velvet curtains, and Mowgli sank
as he looked, for those were the clotted millions of the
sleeping bees. There were other lumps and festoons and
things like decayed tree-trunks studded on the face of the
rock, the old combs of past years, or new cities built in the
shadow of the windless gorge, and huge masses of spongy,
rotten trash had rolled down and stuck among the trees
and creepers that clung to the rock-face. As he listened
he heard more than once the rustle and slide of a honey-
loaded comb turning over or falling away somewhere in
the dark galleries; then a booming of angry wings, and
the sullen drip, drip, drip, of the wasted honey, guttering
along till it lipped over some ledge in the open air and
sluggishly trickled down on the twigs. There was a tiny
little beach, not five feet broad, on one side of the river,
and that was piled high with the rubbish of uncounted
years. There were dead bees, drones, sweepings, and stale
combs, and wings of marauding moths that had strayed in
after honey, all tumbled in smooth piles of the finest black
dust. The mere sharp smell of it was enough to frighten
anything that had no wings, and knew what the Little
People were.

Kaa moved up-stream again till he came to a sandy
bar at the head of the gorge.

'Here is this season's kill,' said he. 'Look!'

On the bank lay the skeletons of a couple of young deer and a buffalo. Mowgli could see that neither wolf nor jackal had touched the bones, which were laid out naturally.

'They came beyond the line; they did not know the Law,' murmured Mowgli, 'and the Little People killed them. Let us go ere they wake.'

'They do not wake till the dawn,' said Kaa. 'Now I will tell thee. A hunted buck from the south, many, many Rains ago, came hither from the south, not knowing the Jungle, a Pack on his trail. Being made blind by fear, he leaped from above, the Pack running by sight, for they were hot and blind on the trail. The sun was high, and the Little People were many and very angry. Many, too, were those of the Pack who leaped into the Waingunga, but they were dead ere they took water. Those who did not leap died also in the rocks above. But the buck lived.'

'How?'

'Because he came first, running for his life, leaping ere the Little People were aware, and was in the river when they gathered to kill. The Pack, following, was altogether lost under the weight of the Little People.'

'The buck lived?' Mowgli repeated slowly.

'At least he did not die *then*, though none waited his coming down with a strong body to hold him safe against the water, as a certain old fat, deaf, yellow Flathead would wait for a Manling—yea, though there were all the dholes of the Dekkan on his trail. What is in thy stomach?' Kaa's head was close to Mowgli's ear; and it was a little time before the boy answered.

'It is to pull the very whiskers of Death, but—Kaa, thou art, indeed, the wisest of all the Jungle.'

'So many have said. Look now, if the dhole follow thee——'

'As surely they will follow. Ho! ho! I have many little thorns under my tongue to prick into their hides.'

'If they follow thee hot and blind, looking only at thy shoulders, those who do not die up above will take water either here or lower down, for the Little People will rise up and cover them. Now the Waingunga is hungry water, and they will have no Kaa to hold them, but will go down, such as live, to the shallows by the Seeonee Lairs, and there thy Pack may meet them by the throat.'

'*Ahai! Eowawa!* Better could not be till the Rains fall in the dry season. There is now only the little matter of the run and the leap. I will make me known to the dholes, so that they shall follow me very closely.'

'Hast thou seen the rocks above thee? From the landward side?'

'Indeed, no. That I had forgotten.'

'Go look. It is all rotten ground, cut and full of holes. One of thy clumsy feet set down without seeing would end the hunt. See, I leave thee here, and for thy sake only I will carry word to the Pack that they may know where to look for the dhole. For myself, I am not of one skin with *any* wolf.'

When Kaa disliked an acquaintance he could be more unpleasant than any of the Jungle People, except perhaps Bagheera. He swam down-stream, and opposite the Rock he came on Phao and Akela listening to the night noises.

'*Hssh!* Dogs,' he said cheerfully. 'The dholes will come down-stream. If ye be not afraid ye can kill them in the shallows.'

'When come they?' said Phao. 'And where is my Man-cub?' said Akela.

'They come when they come,' said Kaa. 'Wait and see. As for *thy* Man-cub, from whom thou hast taken a Word and so laid him open to Death, *thy* Man-cub is with *me*, and if he be not already dead the fault is none of thine, bleached dog! Wait here for the dhole, and be glad that the Man-cub and I strike on thy side.'

Kaa flashed up-stream again, and moored himself in the middle of the gorge, looking upward at the line of the cliff. Presently he saw Mowgli's head move against the stars, and then there was a whizz in the air, the keen, clean *schloop* of a body falling feet first, and next minute the boy was at rest again in the loop of Kaa's body.

'It is no leap by night,' said Mowgli quietly. 'I have jumped twice as far for sport; but that is an evil place above—low bushes and gullies that go down very deep, all full of the Little People. I have put big stones one above the other by the side of three gullies. These I shall throw down with my feet in running, and the Little People will rise up behind me, very angry.'

'That is Man's talk and Man's cunning,' said Kaa. 'Thou art wise, but the Little People are always angry.'

'Nay, at twilight all wings near and far rest for a while. I will play with the dhole at twilight, for the dhole hunts best by day. He follows now Won-tolla's blood-trail.'

'Chil does not leave a dead ox, nor the dhole the blood-trail,' said Kaa.

'Then I will make him a new blood-trail, of his own blood, if I can, and give him dirt to eat. Thou wilt stay here, Kaa, till I come again with my dholes?'

'Ay, but what if they kill thee in the Jungle, or the Little People kill thee before thou canst leap down to the river?'

'When to-morrow comes we will kill for to-morrow,' said Mowgli, quoting a Jungle saying; and again, 'When I am dead it is time to sing the Death Song. Good hunting, Kaa!'

He loosed his arm from the python's neck and went

down the gorge like a log in a freshet, paddling toward the far bank, where he found slack-water, and laughing aloud from sheer happiness. There was nothing Mowgli liked better than, as he himself said, 'to pull the whiskers of Death,' and make the Jungle know that he was their overlord. He had often, with Baloo's help, robbed bees' nests in single trees, and he knew that the Little People hated the smell of wild garlic. So he gathered a small bundle of it, tied it up with a bark string, and then followed Won-tolla's blood-trail, as it ran southerly from the Lairs, for some five miles, looking at the trees with his head on one side, and chuckling as he looked.

'Mowgli the Frog have I been,' said he to himself; 'Mowgli the Wolf have I said that I am. Now Mowgli the Ape must I be before I am Mowgli the Buck. At the end I shall be Mowgli the Man. Ho!' and he slid his thumb along the eighteen-inch blade of his knife.

Won-tolla's trail, all rank with dark blood-spots, ran under a forest of thick trees that grew close together and stretched away north-eastward, gradually growing thinner and thinner to within two miles of the Bee Rocks. From the last tree to the low scrub of the Bee Rocks was open country, where there was hardly cover enough to hide a wolf. Mowgli trotted along under the trees, judging distances between branch and branch, occasionally climbing up a trunk and taking a trial leap from one tree to another till he came to the open ground, which he studied very carefully for an hour. Then he turned, picked up Won-tolla's trail where he had left it, settled himself in a tree with an outrunning branch some eight feet from the ground, and sat still, sharpening his knife on the sole of his foot and singing to himself.

A little before mid-day, when the sun was very warm, he heard the patter of feet and smelt the abominable smell of the dhole-pack as they trotted pitilessly along

Won-tolla's trail. Seen from above, the red dhole does not look half the size of a wolf, but Mowgli knew how strong his feet and jaws were. He watched the sharp bay head of the leader snuffing along the trail, and gave him 'Good hunting!'

The brute looked up, and his companions halted behind him, scores and scores of red dogs with low-hung tails, heavy shoulders, weak quarters, and bloody mouths. The dholes are a very silent people as a rule, and they have no manners even in their own Jungle. Fully two hundred must have gathered below him, but he could see that the leaders sniffed hungrily on Won-tolla's trail, and tried to drag the Pack forward. That would never do, or they would be at the Lairs in broad daylight, and Mowgli meant to hold them under his tree till dusk.

'By whose leave do ye come here?' said Mowgli.

'All Jungles are our Jungle,' was the reply, and the dhole that gave it bared his white teeth. Mowgli looked down with a smile, and imitated perfectly the sharp chitter-chatter of Chikai, the leaping rat of the Dekkan, meaning the dholes to understand that he considered them no better than Chikai. The Pack closed up round the tree-trunk and the leader bayed savagely, calling Mowgli a tree-ape. For an answer Mowgli stretched down one naked leg and wriggled his bare toes just above the leader's head. That was enough, and more than enough, to wake the Pack to stupid rage. Those who have hair between their toes do not care to be reminded of it. Mowgli caught his foot away as the leader leaped up, and said sweetly: 'Dog, red dog! Go back to the Dekkan and eat lizards. Go to Chikai thy brother—dog, dog—red, red dog! There is hair between every toe!' He twiddled his toes a second time.

'Come down ere we starve thee out, hairless ape!' yelled the Pack, and this was exactly what Mowgli wanted. He laid himself down along the branch, his cheek to the bark, his right arm free, and there he told the Pack what he thought and knew about them, their manners, their customs, their mates, and their puppies. There is no speech in the world so rancorous and so stinging as the language the Jungle People use to show scorn and contempt. When you come to think of it you will see how this must be so. As Mowgli told Kaa, he had many little thorns under his tongue, and slowly and deliberately he drove the dholes from silence to growls, from growls to yells, and from yells to hoarse slavery ravings. They tried to answer his taunts, but a cub might as well have tried to answer Kaa in a rage; and all the while Mowgli's right hand lay crooked at his side, ready for action, his feet locked round the branch. The big bay leader had leaped many times in the air, but Mowgli dared not risk a false blow. At last, made furious beyond his natural strength, he bounded up seven or eight feet clear of the ground. Then Mowgli's hand shot out like the head of a tree-snake, and gripped him by the scruff of his neck, and the branch shook with the jar as his weight fell back, almost wrenching Mowgli to the ground. But he never loosed his grip, and inch by inch he hauled the beast, hanging like a drowned jackal, up on the branch. With his left hand he reached for his knife and cut off the red, bushy tail, flinging the dhole back to earth again. That was all he needed. The Pack would not go forward on Won-tolla's trail now till they had killed Mowgli or Mowgli had killed them. He saw them settle down in circles with a quiver of the haunches that meant they were going to stay, and so he climbed to a higher crotch, settled his back comfortably, and went to sleep.

After three or four hours he waked and counted the Pack. They were all there, silent, husky, and dry, with eyes of steel. The sun was beginning to sink. In half an hour the Little People of the Rocks would be ending their labours, and, as you know, the dhole does not fight best in the twilight.

'I did not need such faithful watchers,' he said politely, standing up on a branch, 'but I will remember this. Ye be true dholes, but to my thinking over much of one kind. For that reason I do not give the big lizard-eater his tail again. Art thou not pleased, Red Dog?'

'I myself will tear out thy stomach!' yelled the leader, scratching at the foot of the tree.

'Nay, but consider, wise rat of the Dekkan. There will now be many litters of little tailless red dogs, yea, with raw red stumps that sting when the sand is hot. Go home, Red Dog, and cry that an ape has done this. Ye will not go? Come, then, with me, and I will make you very wise!'

He moved, *Bandar-log* fashion, into the next tree, and so on into the next and the next, the Pack following with lifted hungry heads. Now and then he would pretend to fall, and the Pack would tumble one over the other in their haste to be at the death. It was a curious sight—the boy with the knife that shone in the low sunlight as it sifted through the upper branches, and the silent Pack with their red coats all aflame, huddling and following below. When he came to the last tree he took the garlic and rubbed himself all over carefully, and the dholes yelled with scorn. 'Ape with a wolf's tongue, dost thou think to cover thy scent?' they said. 'We follow to the death.'

'Take thy tail,' said Mowgli, flinging it back along the course he had taken. The Pack instinctively rushed after it. 'And follow now—to the death.'

He had slipped down the tree-trunk, and headed like the wind in bare feet for the Bee Rocks, before the dholes saw what he would do.

They gave one deep howl, and settled down to the long, lobbing canter that can at the last run down anything that runs. Mowgli knew their pack-pace to be much slower than that of the wolves, or he would never have risked a two-mile run in full sight. They were sure that the boy was theirs at last, and he was sure that he held them to play with as he pleased. All his trouble was to keep them sufficiently hot behind him to prevent their turning off too soon. He ran cleanly, evenly, and springily; the tailless leader not five yards behind him; and the Pack tailing out over perhaps a quarter of a mile of ground, crazy and blind with the rage of slaughter. So he kept his distance by ear, reserving his last effort for the rush across the Bee Rocks.

The Little People had gone to sleep in the early twilight, for it was not the season of late blossoming flowers; but as Mowgli's first foot-falls rang hollow on the hollow ground he heard a sound as though all the earth were humming. Then he ran as he had never run in his life before, spurned aside one—two—three of the piles of stones into the dark, sweet-smelling gullies; heard a roar like the roar of the sea in a cave; saw with the tail of his eye the air grow dark behind him; saw the current of the Waingunga far below, and a flat, diamond-shaped head in the water; leaped outward with all his strength, the tailless dhole snapping at his shoulder in mid-air, and dropped feet first to the safety of the river, breathless and triumphant. There was not a sting upon him, for the smell of the garlic had checked the Little People for just the few seconds that he was among them. When he rose Kaa's coils were steadying him and things were bounding over the edge of the cliff—great lumps, it seemed, of clustered bees falling like plummets; but before any lump touched water the bees flew upward and the body of a dhole whirled down-stream. Overhead they could hear furious short yells that were drowned in a roar like breakers—the roar of the wings of the Little People of the Rocks. Some of the dholes, too, had fallen into the gullies that communicated with the underground caves, and there choked and fought and snapped among the tumbled honeycombs, and at last, borne up, even when they were dead, on the heaving waves of bees beneath them, shot out of some hole in the river-face, to roll over on the black rubbish-heaps. There were dholes who had leaped short into the trees on the cliffs, and the bees blotted out their shapes; but the greater number of them, maddened by the stings, had flung themselves into the river; and, as Kaa said, the Waingunga was hungry water.

Kaa held Mowgli fast till the boy had recovered his breath.

'We may not stay here,' he said. 'The Little People are roused indeed. Come!'

Swimming low and diving as often as he could, Mowgli went down the river, knife in hand.

'Slowly, slowly,' said Kaa. 'One tooth does not kill a hundred unless it be a cobra's, and many of the dholes took water swiftly when they saw the Little People rise.'

'The more work for my knife, then. *Phai!* How the Little People follow!' Mowgli sank again. The face of the water was blanketed with wild bees, buzzing sullenly and stinging all they found.

'Nothing was ever yet lost by silence,' said Kaa—no sting could penetrate his scales— 'and thou hast all the long night for the hunting. Hear them howl!'

Nearly half the pack had seen the trap their fellows rushed into, and turning sharp aside had flung themselves into the water where the gorge broke down in steep banks. Their cries of rage and their threats against the 'tree-ape' who had brought them to their shame mixed with the yells and growls of those who had been punished by the Little People. To remain ashore was death, and every dhole knew it. Their pack was swept along the current, down to the deep eddies of the Peace Pool, but even there the angry Little People followed and forced them to the water again. Mowgli could hear the voice of the tailless leader bidding his people hold on and kill out every wolf in Seeonee. But he did not waste his time in listening.

'One kills in the dark behind us!' snapped a dhole. 'Here is tainted water!'

Mowgli had dived forward like an otter, twitched a struggling dhole under water before he could open his mouth, and dark rings rose as the body plopped up, turning on its side. The dholes tried to turn, but the current prevented them, and the Little People darted at the heads and ears, and they could hear the challenge of the Seeonee Pack growing louder and deeper in the gathering darkness. Again Mowgli dived, and again a dhole went under, and rose dead, and again the clamour broke out at the rear of the pack; some howling that it was best to go ashore, others calling on their leader to lead them back to the Dekkan, and others bidding Mowgli show himself and be killed.

'They come to the fight with two stomachs and several voices,' said Kaa. 'The rest is with thy brethren below yonder. The Little People go back to sleep. They have chased us far. Now I, too, turn back, for I am not of one skin with any wolf. Good hunting, Little Brother, and remember the dhole bites low.'

A wolf came running along the bank on three legs, leaping up and down, laying his head sideways close to the ground, hunching his back, and breaking high into the air, as though he were playing with his cubs.

It was Won-tolla, the Outlier, and he said never a word, but continued his horrible sport beside the dholes. They had been long in the water now, and were swimming wearily, their coats drenched and heavy, their bushy tails dragging like sponges, so tired and shaken that they, too, were silent, watching the pair of blazing eyes that moved abreast.

'This is no good hunting,' said one, panting.

'Good hunting!' said Mowgli, as he rose boldly at the brute's side, and sent the long knife home behind the shoulder, pushing hard to avoid his dying snap.

'Art thou there, Man-cub?' said Won-tolla across the water.

'Ask of the dead, Outlier,' Mowgli replied. 'Have none come down-stream? I have filled these dogs' mouths with dirt; I have tricked them in the broad daylight, and their leader lacks his tail, but here be some few for thee still. Whither shall I drive them?'

'I will wait,' said Won-tolla. 'The night is before me.'

Nearer and nearer came the bay of the Seeonee wolves. 'For the Pack, for the Full Pack it is met!' and a bend in the river drove the dholes forward among the sands and shoals opposite the Lairs.

Then they saw their mistake. They should have landed half a mile higher up, and rushed the wolves on dry ground. Now it was too late. The bank was lined with burning eyes, and except for the horrible *pheeal* that had never stopped since sundown, there was no sound in the Jungle. It seemed as though Won-tolla were fawning on them to come ashore; and 'Turn and take hold!' said the leader of the dholes. The entire Pack flung themselves at the shore, threshing and squattering through the shoal water, till the face of the Waingunga was all white and torn, and the great ripples went from side to side, like bow-waves from a boat. Mowgli followed the rush, stabbing and slicing as the dholes, huddled together, rushed up the river-beach in one wave.

Then the long fight began, heaving and straining and splitting and scattering and narrowing and broadening along the red, wet sands, and over and between the tangled tree-roots, and through and among the bushes, and in and out of the grass clumps; for even now the dholes were two to one. But they met wolves fighting for all that made the Pack, and not only the short, high, deep-chested, white-tusked hunters of the Pack, but the anxious-eyed lahinis—the she-wolves of the lair, as the saying is—fighting for their litters, with here and there a yearling wolf, his first coat still half woolly, tugging and grappling by their sides. A wolf, you must know, flies at the throat or snaps at the flank, while a dhole, by preference, bites at the belly; so when the dholes were struggling out of the water and had to raise their heads, the odds were with the wolves. On dry land the wolves suffered; but in the water or ashore, Mowgli's knife came and went without ceasing. The Four had worried their way to his side. Gray Brother, crouched between the boy's knees, was protecting his stomach, while the others guarded his back and either side, or stood over him when the shock of a leaping, yelling dhole who had thrown himself full on the steady blade bore him down. For the rest, it was one tangled confusion—a locked and swaying mob that moved from right to left and from left to right along the bank; and also ground round and round slowly on its own centre. Here would be a heaving mound, like a water-blister in a whirlpool, which would break like a water-blister, and throw up four or five mangled dogs, each striving to get back to the centre; here would be a single wolf borne down by two or three dholes, laboriously dragging them forward, and sinking the while; here a yearling cub would be held up by the pressure round him, though he had been killed early, while his mother, crazed with dumb rage, rolled over and over, snapping, and passing on; and in the middle of the thickest press, perhaps, one wolf and one dhole, forgetting everything else, would be manoeuvring for first hold till they were whirled away by a rush of furious fighters. Once Mowgli passed Akela, a dhole on either flank, and his all but toothless jaws closed over the loins of a third; and once he saw Phao, his teeth set in the throat of a dhole, tugging the unwilling beast forward till the yearlings could finish him. But the bulk of the fight was blind flurry and smother in the dark; hit, trip, and tumble, yelp, groan, and worry-worry-worry, round him and behind him and above him. As the night wore on, the quick, giddy-go-round motion increased. The dholes were cowed and afraid to attack the stronger wolves, but did not yet dare to run away. Mowgli felt that the end was coming soon, and contented himself with striking merely to cripple. The yearlings were growing bolder; there was time now and again to breathe, and pass a word to a friend, and the mere flicker of the knife would sometimes turn a dog aside.

'The meat is very near the bone,' Gray Brother yelled. He was bleeding from a score of flesh-wounds.

'But the bone is yet to be cracked,' said Mowgli. '*Eowawa! Thus* do we do in the Jungle!' The red blade ran like a flame along the side of a dhole whose hind-quarters were hidden by the weight of a clinging wolf.

'My kill!' snorted the wolf through his wrinkled nostrils. 'Leave him to me.'

'Is thy stomach still empty, Outlier?' said Mowgli. Won-tolla was fearfully punished, but his grip had paralysed the dhole, who could not turn round and reach him.

'By the Bull that bought me,' said Mowgli, with a bitter laugh, 'it is the tailless one!' And indeed it was the big bay-coloured leader.

'It is not wise to kill cubs and lahinis,' Mowgli went on philosophically, wiping the blood out of his eyes, 'unless one has also killed the Outlier; and it is in my stomach that this Won-tolla kills thee.'

A dhole leaped to his leader's aid; but before his teeth had found Won-tolla's flank, Mowgli's knife was in his throat, and Gray Brother took what was left.

'And thus do we do in the Jungle,' said Mowgli.

Won-tolla said not a word, only his jaws were closing and closing on the backbone as his life ebbed. The dhole shuddered, his head dropped, and he lay still, and Won-tolla dropped above him.

'*Huh!* The Blood Debt is paid,' said Mowgli. 'Sing the song, Won-tolla.'

'He hunts no more,' said Gray Brother; 'and Akela, too, is silent this long time.'

'The bone is cracked!' thundered Phao, son of Phaona. 'They go! Kill, kill out, O hunters of the Free People!'

Dhole after dhole was slinking away from those dark and bloody sands to the river, to the thick Jungle, up-stream or down-stream as he saw the road clear.

'The debt! The debt!' shouted Mowgli. 'Pay the debt! They have slain the Lone Wolf! Let not a dog go!'

He was flying to the river, knife in hand, to check any dhole who dared to take water, when, from under a mound of nine dead, rose Akela's head and fore-quarters, and Mowgli dropped on his knees beside the Lone Wolf.

'Said I not it would be my last fight?' Akela gasped. 'It is good hunting. And thou, Little Brother?'

'I live, having killed many.'

'Even so. I die, and I would—I would die by thee, Little Brother.'

Mowgli took the terrible scarred head on his knees, and put his arms round the torn neck.

'It is long since the old days of Shere Khan, and a Man-cub that rolled naked in the dust.'

'Nay, nay, I am a wolf. I am of one skin with the Free People,' Mowgli cried. 'It is no will of mine that I am a man.'

'Thou art a man, Little Brother, wolfling of my watching. Thou art a man, or else the Pack had fled before the dhole. My life I owe to thee, and to-day thou hast saved the Pack even as once I saved thee. Hast thou forgotten? All debts are paid now. Go to thine own people. I tell thee again, eye of my eye, this hunting is ended. Go to thine own people.'

'I will never go. I will hunt alone in the Jungle. I have said it.'

'After the summer come the Rains, and after the Rains comes the spring. Go back before thou art driven.'

'Who will drive me?'

'Mowgli will drive Mowgli. Go back to thy people. Go to Man.'

'When Mowgli drives Mowgli I will go,' Mowgli answered.

'There is no more to say,' said Akela. 'Little Brother, canst thou raise me to my feet? I also was a leader of the Free People.'

Very carefully and gently Mowgli lifted the bodies aside, and raised Akela to his feet, both arms round him, and the Lone Wolf drew a long breath, and began the Death Song that a leader of the Pack should sing when he dies. It gathered strength as he went on, lifting and lifting, and ringing far across the river, till it came to the last 'Good hunting!' and Akela shook himself clear of Mowgli for an instant, and, leaping into the air, fell backward dead upon his last and most terrible kill.

Mowgli sat with his head on his knees, careless of anything else, while the remnant of the flying dholes were being overtaken and run down by the merciless lahinis. Little by little the cries died away, and the wolves returned limping, as their wounds stiffened, to take stock of the losses. Fifteen of the Pack, as well as half a dozen lahinis, lay dead by the river, and of the others not one was unmarked. And Mowgli sat through it all till the cold daybreak, when Phao's wet, red muzzle was dropped in his hand, and Mowgli drew back to show the gaunt body of Akela.

'Good hunting!' said Phao, as though Akela were still alive, and then over his bitten shoulder to the others: 'Howl, dogs! A Wolf has died to-night!'

But of all the Pack of two hundred fighting dholes, whose boast was that all Jungles were their Jungle, and that no living thing could stand before them, not one returned to the Dekkan to carry that word.

The Miracle of Purun Bhagat

The night we felt the earth would move
We stole and plucked him by the hand,
Because we loved him with the love
That knows but cannot understand.

And when the roaring hillside broke,
And all our world fell down in rain,
We saved him, we the Little Folk;
But lo! he does not come again!

Mourn now, we saved him for the sake
Of such poor love as wild ones may.
Mourn ye! Our brother will not wake,
And his own kind drive us away!
Dirge of the Langurs.

THERE was once a man in India who was Prime Minister of one of the semi-independent native States in the north-western part of the country. He was a Brahmin, so high-caste that caste ceased to have any particular meaning for him; and his father had been an important official in the gay-coloured tag-rag and bobtail of an old-fashioned Hindu Court. But as Purun Dass grew up he felt that the old order of things was changing, and that if any one wished to get on in the world he must stand well with the English, and imitate all that the English believed to be good. At the same time a native official must keep his own master's favour. This was a difficult game, but the quiet, close-mouthed young Brahmin, helped by a good English education at a Bombay University, played it coolly, and rose, step by step, to be Prime Minister of the kingdom. That is to say, he held more real power than his master the Maharajah.

When the old king—who was suspicious of the English, their railways and telegraphs—died, Purun Dass stood high with his young successor, who had been tutored by an Englishman; and between them, though he always took care that his master should have the credit, they established schools for little girls, made roads, and started State dispensaries and shows of agricultural implements, and published a yearly blue-book on the 'Moral and Material Progress of the State,' and the Foreign Office and the Government of India were delighted. Very few native States take up English progress altogether, for they will not believe, as Purun Dass showed he did, that what was good for the Englishman must be twice as good for the Asiatic. The Prime Minister became the honoured friend of Viceroys, and Governors, and Lieutenant-Governors, and medical missionaries, and common missionaries, and hard-riding English officers who came to shoot in the State preserves, as well as of whole hosts of tourists who travelled up and down India in the cold weather, showing how things ought to be managed. In his spare time he would endow scholarships for the study of medicine and manufactures on strictly English lines, and write letters to the *Pioneer*, the greatest Indian daily paper, explaining his master's aims and objects.

At last he went to England on a visit, and had to pay enormous sums to the priests when he came back; for even so high-caste a Brahmin as Purun Dass lost caste by crossing the black sea. In London he met and talked with every one worth knowing—men whose names go all over the world—and saw a great deal more than he said. He was given honorary degrees by learned universities, and he made speeches and talked of Hindu social reform to English ladies in evening dress, till all London cried, 'This is the most fascinating man we have ever met at dinner since cloths were first laid.'

When he returned to India there was a blaze of glory, for the Viceroy himself made a special visit to confer upon the Maharajah the Grand Cross of the Star of India—all diamonds and ribbons and enamel; and at the same ceremony, while the cannon boomed, Purun Dass was made a Knight Commander of the Order of the Indian Empire; so that his name stood Sir Purun Dass, K.C.I.E.

That evening, at dinner in the big Viceregal tent, he stood up with the badge and the collar of the Order on his breast, and replying to the toast of his master's health, made a speech few Englishmen could have bettered.

Next month, when the city had returned to its sun-baked quiet, he did a thing no Englishman would have dreamed of doing; for, so far as the world's affairs went, he died. The jewelled order of his knighthood went back to the Indian Government, and a new Prime Minister was appointed to the charge of affairs, and a great game of General Post began in all the subordinate appointments. The priests knew what had happened, and the people guessed; but India is the one place in the world where a man can do as he pleases and nobody asks why; and the fact that Dewan Sir Purun Dass, K.C.I.E., had resigned position, palace, and power, and taken up the begging-bowl and ochre-coloured dress of a Sunnyasi, or holy man, was considered nothing extraordinary. He had been, as the Old Law recommends, twenty years a youth, twenty years a fighter,—though he had never carried a weapon in his life,—and twenty years head of a household. He had used his wealth and his power for what he knew both to be worth; he had taken honour when it came his way; he had seen men and cities far and near, and men and cities had stood up and honoured him. Now he would let those things go, as a man drops the cloak he no longer needs.

Behind him, as he walked through the city gates, an antelope skin and brass-handled crutch under his arm, and a begging-bowl of polished brown *coco-de-mer* in his hand, barefoot, alone, with eyes cast on the ground—behind him they were firing salutes from the bastions in honour of his happy successor. Purun Dass nodded. All that life was ended; and he bore it no more ill-will or good-will than a man bears to a colourless dream of the night. He was a Sunnyasi—a houseless, wandering mendicant, depending on his neighbours for his daily bread; and so long as there is a morsel to divide in India, neither priest nor beggar starves. He had never in his life tasted meat, and very seldom eaten even fish. A five-pound note would have covered his personal expenses for food through any one of the many years in which he had been absolute master of millions of money. Even when he was being lionised in London he had held before him his dream of peace and quiet—the long, white, dusty Indian road, printed all over with bare feet, the incessant, slow-moving traffic, and the sharp-smelling wood smoke curling up under the fig-trees in the twilight, where the wayfarers sit at their evening meal.

When the time came to make that dream true the Prime Minister took the proper steps, and in three days you might more easily have found a bubble in the trough of the long Atlantic seas than Purun Dass among the roving, gathering, separating millions of India.

At night his antelope skin was spread where the darkness overtook him—sometimes in a Sunnyasi monastery by the roadside; sometimes by a mud-pillar shrine of Kala

Pir, where the Jogis, who are another misty division of
holy men, would receive him as they do those who know
what castes and divisions are worth; sometimes on the
outskirts of a little Hindu village, where the children
would steal up with the food their parents had prepared;
and sometimes on the pitch of the bare grazing-grounds,
where the flame of his stick fire waked the drowsy camels.
It was all one to Purun Dass—or Purun Bhagat, as he
called himself now. Earth, people, and food were all one.
But unconsciously his feet drew him away northward
and eastward; from the south to Rohtak; from Rohtak
to Kurnool; from Kurnool to ruined Samanah, and then
up-stream along the dried bed of the Gugger river that
fills only when the rain falls in the hills, till one day he
saw the far line of the great Himalayas.

Then Purun Bhagat smiled, for he remembered that his
mother was of Rajput Brahmin birth, from Kulu way—a
Hill-woman, always home-sick for the snows—and that
the least touch of Hill blood draws a man in the end back
to where he belongs.

'Yonder,' said Purun Bhagat, breasting the lower
slopes of the Sewaliks, where the cacti stand up like
seven-branched candlesticks— 'yonder I shall sit down
and get knowledge'; and the cool wind of the Himalayas
whistled about his ears as he trod the road that led to
Simla.

The last time he had come that way it had been in
state, with a clattering cavalry escort, to visit the gentlest
and most affable of Viceroys; and the two had talked for
an hour together about mutual friends in London, and
what the Indian common folk really thought of things.
This time Purun Bhagat paid no calls, but leaned on the
rail of the Mall, watching that glorious view of the Plains
spread out forty miles below, till a native Mohammedan
policeman told him he was obstructing traffic; and Purun

Bhagat salaamed reverently to the Law, because he knew
the value of it, and was seeking for a Law of his own. Then
he moved on, and slept that night in an empty hut at
Chota Simla, which looks like the very last end of the
earth, but it was only the beginning of his journey.

He followed the Himalaya-Thibet road, the little ten-
foot track that is blasted out of solid rock, or strutted
out on timbers over gulfs a thousand feet deep; that
dips into warm, wet, shut-in valleys, and climbs out
across bare, grassy hill-shoulders where the sun strikes
like a burning-glass; or turns through dripping, dark
forests where the tree-ferns dress the trunks from head
to heel, and the pheasant calls to his mate. And he met
Thibetan herdsmen with their dogs and flocks of sheep,
each sheep with a little bag of borax on his back, and
wandering wood-cutters, and cloaked and blanketed
Lamas from Thibet, coming into India on pilgrimage,
and envoys of little solitary Hill-states, posting furiously
on ring-streaked and piebald ponies, or the cavalcade of a
Rajah paying a visit; or else for a long, clear day he would
see nothing more than a black bear grunting and rooting
below in the valley. When he first started, the roar of the
world he had left still rang in his ears, as the roar of a
tunnel rings long after the train has passed through;
but when he had put the Mutteeanee Pass behind him
that was all done, and Purun Bhagat was alone with
himself, walking, wondering, and thinking, his eyes on
the ground, and his thoughts with the clouds.

One evening he crossed the highest pass he had
met till then—it had been a two-day's climb—and
came out on a line of snow-peaks that banded all the
horizon—mountains from fifteen to twenty thousand feet
high, looking almost near enough to hit with a stone,
though they were fifty or sixty miles away. The pass
was crowned with dense, dark forest—deodar, walnut,

wild cherry, wild olive, and wild pear, but mostly deodar, which is the Himalayan cedar; and under the shadow of the deodars stood a deserted shrine to Kali—who is Durga, who is Sitala, who is sometimes worshipped against the smallpox.

Purun Dass swept the stone floor clean, smiled at the grinning statue, made himself a little mud fireplace at the back of the shrine, spread his antelope skin on a bed of fresh pine-needles, tucked his *bairagi*—his brass-handled crutch—under his armpit, and sat down to rest.

Immediately below him the hillside fell away, clean and cleared for fifteen hundred feet, where a little village of stone-walled houses, with roofs of beaten earth, clung to the steep tilt. All round it the tiny terraced fields lay out like aprons of patchwork on the knees of the mountain, and cows no bigger than beetles grazed between the smooth stone circles of the threshing-floors. Looking across the valley, the eye was deceived by the size of things, and could not at first realise that what seemed to be low scrub, on the opposite mountain-flank, was in truth a forest of hundred-foot pines. Purun Bhagat saw an eagle swoop across the gigantic hollow, but the great bird dwindled to a dot ere it was half-way over. A few bands of scattered clouds strung up and down the valley, catching on a shoulder of the hills, or rising up and dying out when they were level with the head of the pass. And 'Here shall I find peace,' said Purun Bhagat.

Now, a Hill-man makes nothing of a few hundred feet up or down, and as soon as the villagers saw the smoke in the deserted shrine, the village priest climbed up the terraced hillside to welcome the stranger.

When he met Purun Bhagat's eyes—the eyes of a man used to control thousands—he bowed to the earth, took the begging-bowl without a word, and returned to the village, saying, 'We have at last a holy man. Never have I seen such a man. He is of the Plains—but pale-coloured—a Brahmin of the Brahmins.' Then all the housewives of the village said, 'Think you he will stay with us?' and each did her best to cook the most savoury meal for the Bhagat. Hill-food is very simple, but with buckwheat and Indian corn, and rice and red pepper, and little fish out of the stream in the valley, and honey from the flue-like hives built in the stone walls, and dried apricots, and turmeric, and wild ginger, and bannocks of flour, a devout woman can make good things, and it was a full bowl that the priest carried to the Bhagat. Was he going to stay? asked the priest. Would he need a *chela*—a disciple—to beg for him? Had he a blanket against the cold weather? Was the food good?

Purun Bhagat ate, and thanked the giver. It was in his mind to stay. That was sufficient, said the priest. Let the begging-bowl be placed outside the shrine, in the hollow made by those two twisted roots, and daily should the Bhagat be fed; for the village felt honoured that such a man—he looked timidly into the Bhagat's face—should tarry among them.

That day saw the end of Purun Bhagat's wanderings. He had come to the place appointed for him—the silence and the space. After this, time stopped, and he, sitting at the mouth of the shrine, could not tell whether he were alive or dead; a man with control of his limbs, or a part of the hills, and the clouds, and the shifting rain and sunlight. He would repeat a Name softly to himself a hundred hundred times, till, at each repetition, he seemed to move more and more out of his body, sweeping up to the doors of some tremendous discovery; but, just as the door was opening, his body would drag him back, and, with grief, he felt he was locked up again in the flesh and bones of Purun Bhagat.

Every morning the filled begging-bowl was laid silently

in the crutch of the roots outside the shrine. Sometimes the priest brought it; sometimes a Ladakhi trader, lodging in the village, and anxious to get merit, trudged up the path; but, more often, it was the woman who had cooked the meal overnight; and she would murmur, hardly above her breath: 'Speak for me before the gods, Bhagat. Speak for such a one, the wife of so-and-so!' Now and then some bold child would be allowed the honour, and Purun Bhagat would hear him drop the bowl and run as fast as his little legs could carry him, but the Bhagat never came down to the village. It was laid out like a map at his feet. He could see the evening gatherings, held on the circle of the threshing-floors, because that was the only level ground; could see the wonderful unnamed green of the young rice, the indigo blues of the Indian corn, the dock-like patches of buckwheat, and, in its season, the red bloom of the amaranth, whose tiny seeds, being neither grain nor pulse, make a food that can be lawfully eaten by Hindus in time of fasts.

When the year turned, the roofs of the huts were all little squares of purest gold, for it was on the roofs that they laid out their cobs of the corn to dry. Hiving and harvest, rice-sowing and husking, passed before his eyes, all embroidered down there on the many-sided plots of fields, and he thought of them all, and wondered what they all led to at the long last.

Even in populated India a man cannot a day sit still before the wild things run over him as though he were a rock; and in that wilderness very soon the wild things, who knew Kali's Shrine well, came back to look at the intruder. The *langurs*, the big gray-whiskered monkeys of the Himalayas, were, naturally, the first, for they are alive with curiosity; and when they had upset the begging-bowl, and rolled it round the floor, and tried their teeth on the brass-handled crutch, and made faces at the antelope skin, they decided that the human being who sat so still was harmless. At evening, they would leap down from the pines, and beg with their hands for things to eat, and then swing off in graceful curves. They liked the warmth of the fire, too, and huddled round it till Purun Bhagat had to push them aside to throw on more fuel; and in the morning, as often as not, he would find a furry ape sharing his blanket. All day long, one or other of the tribe would sit by his side, staring out at the snows, crooning and looking unspeakably wise and sorrowful.

After the monkeys came the *barasingh*, that big deer which is like our red deer, but stronger. He wished to rub off the velvet of his horns against the cold stones of Kali's statue, and stamped his feet when he saw the man at the shrine. But Purun Bhagat never moved, and, little by little, the royal stag edged up and nuzzled his shoulder. Purun Bhagat slid one cool hand along the hot antlers, and the touch soothed the fretted beast, who bowed his head, and Purun Bhagat very softly rubbed and ravelled off the velvet. Afterward, the *barasingh* brought his doe and fawn—gentle things that mumbled on the holy man's blanket—or would come alone at night, his eyes green in the fire-flicker, to take his share of fresh walnuts. At last, the musk-deer, the shyest and almost the smallest of the deerlets, came, too, her big rabbity ears erect; even brindled, silent *mushick-nabha* must needs find out what the light in the shrine meant, and drop out her moose-like nose into Purun Bhagat's lap, coming and going with the shadows of the fire. Purun Bhagat called them all 'my brothers,' and his low call of *'Bhai! Bhai!'* would draw them from the forest at noon if they were within earshot. The Himalayan black bear, moody and suspicious—Sona, who has the V-shaped white mark under his chin—passed that way more than once; and since the Bhagat showed no fear, Sona showed no anger, but watched him, and came closer, and begged a share of the caresses, and a dole of bread or wild berries. Often, in the still dawns, when the Bhagat would climb to the very crest of the pass to watch the red day walking along the peaks of the snows, he would find Sona shuffling and grunting at his heels, thrusting a curious fore-paw under fallen trunks, and bringing it away with a *whoof* of impatience; or his early steps would wake Sona where he lay curled up, and the great brute, rising erect, would think to fight, till he heard the Bhagat's voice and knew his best friend.

Nearly all hermits and holy men who live apart from the big cities have the reputation of being able to work miracles with the wild things, but all the miracle lies in keeping still, in never making a hasty movement, and, for a long time, at least, in never looking directly at a visitor. The villagers saw the outline of the *barasingh* stalking like a shadow through the dark forest behind the shrine; saw the *minaul*, the Himalayan pheasant, blazing in her best colours before Kali's statue; and the *langurs* on their haunches, inside, playing with the walnut shells. Some of the children, too, had heard Sona singing to himself, bear-fashion, behind the fallen rocks, and the Bhagat's reputation as miracle-worker stood firm.

Yet nothing was farther from his mind than miracles. He believed that all things were one big Miracle, and when a man knows that much he knows something to go upon. He knew for a certainty that there was nothing great and nothing little in this world: and day and night he strove to think out his way into the heart of things, back to the place whence his soul had come.

So thinking, his untrimmed hair fell down about his shoulders, the stone slab at the side of the antelope skin was dented into a little hole by the foot of his brass-handled crutch, and the place between the tree-trunks, where the begging-bowl rested day after day, sunk and wore into a hollow almost as smooth as the brown shell itself; and each beast knew his exact place at the fire. The fields changed their colours with the seasons; the threshing-floors filled and emptied, and filled again and again; and again and again, when winter came, the *langurs* frisked among the branches feathered with light snow, till the mother-monkeys brought their sad-eyed little babies up from the warmer valleys with the spring. There were few changes in the village. The priest was older, and many of the little children who used to come with the begging-dish sent their own children now; and when you asked of the villagers how long their holy man had lived in Kali's Shrine at the head of the pass, they answered, 'Always.'

Then came such summer rains as had not been known in the Hills for many seasons. Through three good months the valley was wrapped in cloud and soaking mist—steady, unrelenting downfall, breaking off into thunder-shower after thunder-shower. Kali's Shrine stood above the clouds, for the most part, and there was a whole month in which the Bhagat never caught a glimpse of his village. It was packed away under a white floor of cloud that swayed and shifted and rolled on itself and bulged upward, but never broke from its piers—the streaming flanks of the valley.

All that time he heard nothing but the sound of a million little waters, overhead from the trees, and underfoot along the ground, soaking through the pine-needles, dripping from the tongues of draggled fern, and spouting in newly-torn muddy channels down the slopes. Then the sun came out, and drew forth the good incense of the deodars and the rhododendrons, and that far-off, clean smell which the Hill people call 'the smell of the snows.' The hot sunshine lasted for a week, and then the rains gathered together for their last downpour, and the water fell in sheets that flayed off the skin of the ground and leaped back in mud. Purun Bhagat heaped his fire high that night, for he was sure his brothers would need warmth; but never a beast came to the shrine, though he called and called till he dropped asleep, wondering what had happened in the woods.

It was in the black heart of the night, the rain drumming like a thousand drums, that he was roused by a plucking at his blanket, and, stretching out, felt the little hand of a *langur*. 'It is better here than in the trees,' he said sleepily, loosening a fold of blanket; 'take it and be warm.' The monkey caught his hand and pulled hard. 'Is it food, then?' said Purun Bhagat. 'Wait awhile, and I will prepare some.' As he kneeled to throw fuel on the fire the *langur* ran to the door of the shrine, crooned and ran back again, plucking at the man's knee.

'What is it? What is thy trouble, Brother?' said Purun Bhagat, for the *langur*'s eyes were full of things that he could not tell. 'Unless one of thy caste be in a trap—and none set traps here—I will not go into that weather. Look, Brother, even the *barasingh* comes for shelter!'

The deer's antlers clashed as he strode into the shrine, clashed against the grinning statue of Kali. He lowered them in Purun Bhagat's direction and stamped uneasily, hissing through his half-shut nostrils.

'Hai! Hai! Hai!' said the Bhagat, snapping his fingers, 'Is *this* payment for a night's lodging?' But the deer pushed him toward the door, and as he did so Purun Bhagat heard the sound of something opening with a sigh, and saw two slabs of the floor draw away from each other, while the sticky earth below smacked its lips.

'Now I see,' said Purun Bhagat. 'No blame to my brothers that they did not sit by the fire to-night. The mountain is falling. And yet—why should I go?' His eye fell on the empty begging-bowl, and his face changed. 'They have given me good food daily since—since I came, and, if I am not swift, to-morrow there will not be one mouth in the valley. Indeed, I must go and warn them below. Back there, Brother! Let me get to the fire.'

The *barasingh* backed unwillingly as Purun Bhagat drove a pine torch deep into the flame, twirling it till it was well lit. 'Ah! ye came to warn me,' he said, rising. 'Better than that we shall do; better than that. Out, now, and lend me thy neck, Brother, for I have but two feet.'

He clutched the bristling withers of the *barasingh* with his right hand, held the torch away with his left, and stepped out of the shrine into the desperate night. There was no breath of wind, but the rain nearly drowned the flare as the great deer hurried down the slope, sliding on his haunches. As soon as they were clear of the forest more of the Bhagat's brothers joined them. He heard, though he could not see, the *langurs* pressing about him, and behind them the *uhh! uhh!* of Sona. The rain matted his long white hair into ropes; the water splashed beneath his bare feet, and his yellow robe clung to his frail old body, but he stepped down steadily, leaning against the *barasingh*. He was no longer a holy man, but Sir Purun Dass, K.C.I.E., Prime Minister of no small State, a man accustomed to command, going out to save life. Down the steep, plashy path they poured all together, the Bhagat and his brothers, down and down till the deer's feet clicked and stumbled on the wall of a threshing-floor, and he snorted because he smelt Man. Now they were at the head of the one crooked village street, and the Bhagat beat with his crutch on the barred windows of the blacksmith's house, as his torch blazed up in the shelter of the eaves. 'Up and out!' cried Purun Bhagat; and he did not know his own voice, for it was years since he had spoken aloud to a man. 'The hill falls! The hill is falling! Up and out, oh, you within!'

'It is our Bhagat,' said the blacksmith's wife. 'He stands among his beasts. Gather the little ones and give the call.'

It ran from house to house, while the beasts, cramped in the narrow way, surged and huddled round the Bhagat, and Sona puffed impatiently.

The people hurried into the street—they were no more than seventy souls all told—and in the glare of the torches they saw their Bhagat holding back the terrified *barasingh*, while the monkeys plucked piteously at his skirts, and Sona sat on his haunches and roared.

'Across the valley and up the next hill!' shouted Purun Bhagat. 'Leave none behind! We follow!'

Then the people ran as only Hill folk can run, for they knew that in a landslip you must climb for the highest ground across the valley. They fled, splashing through the little river at the bottom, and panted up the terraced fields on the far side, while the Bhagat and his brethren followed. Up and up the opposite mountain they climbed, calling to each other by name—the roll-call of the village—and at their heels toiled the big *barasingh*, weighted by the failing strength of Purun Bhagat. At last the deer stopped in the shadow of a deep pine-wood, five hundred feet up the hillside. His instinct, that had warned him of the coming slide, told him he would be safe here.

Purun Bhagat dropped fainting by his side, for the chill of the rain and that fierce climb were killing him; but first he called to the scattered torches ahead, 'Stay and count your numbers'; then, whispering to the deer as he saw the lights gather in a cluster: 'Stay with me, Brother. Stay—till—I—go!'

There was a sigh in the air that grew to a mutter, and a mutter that grew to a roar, and a roar that passed all sense of hearing, and the hillside on which the villagers stood was hit in the darkness, and rocked to the blow. Then a note as steady, deep, and true as the deep C of the organ drowned everything for perhaps five minutes, while the very roots of the pines quivered to it. It died away, and the sound of the rain falling on miles of hard ground and grass changed to the muffled drum of water on soft earth. That told its own tale.

Never a villager—not even the priest—was bold enough to speak to the Bhagat who had saved their lives. They crouched under the pines and waited till the day. When it came they looked across the valley and saw that what had been forest, and terraced field, and track-threaded grazing-ground was one raw, red, fan-shaped smear, with a few trees flung head-down on the scarp. That red ran high up the hill of their refuge, damming back the little river, which had begun to spread into a brick-coloured lake. Of the village, of the road to the shrine, of the shrine itself, and the forest behind, there was no trace. For one mile in width and two thousand feet in sheer depth the mountain-side had come away bodily, planed clean from head to heel.

And the villagers, one by one, crept through the wood to pray before their Bhagat. They saw the *barasingh* standing over him, who fled when they came near, and they heard the *langurs* wailing in the branches, and Sona moaning up the hill; but their Bhagat was dead, sitting cross-legged, his back against a tree, his crutch under his armpit, and his face turned to the north-east.

The priest said: 'Behold a miracle after a miracle, for in this very attitude must all Sunnyasis be buried! Therefore where he now is we will build the temple to our holy man.'

They built the temple before a year was ended—a little stone-and-earth shrine—and they called the hill the Bhagat's hill, and they worship there with lights and flowers and offerings to this day. But they do not know that the saint of their worship is the late Sir Purun Dass, K.C.I.E., D.C.L., Ph.D., etc., once Prime Minister of the progressive and enlightened State of Mohiniwala, and honorary or corresponding member of more learned and scientific societies than will ever do any good in this world or the next.

In the Rukh

The Only Son lay down again and dreamed that he dreamed a dream.
The last ash dropped from the dying fire with the click of a falling spark,
And the Only Son woke up again and called across the dark:—
'Now, was I born of womankind and laid in a mother's breast?
For I have dreamed of a shaggy hide whereon I went to rest.
And was I born of womankind and laid on a father's arm?
For I have dreamed of long white teeth that guarded me from harm.
Oh, was I born of womankind and did I play alone?
For I have dreamed of playmates twain that bit me to the bone.
And did I break the barley bread and steep it in the tyre?
For I have dreamed of a youngling kid new riven from the byre.
An hour it lacks and an hour it lacks to the rising of the moon—
But I can see the black roof-beams as plain as it were noon!
'Tis a league and a league to the Lena Falls where the trooping sambhur go,
But I can hear the little fawn that bleats behind the doe!
'Tis a league and a league to the Lena Falls where the crop and the
  upland meet,
But I can smell the warm wet wind that whispers through the wheat!'
                                          The Only Son.

OF the wheels of public service that turn under the
Indian Government, there is none more important than
the Department of Woods and Forests. The reboisement
of all India is in its hands; or will be when Government
has the money to spend. Its servants wrestle with
wandering sand-torrents and shifting dunes: wattling
them at the sides, damming them in front, and pegging
them down atop with coarse grass and spindling pine
after the rules of Nancy. They are responsible for all
the timber in the State forests of the Himalayas, as well
as for the denuded hillsides that the monsoons wash into
dry gullies and aching ravines; each cut a mouth crying
aloud what carelessness can do. They experiment with

battalions of foreign trees, and coax the blue gum to take root and, perhaps, dry up the Canal fever. In the plains the chief part of their duty is to see that the belt fire-lines in the forest reserves are kept clean, so that when drought comes and the cattle starve, they may throw the reserve open to the villager's herds and allow the man himself to gather sticks. They poll and lop for the stacked railway-fuel along the lines that burn no coal; they calculate the profit of their plantations to five points of decimals; they are the doctors and midwives of the huge teak forests of Upper Burma, the rubber of the Eastern Jungles, and the gall-nuts of the South; and they are always hampered by lack of funds. But since a Forest Officer's business takes him far from the beaten roads and the regular stations, he learns to grow wise in more than wood-lore alone; to know the people and the polity of the jungle; meeting tiger, bear, leopard, wild-dog, and all the deer, not once or twice after days of beating, but again and again in the execution of his duty. He spends much time in saddle or under canvas—the friend of newly-planted trees, the associate of uncouth rangers and hairy trackers—till the woods, that show his care, in turn set their mark upon him, and he ceases to sing the naughty French songs he learned at Nancy, and grows silent with the silent things of the underbrush.

Gisborne of the Woods and Forests had spent four years in the Service. At first he loved it without comprehension, because it led him into the open on horseback and gave him authority. Then he hated it furiously, and would have given a year's pay for one month of such society as India affords. That crisis over, the forests took him back again, and he was content to serve them, to deepen and widen his fire-lines, to watch the green mist of his new plantation against the older foliage, to dredge out the choked stream, and to follow and strengthen the last struggle of the forest where it broke down and died among the long pig-grass. On some still day that grass would be burned off, and a hundred beasts that had their homes there would rush out before the pale flames at high noon. Later, the forest would creep forward over the blackened ground in orderly lines of saplings, and Gisborne, watching, would be well pleased. His bungalow, a thatched white-walled cottage of two rooms, was set at one end of the great *rukh* and overlooking it. He made no pretence at keeping a garden, for the *rukh* swept up to his door, curled over in a thicket of bamboo, and he rode from his verandah into its heart without the need of any carriage-drive.

Abdul Gafur, his fat Mohammedan butler, fed him when he was at home, and spent the rest of the time gossiping with the little band of native servants whose huts lay behind the bungalow. There were two grooms, a cook, a water-carrier, and a sweeper, and that was all. Gisborne cleaned his own guns and kept no dog. Dogs scared the game, and it pleased the man to be able to say where the subjects of his kingdom would drink at moonrise, eat before dawn, and lie up in the day's heat. The rangers and forest-guards lived in little huts far away in the *rukh*, only appearing when one of them had been injured by a falling tree or a wild beast. Thus Gisborne was alone.

In spring the *rukh* put out few new leaves, but lay dry and still untouched by the finger of the year, waiting for rain. Only there was then more calling and roaring in the dark on a quiet night; the tumult of a battle-royal among the tigers, the bellowing of arrogant buck, or the steady wood-chopping of an old boar sharpening his tushes against a bole. Then Gisborne laid aside his little-used gun altogether, for it was to him a sin to kill. In summer, through the furious May heats, the *rukh* reeled in the

haze, and Gisborne watched for the first sign of curling
smoke that should betray a forest fire. Then came the
Rains with a roar, and the *rukh* was blotted out in fetch
after fetch of warm mist, and the broad leaves drummed
the night through under the big drops; and there was a
noise of running water, and of juicy green stuff crackling
where the wind struck it, and the lightning wove patterns
behind the dense matting of the foliage, till the sun
broke loose again and the *rukh* stood with hot flanks
smoking to the newly-washed sky. Then the heat and
the dry cold subdued everything to tiger-colour again.
So Gisborne learned to know his *rukh* and was very
happy. His pay came month by month, but he had very
little need for money. The currency notes accumulated
in the drawer where he kept his home-letters and the
recapping-machine. If he drew anything, it was to make
a purchase from the Calcutta Botanical Gardens, or to
pay a ranger's widow a sum that the Government of
India would never have sanctioned for her man's death.

Payment was good, but vengeance was also necessary,
and he took that when he could. One night of many nights
a runner, breathless and gasping, came to him with the
news that a forest-guard lay dead by the Kanye stream,
the side of his head smashed in as though it had been
an egg-shell. Gisborne went out at dawn to look for the
murderer. It is only travellers and now and then young
soldiers who are known to the world as great hunters.
The Forest Officers take their *shikar* as part of the day's
work, and no one hears of it. Gisborne went on foot to the
place of the kill: the widow was wailing over the corpse as
it lay on a bedstead, while two or three men were looking
at footprints on the moist ground. 'That is the Red One,'
said a man. 'I knew he would turn to man in time, but
surely there is game enough even for him. This must
have been done for devilry.'

'The Red One lies up in the rocks at the back of the *sal* trees,' said Gisborne. He knew the tiger under suspicion.

'Not now, Sahib, not now. He will be raging and ranging to and fro. Remember that the first kill is a triple kill always. Our blood makes them mad. He may be behind us even as we speak.'

'He may have gone to the next hut,' said another. 'It is only four *koss*. Wallah, who is this?'

Gisborne turned with the others. A man was walking down the dried bed of the stream, naked except for the loin-cloth, but crowned with a wreath of the tasselled blossoms of the white convolvulus creeper. So noiselessly did he move over the little pebbles, that even Gisborne, used to the soft-footedness of trackers, started.

'The tiger that killed,' he began, without any salute, 'has gone to drink, and now he is asleep under a rock beyond that hill.' His voice was clear and bell-like, utterly different from the usual whine of the native, and his face as he lifted it in the sunshine might have been that of an angel strayed among the woods. The widow ceased wailing above the corpse and looked round-eyed at the stranger, returning to her duty with double strength.

'Shall I show the Sahib?' he said simply.

'If thou art sure—' Gisborne began.

'Sure indeed. I saw him only an hour ago—the dog. It is before his time to eat man's flesh. He has yet a dozen sound teeth in his evil head.'

The men kneeling above the footprints slunk off quietly, for fear that Gisborne should ask them to go with him, and the young man laughed a little to himself.

'Come, Sahib,' he cried, and turned on his heel, walking before his companion.

'Not so fast. I cannot keep that pace,' said the white man. 'Halt there. Thy face is new to me.'

'That may be. I am but newly come into this forest.'

'From what village?'

'I am without a village. I came from over there.' He flung out his arm towards the north.

'A gipsy then?'

'No, Sahib. I am a man without caste, and for matter of that without a father.'

'What do men call thee?'

'Mowgli, Sahib. And what is the Sahib's name?'

'I am the warden of this *rukh*—Gisborne is my name.'

'How? Do they number the trees and the blades of grass here?'

'Even so; lest such gipsy fellows as thou set them afire.'

'I! I would not hurt the jungle for any gift. That is my home.'

He turned to Gisborne with a smile that was irresistible, and held up a warning hand.

'Now, Sahib, we must go a little quietly. There is no need to wake the dog, though he sleeps heavily enough. Perhaps it were better if I went forward alone and drove him down wind to the Sahib.'

'Allah! Since when have tigers been driven to and fro like cattle by naked men?' said Gisborne, aghast at the man's audacity.

He laughed again softly. 'Nay, then, come along with me and shoot him in thy own way with the big English rifle.'

Gisborne stepped in his guide's track, twisted, crawled, and clomb and stooped and suffered through all the many agonies of a jungle-stalk. He was purple and dripping with sweat when Mowgli at the last bade him raise his head and peer over a blue baked rock near a tiny hill pool. By the waterside lay the tiger extended and at ease, lazily licking clean again an enormous elbow and fore-paw. He was old, yellow-toothed, and not a little mangy, but in that setting and sunshine, imposing enough.

Gisborne had no false ideas of sport where the man-eater was concerned. This thing was vermin, to be killed as speedily as possible. He waited to recover his breath, rested the rifle on the rock and whistled. The brute's head turned slowly not twenty feet from the rifle-mouth, and Gisborne planted his shots, business-like, one behind the shoulder and the other a little below the eye. At that range the heavy bones were no guard against the rending bullets.

'Well, the skin was not worth keeping at any rate,' said he, as the smoke cleared away and the beast lay kicking and gasping in the last agony.

'A dog's death for a dog,' said Mowgli quietly. 'Indeed there is nothing in that carrion worth taking away.'

'The whiskers. Dost thou not take the whiskers?' said Gisborne, who knew how the rangers valued such things.

'I? Am I a lousy *shikarri* of the jungle to paddle with a tiger's muzzle? Let him lie. Here come his friends already.'

A dropping kite whistled shrilly overhead, as Gisborne snapped out the empty shells, and wiped his face.

'And if thou art not a *shikarri*, where didst thou learn thy knowledge of the tiger-folk?' said he. 'No tracker could have done better.'

'I hate all tigers,' said Mowgli curtly. 'Let the Sahib give me his gun to carry. Arré, it is a very fine one. And where does the Sahib go now?'

'To my house.'

'May I come? I have never yet looked within a white man's house.'

Gisborne returned to his bungalow, Mowgli striding noiselessly before him, his brown skin glistening in the sunlight.

He stared curiously at the verandah and the two chairs there, fingered the split bamboo shade curtains with suspicion, and entered, looking always behind him. Gisborne loosed a curtain to keep out the sun. It dropped with a clatter, but almost before it touched the flagging of the verandah Mowgli had leaped clear, and was standing with heaving chest in the open.

'It is a trap,' he said quickly.

Gisborne laughed. 'White men do not trap men. Indeed thou art altogether of the jungle.'

'I see,' said Mowgli, 'it has neither catch nor fall. I—I never beheld these things till to-day.'

He came in on tiptoe and stared with large eyes at the furniture of the two rooms. Abdul Gafur, who was laying lunch, looked at him with deep disgust.

'So much trouble to eat, and so much trouble to lie down after you have eaten!' said Mowgli with a grin. 'We do better in the jungle. It is very wonderful. There are very many rich things here. Is the Sahib not afraid that he may be robbed? I have never seen such wonderful things.' He was staring at a dusty Benares brass plate on a rickety bracket.

'Only a thief from the jungle would rob here,' said Abdul Gafur, setting down a plate with a clatter. Mowgli opened his eyes wide and stared at the white-bearded Mohammedan.

'In my country when goats bleat very loud we cut their throats,' he returned cheerfully. 'But have no fear, thou. I am going.'

He turned and disappeared into the *rukh*. Gisborne looked after him with a laugh that ended in a little sigh. There was not much outside his regular work to interest the Forest Officer, and this son of the forest, who seemed to know tigers as other people know dogs, would have been a diversion.

'He's a most wonderful chap,' thought Gisborne; 'he's like the illustrations in the Classical Dictionary. I wish I could have made him a gun-boy. There's no fun in shikarring alone, and this fellow would have been a perfect *shikarri*. I wonder what in the world he is.'

That evening he sat on the verandah under the stars, smoking as he wondered. A puff of smoke curled from the pipe-bowl. As it cleared he was aware of Mowgli sitting with arms crossed on the verandah edge. A ghost could not have drifted up more noiselessly. Gisborne started and let the pipe drop.

'There is no man to talk to out there in the *rukh*,' said Mowgli; 'I came here, therefore.' He picked up the pipe and returned it to Gisborne.

'Oh,' said Gisborne, and after a long pause, 'What news is there in the *rukh*? Hast thou found another tiger?'

'The nilghai are changing their feeding-ground against the new moon, as is their custom. The pig are feeding near the Kanye river now, because they will not feed with the nilghai, and one of their sows has been killed by a leopard in the long grass at the water-head. I do not know any more.'

'And how didst thou know all these things?' said Gisborne, leaning forward and looking at the eyes that glittered in the starlight.

'How should I not know? The nilghai has his custom and his use, and a child knows that pig will not feed with him.'

'I do not know this,' said Gisborne.

'Tck! Tck! And thou art in charge—so the men of the huts tell me—in charge of all this *rukh*.' He laughed to himself.

'It is well enough to talk and to tell child's tales,' Gisborne retorted, nettled at the chuckle. 'To say that this and that goes on in the *rukh*. No man can deny thee.'

'As for the sow's carcase, I will show thee her bones to-morrow,' Mowgli returned, absolutely unmoved. 'Touching the matter of the nilghai, if the Sahib will sit here very still I will drive one nilghai up to this place, and by listening to the sounds carefully, the Sahib can tell whence that nilghai has been driven.'

'Mowgli, the jungle has made thee mad,' said Gisborne. 'Who can drive nilghai?'

'Still—sit still, then. I go.'

'Gad, the man's a ghost!' said Gisborne; for Mowgli had faded out into the darkness and there was no sound of feet. The *rukh* lay out in great velvety folds in the uncertain shimmer of the stardust—so still that the least little wandering wind among the tree-tops came up as the sigh of a child sleeping equably. Abdul Gafur in the cook-house was clicking plates together.

'Be still there!' shouted Gisborne, and composed himself to listen as a man can who is used to the stillness of the *rukh*. It had been his custom, to preserve his self-respect in his isolation, to dress for dinner each night, and the stiff white shirt-front creaked with his regular breathing till he shifted a little sideways. Then the tobacco of a somewhat foul pipe began to purr, and he threw the pipe from him. Now, except for the night-breath in the *rukh*, everything was dumb.

From an inconceivable distance, and drawled through immeasurable darkness, came the faint, faint echo of a wolf's howl. Then silence again for, it seemed, long hours. At last, when his legs below the knees had lost all feeling, Gisborne heard something that might have been a crash far off through the undergrowth. He doubted till it was repeated again and yet again.

'That's from the west,' he muttered; 'there's something on foot there.' The noise increased—crash on

crash, plunge on plunge—with the thick grunting of a
hotly pressed nilghai, flying in panic terror and taking
no heed to his course.

A shadow blundered out from between the tree-trunks,
wheeled back, turned again grunting, and with a clatter
on the bare ground dashed up almost within reach of
his hand. It was a bull nilghai, dripping with dew—his
withers hung with a torn trail of creeper, his eyes shining
in the light from the house. The creature checked at sight
of the man, and fled along the edge of the *rukh* till he
melted in the darkness. The first idea in Gisborne's
bewildered mind was the indecency of thus dragging out
for inspection the big blue bull of the *rukh*—the putting
him through his paces in the night which should have
been his own.

Then said a smooth voice at his ear as he stood staring:

'He came from the water-head where he was leading
the herd. From the west he came. Does the Sahib believe
now, or shall I bring up the herd to be counted? The Sahib
is in charge of this *rukh*.'

Mowgli had reseated himself on the verandah, breathing a little quickly. Gisborne looked at him with open
mouth. 'How was that accomplished?' he said.

'The Sahib saw. The bull was driven—driven as a
buffalo is. Ho! ho! He will have a fine tale to tell when
he returns to the herd.'

'That is a new trick to me. Canst thou run as swiftly
as the nilghai, then?'

'The Sahib has seen. If the Sahib needs more knowledge
at any time of the movings of the game, I, Mowgli, am
here. This is a good *rukh*, and I shall stay.'

'Stay then, and if thou hast need of a meal at any
time my servants shall give thee one.'

'Yes, indeed, I am fond of cooked food,' Mowgli
answered quickly. 'No man may say that I do not eat

boiled and roast as much as any other man. I will come
for that meal. Now, on my part, I promise that the Sahib
shall sleep safely in his house by night, and no thief shall
break in to carry away his so rich treasures.'

The conversation ended itself on Mowgli's abrupt
departure. Gisborne sat long smoking, and the upshot
of his thoughts was that in Mowgli he had found at last
that ideal ranger and forest-guard for whom he and the
Department were always looking.

'I must get him into the Government service somehow. A man who can drive nilghai would know more
about the *rukh* than fifty men. He's a miracle—a *lusus
naturae*—but a forest-guard he must be if he'll only settle
down in one place,' said Gisborne.

Abdul Gafur's opinion was less favourable. He confided
to Gisborne at bedtime that strangers from God-knew-
where were more than likely to be professional thieves,
and that he personally did not approve of naked out-
castes who had not the proper manner of addressing
white people. Gisborne laughed and bade him go to his
quarters, and Abdul Gafur retreated growling. Later in
the night he found occasion to rise up and beat his
thirteen-year-old daughter. Nobody knew the cause of
dispute, but Gisborne heard the cry.

Through the days that followed Mowgli came and
went like a shadow. He had established himself and
his wild house-keeping close to the bungalow, but on
the edge of the *rukh*, where Gisborne, going out on
to the verandah for a breath of cool air, would see
him sometimes sitting in the moonlight, his forehead
on his knees, or lying out along the fling of a branch,
closely pressed to it as some beast of the night. Thence
Mowgli would throw him a salutation and bid him sleep
at ease, or descending would weave prodigious stories of
the manners of the beasts in the *rukh*. Once he wandered

into the stables and was found looking at the horses with
deep interest.

'That,' said Abdul Gafur pointedly, 'is sure sign that
some day he will steal one. Why, if he lives about this
house, does he not take an honest employment? But
no, he must wander up and down like a loose camel,
turning the heads of fools and opening the jaws of the
unwise to folly.' So Abdul Gafur would give harsh orders
to Mowgli when they met, would bid him fetch water and
pluck fowls, and Mowgli, laughing unconcernedly, would
obey.

'He has no caste,' said Abdul Gafur. 'He will do
anything. Look to it, Sahib, that he does not do too
much. A snake is a snake, and a jungle-gipsy is a thief
till the death.'

'Be silent, then,' said Gisborne. 'I allow thee to cor-
rect thy own household if there is not too much noise,
because I know thy customs and use. My custom thou
dost not know. The man is without doubt a little
mad.'

'Very little mad indeed,' said Abdul Gafur. 'But we
shall see what comes thereof.'

A few days later on his business took Gisborne into
the *rukh* for three days. Abdul Gafur being old and fat
was left at home. He did not approve of lying up in
rangers' huts, and was inclined to levy contributions
in his master's name of grain and oil and milk from
those who could ill afford such benevolences. Gisborne
rode off early one dawn a little vexed that his man of
the woods was not at the verandah to accompany him.
He liked him—liked his strength, fleetness, and silence
of foot, and his ever-ready open smile; his ignorance of
all forms of ceremony and salutations, and the child-like
tales that he would tell (and Gisborne would credit now)
of what the game was doing in the *rukh*. After an hour's

riding through the greenery, he heard a rustle behind him, and Mowgli trotted at his stirrup.

'We have a three days' work toward,' said Gisborne, 'among the new trees.'

'Good,' said Mowgli. 'It is always good to cherish young trees. They make cover if the beasts leave them alone. We must shift the pig again.'

'Again? How?' Gisborne smiled.

'Oh, they were rooting and tusking among the young *sal* last night, and I drove them off. Therefore I did not come to the verandah this morning. The pig should not be on this side of the *rukh* at all. We must keep them below the head of the Kanye river.'

'If a man could herd clouds he might do that thing; but, Mowgli, if as thou sayest, thou art herder in the *rukh* for no gain and for no pay——'

'It is the Sahib's *rukh*,' said Mowgli, quickly looking up. Gisborne nodded thanks and went on: 'Would it not be better to work for pay from the Government? There is a pension at the end of long service.'

'Of that I have thought,' said Mowgli, 'but the rangers live in huts with shut doors, and all that is all too much a trap to me. Yet I think——'

'Think well then and tell me later. Here we will stay for breakfast.'

Gisborne dismounted, took his morning meal from his home-made saddle-bags, and saw the day open hot above the *rukh*. Mowgli lay in the grass at his side staring up to the sky.

Presently he said in a lazy whisper: 'Sahib, is there any order at the bungalow to take out the white mare to-day?'

'No, she is fat and old and a little lame besides. Why?'

'She is being ridden now and *not* slowly on the road that runs to the railway line.'

'Bah, that is two *koss* away. It is a woodpecker.'

Mowgli put up his forearm to keep the sun out of his eyes.

'The road curves in with a big curve from the bungalow. It is not more than a *koss*, at the farthest, as the kite goes; and sound flies with the birds. Shall we see?'

'What folly! To run a *koss* in this sun to see a noise in the forest.'

'Nay, the pony is the Sahib's pony. I meant only to bring her here. If she is not the Sahib's pony, no matter. If she is, the Sahib can do what he wills. She is certainly being ridden hard.'

'And how wilt thou bring her here, madman?'

'Has the Sahib forgotten? By the road of the nilghai and no other.'

'Up then and run if thou art so full of zeal.'

'Oh, I do not run!' He put out his hand to sign for silence, and still lying on his back called aloud thrice—with a deep gurgling cry that was new to Gisborne.

'She will come,' he said at the end. 'Let us wait in the shade.' The long eyelashes drooped over the wild eyes as Mowgli began to doze in the morning hush. Gisborne waited patiently: Mowgli was surely mad, but as entertaining a companion as a lonely Forest Officer could desire.

'Ho! ho!' said Mowgli lazily, with shut eyes. 'He has dropped off. Well, first the mare will come and then the man.' Then he yawned as Gisborne's pony stallion neighed. Three minutes later Gisborne's white mare, saddled, bridled, but riderless, tore into the glade where they were sitting, and hurried to her companion.

'She is not very warm,' said Mowgli, 'but in this heat the sweat comes easily. Presently we shall see her rider, for a man goes more slowly than a horse—especially if he chance to be a fat man and old.'

'Allah! This is the devil's work,' cried Gisborne leaping to his feet, for he heard a yell in the jungle.

'Have no care, Sahib. He will not be hurt. He also will say that it is devil's work. Ah! Listen! Who is that?'

It was the voice of Abdul Gafur in an agony of terror, crying out upon unknown things to spare him and his gray hairs.

'Nay, I cannot move another step,' he howled. 'I am old and my turban is lost. Arré! Arré! But I will move. Indeed I will hasten. I will run! Oh, Devils of the Pit, I am a Mussulman!'

The undergrowth parted and gave up Abdul Gafur, turbanless, shoeless, with his waist-cloth unbound, mud and grass in his clutched hands, and his face purple. He saw Gisborne, yelled anew, and pitched forward, exhausted and quivering, at his feet. Mowgli watched him with a sweet smile.

'This is no joke,' said Gisborne sternly. 'The man is like to die, Mowgli.'

'He will not die. He is only afraid. There was no need that he should have come out of a walk.'

Abdul Gafur groaned and rose up, shaking in every limb.

'It was witchcraft—witchcraft and devildom!' he sobbed, fumbling with his hand in his breast. 'Because of my sin I have been whipped through the woods by devils. It is all finished. I repent. Take them, Sahib!' He held out a roll of dirty paper.

'What is the meaning of this, Abdul Gafur?' said Gisborne, already knowing what would come.

'Put me in the jail-khana—the notes are all here—but lock me up safely that no devils may follow. I have sinned against the Sahib and his salt which I have eaten; and but for those accursed wood-demons, I might have bought land afar off and lived in peace all my days.'

He beat his head upon the ground in an agony of despair and mortification. Gisborne turned the roll of notes over and over. It was his accumulated back-pay for the last nine months—the roll that lay in the drawer with the home-letters and the recapping machine. Mowgli watched Abdul Gafur, laughing noiselessly to himself. 'There is no need to put me on the horse again. I will walk home slowly with the Sahib, and then he can send me under guard to the jail-khana. The Government gives many years for this offence,' said the butler sullenly.

Loneliness in the *rukh* affects very many ideas about very many things. Gisborne stared at Abdul Gafur, remembering that he was a very good servant, and that a new butler must be broken into the ways of the house from the beginning, and at the best would be a new face and a new tongue.

'Listen, Abdul Gafur,' he said. 'Thou hast done great wrong, and altogether lost thy *izzat* and thy reputation. But I think that this came upon thee suddenly.'

'Allah! I had never desired the notes before. The Evil took me by the throat while I looked.'

'That also I can believe. Go then back to my house, and when I return I will send the notes by a runner to the Bank, and there shall be no more said. Thou art too old for the jail-khana. Also thy household is guiltless.'

For answer Abdul Gafur sobbed between Gisborne's cowhide riding-boots.

'Is there no dismissal then?' he gulped.

'That we shall see. It hangs upon thy conduct when we return. Get upon the mare and ride slowly back.'

'But the devils! The *rukh* is full of devils.'

'No matter, my father. They will do thee no more harm unless, indeed, the Sahib's orders be not obeyed,' said Mowgli. 'Then, perchance, they may drive thee home—by the road of the nilghai.'

Abdul Gafur's lower jaw dropped as he twisted up his waist-cloth, staring at Mowgli.

'Are they *his* devils? His devils! And I had thought to return and lay the blame upon this warlock!'

'That was well thought of, Huzrut; but before we make a trap we see first how big the game is that may fall into it. Now I thought no more than that a man had taken one of the Sahib's horses. I did not know that the design was to make me a thief before the Sahib, or my devils had haled thee here by the leg. It is not too late now.'

Mowgli looked inquiringly at Gisborne; but Abdul Gafur waddled hastily to the white mare, scrambled on her back and fled, the woodways crashing and echoing behind them.

'That was well done,' said Mowgli. 'But he will fall again unless he holds by the mane.'

'Now it is time to tell me what these things mean,' said Gisborne a little sternly. 'What is this talk of thy devils? How can men be driven up and down the *rukh* like cattle? Give answer.'

'Is the Sahib angry because I have saved him his money?'

'No, but there is trick-work in this that does not please me.'

'Very good. Now if I rose and stepped three paces into the *rukh* there is no one, not even the Sahib, could find me till I chose. As I would not willingly do this, so I would not willingly tell. Have patience a little, Sahib, and some day I will show thee everything, for, if thou wilt, some day we will drive the buck together. There is no devil-work in the matter at all. Only . . . I know the *rukh* as a man knows the cooking-place in his house.'

Mowgli was speaking as he would speak to an impatient child. Gisborne, puzzled, baffled, and a great deal annoyed, said nothing, but stared on the ground and thought. When he looked up the man of the woods had gone.

'It is not good,' said a level voice from the thicket, 'for friends to be angry. Wait till the evening, Sahib, when the air cools.'

Left to himself thus, dropped as it were in the heart of the *rukh*, Gisborne swore, then laughed, remounted his pony, and rode on. He visited a ranger's hut, overlooked a couple of new plantations, left some orders as to the burning of a patch of dry grass, and set out for a camping-ground of his own choice, a pile of splintered rocks roughly roofed over with branches and leaves, not far from the banks of the Kanye stream. It was twilight when he came in sight of his resting-place, and the *rukh* was waking to the hushed ravenous life of the night.

A camp-fire flickered on the knoll, and there was the smell of a very good dinner in the wind.

'Um,' said Gisborne, 'that's better than cold meat at any rate. Now the only man who'd be likely to be here'd be Muller, and, officially, he ought to be looking over the Changamanga *rukh*. I suppose that's why he's on my ground.'

The gigantic German who was the head of the Woods and Forests of all India, Head Ranger from Burma to Bombay, had a habit of flitting bat-like without warning from one place to another, and turning up exactly where he was least looked for. His theory was that sudden visitations, the discovery of shortcomings and a word-of-mouth upbraiding of a subordinate were infinitely better than the slow processes of correspondence, which might end in a written and official reprimand—a thing in after years to be counted against a Forest Officer's record. As he explained it: 'If I only talk to my boys like a Dutch uncle, dey say, "It was only dot damned old Muller," and dey do better next dime. But if my fat-head clerk he write and say dot Muller der Inspecdor-General fail to onderstand and is much annoyed, first dot does no goot because I am not dere, and, second, der fool dot comes after me he may say to my best boys: "Look here, you haf been wigged by my bredecessor." I tell you der big brass-hat pizness does not make der trees grow.'

Muller's deep voice was coming out of the darkness behind the firelight as he bent over the shoulders of his pet cook. 'Not so much sauce, you son of Belial! Worcester sauce he is a gondiment and not a fluid. Ah, Gisborne, you haf come to a very bad dinner. Where is your camp?' and he walked up to shake hands.

'I'm the camp, sir,' said Gisborne. 'I didn't know you were about here.'

Muller looked at the young man's trim figure. 'Goot! This is very goot! One horse and some cold things to eat. When I was young I did my camp so. Now you shall dine with me. I went into Headquarters to make up my rebort last month. I haf written half—ho! ho!—and der rest I haf leaved to my glerks and come out for a walk. Der Government is mad about dose reborts. I dold der Viceroy so at Simla.'

Gisborne chuckled, remembering the many tales that were told of Muller's conflicts with the Supreme Government. He was the chartered libertine of all the offices, for as a Forest Officer he had no equal.

'If I find you, Gisborne, sitting in your bungalow und hatching reborts to me about der blantations instead of riding der blantations, I will dransfer you to der middle of der Bikaneer Desert to reforest *him*. I am sick of reborts und chewing paper when we should do our work.'

'There's not much danger of my wasting time over my annuals. I hate them as much as you do, sir.'

The talk went over at this point to professional matters.

Muller had some questions to ask, and Gisborne orders and hints to receive, till dinner was ready. It was the most civilised meal Gisborne had eaten for months. No distance from the base of supplies was allowed to interfere with the work of Muller's cook; and that table spread in the wilderness began with devilled small fresh-water fish, and ended with coffee and cognac.

'Ah!' said Muller at the end, with a sigh of satisfaction as he lighted a cheroot and dropped into his much worn camp-chair. 'When I am making reborts I am Freethinker und Atheist, but here in der *rukh* I am more than Christian. I am Bagan also.' He rolled the cheroot-butt luxuriously under his tongue, dropped his hands on his knees, and stared before him into the dim shifting heart of the *rukh*, full of stealthy noises; the snapping of twigs like the snapping of the fire behind him; the sigh and rustle of a heat-bended branch recovering her straightness in the cool night; the incessant mutter of the Kanye stream, and the undernote of the many-peopled grass uplands out of sight beyond a swell of hill. He blew out a thick puff of smoke, and began to quote Heine to himself.

'Yes, it is very goot. Very goot. "Yes, I work miracles, and, by Gott, dey come off too." I remember when dere was no *rukh* more big than your knee, from here to der plough-lands, und in drought-time der cattle ate bones of dead cattle up and down. Now der trees haf come back. Dey were planted by a Freethinker, because he know just de cause dot made der effect. But der trees dey had der cult of der old gods—"und der Christian Gods howl loudly." Dey could not live in der *rukh*, Gisborne.'

A shadow moved in one of the bridle-paths—moved and stepped out into the starlight.

'I haf said true. Hush! Here is Faunus himself come to see der Insbector-General. Himmel, he is der god! Look!'

It was Mowgli, crowned with his wreath of white flowers and walking with a half-peeled branch—Mowgli, very mistrustful of the fire-light and ready to fly back to the thicket on the least alarm.

'That's a friend of mine,' said Gisborne. 'He's looking for me. Ohé, Mowgli!'

Muller had barely time to gasp before the man was at Gisborne's side, crying: 'I was wrong to go. I was wrong, but I did not know then that the mate of him that was killed by this river was awake looking for thee. Else I should not have gone away. She tracked thee from the back-ranges, Sahib.'

'He is a little mad,' said Gisborne, 'and he speaks of all the beasts about here as if he was a friend of theirs.'

'Of course—of course. If Faunus does not know, who should know?' said Muller gravely. 'What does he say about tigers—dis god who knows you so well?'

Gisborne relighted his cheroot, and before he had finished the story of Mowgli and his exploits it was burned down to moustache-edge. Muller listened without interruption. 'Dot is not madness,' he said at last when Gisborne had described the driving of Abdul Gafur. 'Dot is not madness at all.'

'What is it, then? He left me in a temper this morning because I asked him to tell how he did it. I fancy the chap's possessed in some way.'

'No, dere is no bossession, but it is most wonderful. Normally they die young—dese beople. Und you say now dot your thief-servant did not say what drove der pony, and of course der nilghai he could not speak.'

'No, but, confound it, there wasn't anything. I listened, and I can hear most things. The bull and the man simply came headlong—mad with fright.'

For answer Muller looked Mowgli up and down from

head to foot, then beckoned him nearer. He came as a buck treads a tainted trail.

'There is no harm,' said Muller in the vernacular. 'Hold out an arm.'

He ran his hand down to the elbow, felt that, and nodded. 'So I thought. Now the knee.' Gisborne saw him feel the knee-cap and smile. Two or three white scars just above the ankle caught his eye.

'Those came when thou wast very young?' he said.

'Ay,' Mowgli answered with a smile. 'They were love-tokens from the little ones.' Then to Gisborne over his shoulder. 'This Sahib knows everything. Who is he?'

'That comes after, my friend. Now where are *they*?' said Muller.

Mowgli swept his hand round his head in a circle.

'So! And thou canst drive nilghai? See! There is my mare in her pickets. Canst thou bring her to me without frightening her?'

'Can I bring the mare to the Sahib without frightening her!' Mowgli repeated, raising his voice a little above its normal pitch. 'What is more easy if the heel-ropes are loose?'

'Loosen the head and heel-pegs,' shouted Muller to the groom. They were hardly out of the ground before the mare, a huge black Australian, flung up her head and cocked her ears.

'Careful! I do not wish her driven into the *rukh*,' said Muller.

Mowgli stood still fronting the blaze of the fire—in the very form and likeness of that Greek god who is so lavishly described in the novels. The mare whickered, drew up one hind leg, found that the heel-ropes were free, and moved swiftly to her master, on whose bosom she dropped her head, sweating lightly.

'She came of her own accord. My horses will do that,' cried Gisborne.

'Feel if she sweats,' said Mowgli.

Gisborne laid a hand on the damp flank.

'It is enough,' said Muller.

'It is enough,' Mowgli repeated, and a rock behind him threw back the word.

'That's uncanny, isn't it?' said Gisborne.

'No, only wonderful—most wonderful. Still you do not know, Gisborne?'

'I confess I don't.'

'Well then, I shall not tell. He says dot some day he will show you what it is. It would be gruel if I told. But why he is not dead I do not understand. Now listen thou.' Muller faced Mowgli, and returned to the vernacular. 'I am the head of all the *rukhs* in the country of India and others across the Black Water. I do not know how many men be under me—perhaps five thousand, perhaps ten. Thy business is this,—to wander no more up and down the *rukh* and drive beasts for sport or for show, but to take service under me, who am the Government in the matter of Woods and Forests, and to live in this *rukh* as a forest-guard; to drive the villagers' goats away when there is no order to feed them in the *rukh*; to admit them when there is an order; to keep down, as thou canst keep down, the boar and the nilghai when they become too many; to tell Gisborne Sahib how and where tigers move, and what game there is in the forests; and to give sure warning of all the fires in the *rukh*, for thou canst give warning more quickly than any other. For that work there is a payment each month in silver, and at the end, when thou hast gathered a wife and cattle and, maybe, children, a pension. What answer?'

'That's just what I——' Gisborne began.

'My Sahib spoke this morning of such a service. I walked all day alone considering the matter, and my answer is ready here. I serve, *if* I serve in this *rukh* and no other: *with* Gisborne Sahib and with no other.'

'It shall be so. In a week comes the written order that pledges the honour of the Government for the pension. After that thou wilt take up thy hut where Gisborne Sahib shall appoint.'

'I was going to speak to you about it,' said Gisborne.

'I did not want to be told when I saw dot man. Dere will never be a forest-guard like him. He is a miracle. I tell you, Gisborne, some day you will find it so. Listen, he is blood-brother to every beast in der *rukh!*'

'I should be easier in my mind if I could understand him.'

'Dot will come. Now I tell you dot only once in my service, and dot is thirty years, haf I met a boy dot began as this man began. Und he died. Sometimes you hear of dem in der census reports, but dey all die. Dis man haf lived, and he is an anachronism, for he is before der Iron Age, and der Stone Age. Look here, he is at der beginnings of der history of man—Adam in der Garden, und now we want only an Eva! No! He is older than dot child-tale, shust as der *rukh* is older dan der gods. Gisborne, I am a Bagan now, once for all.'

Through the rest of the long evening Muller sat smoking and smoking, and staring and staring into the darkness, his lips moving in multiplied quotations, and great wonder upon his face. He went to his tent, but presently came out again in his majestic pink sleeping-suit, and the last words that Gisborne heard him address to the *rukh* through the deep hush of midnight were these, delivered with immense emphasis:—

'Dough we shivt und bedeck und bedrape us,
    Dou art noble und nude und andeek;
Libidina dy moder, Briapus
    Dy fader, a God und a Greek.

Now I know dot, Bagan *or* Christian, I shall nefer know der inwardness of der *rukh!*'

It was midnight in the bungalow a week later when Abdul Gafur, ashy gray with rage, stood at the foot of Gisborne's bed and whispering bade him awake.

'Up, Sahib,' he stammered. 'Up and bring thy gun. Mine honour is gone. Up and kill before any see.'

The old man's face had changed, so that Gisborne stared stupidly.

'It was for this, then, that that jungle outcaste helped me to polish the Sahib's table, and drew water and plucked fowls. They have gone off together for all my beatings, and now he sits among his devils dragging her soul to the Pit. Up, Sahib, and come with me!'

He thrust a rifle into Gisborne's half-wakened hand and almost dragged him from the room on to the verandah.

'They are there in the *rukh*; even within gunshot of the house. Come softly with me.'

'But what is it? What is the trouble, Abdul?'

'Mowgli, and his devils. Also my own daughter,' said Abdul Gafur. Gisborne whistled and followed his guide. Not for nothing, he knew, had Abdul Gafur beaten his daughter of nights, and not for nothing had Mowgli helped in the housework a man whom his own powers, whatever those were, had convicted of theft. Also, a forest wooing goes quickly.

There was the breathing of a flute in the *rukh*, as it might have been the song of some wandering wood-god, and, as they came nearer, a murmur of voices. The path ended in a little semicircular glade walled partly by high grass and partly by trees. In the centre, upon a fallen trunk, his back to the watchers and his arm round the neck of Abdul Gafur's daughter, sat Mowgli, newly crowned with flowers, playing upon a rude bamboo flute, to whose music four huge wolves danced solemnly on their hind legs.

'Those are his devils,' Abdul Gafur whispered. He held a bunch of cartridges in his hand. The beasts dropped to a long-drawn quavering note and lay still with steady green eyes, glaring at the girl.

'Behold,' said Mowgli, laying aside the flute. 'Is there anything of fear in that? I told thee, little Stout-heart, that there was not, and thou didst believe. Thy father said—and oh, if thou couldst have seen thy father being driven by the road of the nilghai!—thy father said that they were devils; and by Allah, who is thy God, I do not wonder that he so believed.'

The girl laughed a little rippling laugh, and Gisborne heard Abdul grind his few remaining teeth. This was not at all the girl that Gisborne had seen with a half-eye slinking about the compound veiled and silent, but another—a woman full blown in a night as the orchid puts out in an hour's moist heat.

'But they are my playmates and my brothers, children of that mother that gave me suck, as I told thee behind the cook-house,' Mowgli went on. 'Children of the father that lay between me and the cold at the mouth of the cave when I was a little naked child. Look'—a wolf raised his gray jowl, slavering at Mowgli's knee—'my brother knows that I speak of them. Yes, when I was a little child he was a cub rolling with me on the clay.'

'But thou hast said that thou art human-born,' cooed the girl, nestling closer to the shoulder. 'Thou art human-born?'

'Said! Nay, I know that I am human-born, because

my heart is in thy hold, little one.' Her head dropped under Mowgli's chin. Gisborne put up a warning hand to restrain Abdul Gafur, who was not in the least impressed by the wonder of the sight.

'But I was a wolf among wolves none the less till a time came when Those of the jungle bade me go because I was a man.'

'Who bade thee go? That is not like a true man's talk.'

'The very beasts themselves. Little one, thou wouldst never believe that telling, but so it was. The beasts of the jungle bade me go, but these four followed me because I was their brother. Then was I a herder of cattle among men, having learned their language. Ho! ho! The herds paid toll to my brothers, till a woman, an old woman, beloved, saw me playing by night with my brethren in the crops. They said that I was possessed of devils, and drove me from that village with sticks and stones, and the four came with me by stealth and not openly. That was when I had learned to eat cooked meat and to talk boldly. From village to village I went, heart of my heart, a herder of cattle, a tender of buffaloes, a tracker of game, but there was no man that dared lift a finger against me twice.' He stooped down and patted one of the heads. 'Do thou also like this. There is neither hurt nor magic in them. See, they know thee.'

'The woods are full of all manner of devils,' said the girl with a shudder.

'A lie. A child's lie,' Mowgli returned confidently. 'I have lain out in the dew under the stars and in the dark night, and I know. The jungle is my house. Shall a man fear his own roof-beams or a woman her man's hearth? Stoop down and pat them.'

'They are dogs and unclean,' she murmured, bending forward with averted head.

'Having eaten the fruit, now we remember the Law!'

said Abdul Gafur bitterly. 'What is the need of this waiting, Sahib? Kill!'

'H'sh, thou. Let us learn what has happened,' said Gisborne.

'That is well done,' said Mowgli, slipping his arm round the girl again. 'Dogs or no dogs, they were with me through a thousand villages.'

'Ahi, and where was thy heart then? Through a thousand villages. Thou hast seen a thousand maids. I—that am—that am a maid no more, have I thy heart?'

'What shall I swear by? By Allah, of whom thou speakest?'

'Nay, by the life that is in thee, and I am well content. Where was thy heart in those days?'

Mowgli laughed a little. 'In my belly, because I was young and always hungry. So I learned to track and to hunt, sending and calling my brothers back and forth as a king calls his armies. Therefore I drove the nilghai for the foolish young Sahib, and the big fat mare for the big fat Sahib, when they questioned my power. It were as easy to have driven the men themselves. Even now,'—his voice lifted a little—'even now I know that behind me stand thy father and Gisborne Sahib. Nay, do not run, for no ten men dare move a pace forward. Remembering that thy father beat thee more than once, shall I give the word and drive him again in rings through the *rukh*?' A wolf stood up with bared teeth.

Gisborne felt Abdul Gafur tremble at his side. Next, his place was empty, and the fat man was skimming down the glade.

'Remains only Gisborne Sahib,' said Mowgli, still without turning; 'but I have eaten Gisborne Sahib's bread, and presently I shall be in his service, and my brothers will be his servants to drive game and carry the news. Hide thou in the grass.'

The girl fled, the tall grass closed behind her and the guardian wolf that followed, and Mowgli turning with his three retainers faced Gisborne as the Forest Officer came forward.

'That is all the magic,' he said, pointing to the three. 'The fat Sahib knew that we who are bred among wolves run on our elbows and our knees for a season. Feeling my arms and legs, he felt the truth which thou didst not know. Is it so wonderful, Sahib?'

'Indeed it is all more wonderful than magic. These then drove the nilghai?'

'Ay, as they would drive Eblis if I gave the order. They are my eyes and feet to me.'

'Look to it, then, that Eblis does not carry a double rifle. They have yet something to learn, thy devils, for they stand one behind the other, so that two shots would kill the three.'

'Ah, but they know they will be thy servants as soon as I am a forest-guard.'

'Guard or no guard, Mowgli, thou hast done a great shame to Abdul Gafur. Thou hast dishonoured his house and blackened his face.'

'For that, it was blackened when he took thy money, and made blacker still when he whispered in thy ear a little while since to kill a naked man. I myself will talk to Abdul Gafur, for I am a man of the Government service, with a pension. He shall make the marriage by whatsoever rite he will, or he shall run once more. I will speak to him in the dawn. For the rest, the Sahib has his house and this is mine. It is time to sleep again, Sahib.'

Mowgli turned on his heel and disappeared into the grass, leaving Gisborne alone. The hint of the wood-god was not to be mistaken; and Gisborne went back to the bungalow, where Abdul Gafur, torn by rage and fear, was raving in the verandah.

'Peace, peace,' said Gisborne, shaking him, for he looked as though he were going to have a fit. 'Muller Sahib has made the man a forest-guard, and as thou knowest, there is a pension at the end of that business, and it is Government service.'

'He is an outcaste—a *mlech*—a dog among dogs; an eater of carrion! What pension can pay for that?'

'Allah knows; and thou hast heard that the mischief is done. Wouldst thou blaze it to all the other servants? Make the *shadi* swiftly, and the girl will make him a Mussulman. He is very comely. Canst thou wonder that after thy beatings she went to him?'

'Did he say that he would chase me with his beasts?'

'So it seemed to me. If he be a wizard, he is at least a very strong one.'

Abdul Gafur thought awhile, and then broke down and howled, forgetting that he was a Mussulman:—

'Thou art a Brahmin. I am thy cow. Make thou the matter plain, and save my honour if it can be saved!'

A second time then Gisborne plunged into the *rukh* and called Mowgli. The answer came from high overhead, and in no submissive tones.

'Speak softly,' said Gisborne, looking up. 'There is yet time to strip thee of thy place and hunt thee with thy wolves. The girl must go back to her father's house to-night. To-morrow there will be the *shadi*, by the Mussulman law, and then thou canst take her away. Bring her to Abdul Gafur.'

'I hear.' There was a murmur of two voices conferring among the leaves. 'Also, we will obey—for the last time.'

A year later Muller and Gisborne were riding through the *rukh* together, talking of their business. They came out among the rocks near the Kanye stream; Muller riding a little in advance. Under the shade of a thorn thicket sprawled a naked brown baby, and from the brake immediately behind him peered the head of a gray wolf. Gisborne had just time to strike up Muller's rifle, and the bullet tore spattering through the branches above.

'Are you mad?' thundered Muller. 'Look!'

'I see,' said Gisborne quietly. 'The mother's somewhere near. You'll wake the whole pack, by Jove!'

The bushes parted once more, and a woman unveiled snatched up the child.

'Who fired, Sahib?' she cried to Gisborne.

'This Sahib. He had not remembered thy man's people.'

'Not remembered? But indeed it may be so, for we who live with them forget that they are strangers at all. Mowgli is down the stream catching fish. Does the Sahib wish to see him? Come out, ye lacking manners. Come out of the bushes, and make your service to the Sahibs.'

Muller's eyes grew rounder and rounder. He swung himself off the plunging mare and dismounted, while the jungle gave up four wolves who fawned round Gisborne. The mother stood nursing her child and spurning them aside as they brushed against her bare feet.

'You were quite right about Mowgli,' said Gisborne. 'I meant to have told you, but I've got so used to these fellows in the last twelve months that it slipped my mind.'

'Oh, don't apologise,' said Muller. 'It's nothing. Gott in Himmel! "Und I work miracles—und dey come off too!"'

The Lost Legion

WHEN the Indian Mutiny broke out, and a little time
before the siege of Delhi, a regiment of Native Irregular
Horse was stationed at Peshawur on the frontier of India.
That regiment caught what John Lawrence called at the
time 'the prevalent mania,' and would have thrown in
its lot with the mutineers had it been allowed to do
so. The chance never came, for, as the regiment swept
off down south, it was headed up by a remnant of an
English corps into the hills of Afghanistan, and there
the newly-conquered tribesmen turned against it as
wolves turn against buck. It was hunted for the sake
of its arms and accoutrements from hill to hill, from
ravine to ravine, up and down the dried beds of rivers
and round the shoulders of bluffs, till it disappeared as
water sinks in the sand—this officerless, rebel regiment.
The only trace left of its existence to-day is a nominal roll
drawn up in neat round hand and countersigned by an
officer who called himself 'Adjutant, late——Irregular
Cavalry.' The paper is yellow with years and dirt, but
on the back of it you can still read a pencil note by
John Lawrence, to this effect: 'See that the two native
officers who remained loyal are not deprived of their
estates.—J.L.' Of six hundred and fifty sabres only two
stood strain, and John Lawrence in the midst of all the
agony of the first months of the Mutiny found time to
think about their merits.

That was more than thirty years ago, and the tribesmen across the Afghan border who helped to annihilate
the regiment are now old men. Sometimes a graybeard
speaks of his share in the massacre. 'They came,' he will
say, 'across the border, very proud, calling upon us to rise
and kill the English, and go down to the sack of Delhi.
But we who had just been conquered by the same English
knew that they were over bold, and that the Government
could account easily for those down-country dogs. This
Hindustani regiment, therefore, we treated with fair
words, and kept standing in one place till the redcoats
came after them very hot and angry. Then this regiment
ran forward a little more into our hills to avoid the wrath
of the English, and we lay upon their flanks watching
from the sides of the hills till we were well assured that
their path was lost behind them. Then we came down, for
we desired their clothes, and their bridles, and their rifles,
and their boots—more especially their boots. That was a
great killing—done slowly.' Here the old man will rub his
nose, and shake his long snaky locks, and lick his bearded
lips, and grin till the yellow tooth-stumps show. 'Yes, we
killed them because we needed their gear, and we knew
that their lives had been forfeited to God on account of
their sin—the sin of treachery to the salt which they had
eaten. They rode up and down the valleys, stumbling and
rocking in their saddles, and howling for mercy. We drove
them slowly like cattle till they were all assembled in one
place, the flat wide valley of Sheor Kôt. Many had died
from want of water, but there still were many left, and
they could not make any stand. We went among them,
pulling them down with our hands two at a time, and
our boys killed them who were new to the sword. My
share of the plunder was such and such—so many guns,
and so many saddles. The guns were good in those days.
Now we steal the Government rifles, and despise smooth

barrels. Yes, beyond doubt we wiped that regiment from
off the face of the earth, and even the memory of the deed
is now dying. But men say—— '

At this point the tale would stop abruptly, and it was
impossible to find out what men said across the border.
The Afghans were always a secretive race, and vastly
preferred doing something wicked to saying anything at
all. They would be quiet and well-behaved for months,
till one night, without word or warning, they would rush
a police-post, cut the throats of a constable or two, dash
through a village, carry away three or four women, and
withdraw, in the red glare of burning thatch, driving the
cattle and goats before them to their own desolate hills.
The Indian Government would become almost tearful
on these occasions. First it would say, 'Please be good
and we'll forgive you.' The tribe concerned in the latest
depredation would collectively put its thumb to its nose
and answer rudely. Then the Government would say:
'Hadn't you better pay up a little money for those few
corpses you left behind you the other night?' Here the
tribe would temporise, and lie and bully, and some of
the younger men, merely to show contempt of authority,
would raid another police-post and fire into some frontier
mud fort, and, if lucky, kill a real English officer. Then
the Government would say: 'Observe; if you really persist
in this line of conduct you will be hurt.' If the tribe knew
exactly what was going on in India, it would apologise or
be rude, according as it learned whether the Government
was busy with other things, or able to devote its full
attention to their performances. Some of the tribes knew
to one corpse how far to go. Others became excited, lost
their heads, and told the Government to come on. With
sorrow and tears, and one eye on the British taxpayer at
home, who insisted on regarding these exercises as brutal
wars of annexation, the Government would prepare an

expensive little field-brigade and some guns, and send all up into the hills to chase the wicked tribe out of the valleys, where the corn grew, into the hill-tops where there was nothing to eat. The tribe would turn out in full strength and enjoy the campaign, for they knew that their women would never be touched, that their wounded would be nursed, not mutilated, and that as soon as each man's bag of corn was spent they could surrender and palaver with the English General as though they had been a real enemy. Afterwards, years afterwards, they would pay the blood-money, driblet by driblet, to the Government and tell their children how they had slain the redcoats by thousands. The only drawback to this kind of picnic-war was the weakness of the redcoats for solemnly blowing up with powder their fortified towers and keeps. This the tribes always considered mean.

Chief among the leaders of the smaller tribes—the little clans who knew to a penny the expense of moving white troops against them—was a priest-bandit-chief whom we will call the Gulla Kutta Mullah. His enthusiasm for border murder as an art was almost dignified. He would cut down a mail-runner from pure wantonness, or bombard a mud fort with rifle fire when he knew that our men needed to sleep. In his leisure moments he would go on circuit among his neighbours, and try to incite other tribes to devilry. Also, he kept a kind of hotel for fellow-outlaws in his own village, which lay in a valley called Bersund. Any respectable murderer on that section of the frontier was sure to lie up at Bersund, for it was reckoned an exceedingly safe place. The sole entry to it ran through a narrow gorge which could be converted into a death-trap in five minutes. It was surrounded by high hills, reckoned inaccessible to all save born mountaineers, and here the Gulla Kutta Mullah lived in great state, the head of a colony of mud and stone huts, and in each mud hut hung some portion of a red uniform and the plunder of dead men. The Government particularly wished for his capture, and once invited him formally to come out and be hanged on account of a few of the murders in which he had taken a direct part. He replied:—

'I am only twenty miles, as the crow flies, from your border. Come and fetch me.'

'Some day we will come,' said the Government, 'and hanged you will be.'

The Gulla Kutta Mullah let the matter from his mind. He knew that the patience of the Government was as long as a summer day; but he did not realise that its arm was as long as a winter night. Months afterwards, when there was peace on the border, and all India was quiet, the Indian Government turned in its sleep and remembered the Gulla Kutta Mullah at Bersund with his thirteen outlaws. The movement against him of one single regiment—which the telegrams would have translated as war—would have been highly impolitic. This was a time for silence and speed, and, above all, absence of bloodshed.

You must know that all along the north-west frontier of India there is spread a force of some thirty thousand foot and horse, whose duty it is quietly and unostentatiously to shepherd the tribes in front of them. They move up and down, and down and up, from one desolate little post to another; they are ready to take the field at ten minutes' notice; they are always half in and half out of a difficulty somewhere along the monotonous line; their lives are as hard as their own muscles, and the papers never say anything about them. It was from this force that the Government picked its men.

One night at a station where the mounted Night Patrol fire as they challenge, and the wheat rolls in great blue-green waves under our cold northern moon,

the officers were playing billiards in the mud-walled
club-house, when orders came to them that they were to
go on parade at once for a night-drill. They grumbled, and
went to turn out their men—a hundred English troops,
let us say, two hundred Goorkhas, and about a hundred
cavalry of the finest native cavalry in the world.

When they were on the parade-ground, it was explained
to them in whispers that they must set off at once across
the hills to Bersund. The English troops were to post
themselves round the hills at the side of the valley; the
Goorkhas would command the gorge and the death-trap,
and the cavalry would fetch a long march round and get to
the back of the circle of hills, whence, if there were any difficulty, they could charge down on the Mullah's men. But
orders were very strict that there should be no fighting
and no noise. They were to return in the morning with
every round of ammunition intact, and the Mullah and
the thirteen outlaws bound in their midst. If they were
successful, no one would know or care anything about
their work; but failure meant probably a small border
war, in which the Gulla Kutta Mullah would pose as a
popular leader against a big bullying power, instead of a
common border murderer.

Then there was silence, broken only by the clicking
of the compass-needles and snapping of watch-cases,
as the heads of columns compared bearings and made
appointments for the rendezvous. Five minutes later
the parade-ground was empty; the green coats of the
Goorkhas and the overcoats of the English troops had
faded into the darkness, and the cavalry were cantering
away in the face of a blinding drizzle.

What the Goorkhas and the English did will be seen
later on. The heavy work lay with the horses, for they
had to go far and pick their way clear of habitations.
Many of the troopers were natives of that part of the

world, ready and anxious to fight against their kin, and
some of the officers had made private and unofficial
excursions into those hills before. They crossed the
border, found a dried river bed, cantered up that, walked
through a stony gorge, risked crossing a low hill under
cover of the darkness, skirted another hill, leaving their
hoof-marks deep in some ploughed ground, felt their way
along another watercourse, ran over the neck of a spur,
praying that no one would hear their horses grunting,
and so worked on in the rain and the darkness, till they
had left Bersund and its crater of hills a little behind
them, and to the left, and it was time to swing round.
The ascent commanding the back of Bersund was steep,
and they halted to draw breath in a broad level valley
below the height. That is to say, the men reined up, but
the horses, blown as they were, refused to halt. There
was unchristian language, the worse for being delivered
in a whisper, and you heard the saddles squeaking in the
darkness as the horses plunged.

The subaltern at the rear of one troop turned in
his saddle and said very softly:—

'Carter, what the blessed heavens are you doing
at the rear? Bring your men up, man.'

There was no answer, till a trooper replied:—

'Carter Sahib is forward—not there. There is nothing
behind us.'

'There is,' said the subaltern. 'The squadron's walking
on its own tail.'

Then the Major in command moved down to the rear
swearing softly and asking for the blood of Lieutenant
Halley—the subaltern who had just spoken.

'Look after your rearguard,' said the Major. 'Some
of your infernal thieves have got lost. They're at the
head of the squadron, and you're a several kinds of
idiot.'

'Shall I tell off my men, sir?' said the subaltern sulkily, for he was feeling wet and cold.

'Tell 'em off!' said the Major. '*Whip* 'em off, by Gad! You're squandering them all over the place. There's a troop behind you *now!*'

'So I was thinking,' said the subaltern calmly. 'I have all my men here, sir. Better speak to Carter.'

'Carter Sahib sends salaam and wants to know why the regiment is stopping,' said a trooper to Lieutenant Halley.

'Where under heaven *is* Carter?' said the Major.

'Forward with his troop,' was the answer.

'Are we walking in a ring, then, or are we the centre of a blessed brigade?' said the Major.

By this time there was silence all along the column. The horses were still; but, through the drive of the fine rain, men could hear the feet of many horses moving over stony ground.

'We're being stalked,' said Lieutenant Halley.

'They've no horses here. Besides they'd have fired before this,' said the Major. 'It's—it's villagers' ponies.'

'Then our horses would have neighed and spoilt the attack long ago. They must have been near us for half an hour,' said the subaltern.

'Queer that we can't smell the horses,' said the Major, damping his finger and rubbing it on his nose as he sniffed up wind.

'Well, it's a bad start,' said the subaltern, shaking the wet from his overcoat. 'What shall we do, sir?'

'Get on,' said the Major. 'We shall catch it to-night.'

The column moved forward very gingerly for a few paces. Then there was an oath, a shower of blue sparks as shod hooves crashed on small stones, and a man rolled over with a jangle of accoutrements that would have waked the dead.

'Now we've gone and done it,' said Lieutenant Halley. 'All the hillside awake, and all the hillside to climb in the face of musketry-fire. This comes of trying to do night-hawk work.'

The trembling trooper picked himself up, and tried to explain that his horse had fallen over one of the little cairns that are built of loose stones on the spot where a man has been murdered. There was no need for reasons. The Major's big Australian charger blundered next, and the column came to a halt in what seemed to be a very graveyard of little cairns all about two feet high. The manoeuvres of the squadron are not reported. Men said that it felt like mounted quadrilles without training and without the music; but at last the horses, breaking rank and choosing their own way, walked clear of the cairns, till every man of the squadron re-formed and drew rein a few yards up the slope of the hill. Then, according to Lieutenant Halley, there was another scene very like the one which has been described. The Major and Carter insisted that all the men had not joined rank, and that there were more of them in the rear clicking and blundering among the dead men's cairns. Lieutenant Halley told off his own troopers again and resigned himself to wait. Later on he told me:—

'I didn't much know, and I didn't much care what was going on. The row of that trooper falling ought to have scared half the country, and I would take my oath that we were being stalked by a full regiment in the rear, and *they* were making row enough to rouse all Afghanistan. I sat tight, but nothing happened.'

The mysterious part of the night's work was the silence on the hillside. Everybody knew that the Gulla Kutta Mullah had his outpost huts on the reverse side of the hill, and everybody expected by the time that the Major had sworn himself into a state of quiet that the watchmen there would open fire. When nothing occurred, they said that the gusts of the rain had deadened the sound of the horses, and thanked Providence. At last the Major satisfied himself (a) that he had left no one behind among the cairns, and (b) that he was not being taken in the rear by a large and powerful body of cavalry. The men's tempers were thoroughly spoiled, the horses were lathered and unquiet, and one and all prayed for the daylight.

They set themselves to climb up the hill, each man leading his mount carefully. Before they had covered the lower slopes or the breastplates had begun to tighten, a thunderstorm came up behind, rolling across the low hills and drowning any noise less than that of cannon. The first flash of the lightning showed the bare ribs of the ascent, the hill-crest standing steely blue against the black sky, the little falling lines of the rain, and, a few yards to their left flank, an Afghan watch-tower, two-storied, built of stone, and entered by a ladder from the upper story. The ladder was up, and a man with a rifle was leaning from the window. The darkness and the thunder rolled down in an instant, and, when the lull followed, a voice from the watch-tower cried, 'Who goes there?'

The cavalry were very quiet, but each man gripped his carbine and stood beside his horse. Again the voice called, 'Who goes there?' and in a louder key, 'O, brothers, give the alarm!' Now, every man in the cavalry would have died in his long boots sooner than have asked for quarter; but it is a fact that the answer to the second call was a long wail of 'Marf karo! Marf karo!' which means, 'Have mercy! Have mercy!' It came from the climbing regiment.

The cavalry stood dumbfounded, till the big troopers had time to whisper one to another: 'Mir Khan, was that the voice? Abdullah, didst *thou* call?' Lieutenant Halley

stood beside his charger and waited. So long as no firing
was going on he was content. Another flash of lightning
showed the horses with heaving flanks and nodding
heads, the men, white eye-balled, glaring beside them,
and the stone watch-tower to the left. This time there
was no head at the window, and the rude iron-clamped
shutter that could turn a rifle bullet was closed.

'Go on, men,' said the Major. 'Get up to the top
at any rate.' The squadron toiled forward, the horses
wagging their tails and the men pulling at the bridles,
the stones rolling down the hillside and the sparks flying.
Lieutenant Halley declares that he never heard a squadron make so much noise in his life. They scrambled up,
he said, as though each horse had eight legs and a spare
horse to follow him. Even then there was no sound from
the watch-tower, and the men stopped exhausted on the
ridge that overlooked the pit of darkness in which the
village of Bersund lay. Girths were loosed, curb-chains
shifted, and saddles adjusted, and the men dropped down
among the stones. Whatever might happen now, they had
the upper ground of any attack.

The thunder ceased, and with it the rain, and the soft
thick darkness of a winter night before the dawn covered
them all. Except for the sound of falling water among
the ravines below, everything was still. They heard the
shutter of the watch-tower below them thrown back with
a clang, and the voice of the watcher calling: 'Oh, Hafiz
Ullah!'

The echoes took up the call, 'La-la-la!' And an answer
came from the watch-tower hidden round the curve of
the hill, 'What is it, Shahbaz Khan?'

Shahbaz Khan replied in the high-pitched voice of
the mountaineer: 'Hast thou seen?'

The answer came back: 'Yes. God deliver us from
all evil spirits!'

There was a pause, and then: 'Hafiz Ullah, I am alone! Come to me!'

'Shahbaz Khan, I am alone also; but I dare not leave my post!'

'That is a lie; thou art afraid.'

A longer pause followed, and then: 'I am afraid. Be silent! They are below us still. Pray to God and sleep.'

The troopers listened and wondered, for they could not understand what save earth and stone could lie below the watch-towers.

Shahbaz Khan began to call again: 'They are below us. I can see them. For the pity of God come over to me, Hafiz Ullah! My father slew ten of them. Come over!'

Hafiz Ullah answered in a very loud voice, 'Mine was guiltless. Hear, ye Men of the Night, neither my father nor my blood had any part in that sin. Bear thou thy own punishment, Shahbaz Khan.'

'Oh, some one ought to stop those two chaps crowing away like cocks there,' said Lieutenant Halley, shivering under his rock.

He had hardly turned round to expose a new side of him to the rain before a bearded, long-locked, evil-smelling Afghan rushed up the hill, and tumbled into his arms. Halley sat upon him, and thrust as much of a sword-hilt as could be spared down the man's gullet. 'If you cry out, I kill you,' he said cheerfully.

The man was beyond any expression of terror. He lay and quaked, grunting. When Halley took the sword-hilt from between his teeth, he was still inarticulate, but clung to Halley's arm, feeling it from elbow to wrist.

'The Rissala! The dead Rissala!' he gasped. 'It is down there!'

'No; the Rissala, the very much alive Rissala. It is up here,' said Halley, unshipping his watering-bridle, and fastening the man's hands. 'Why were you in the towers so foolish as to let us pass?'

'The valley is full of the dead,' said the Afghan. 'It is better to fall into the hands of the English than the hands of the dead. They march to and fro below there. I saw them in the lightning.'

He recovered his composure after a little, and whispering, because Halley's pistol was at his stomach said: 'What is this? There is no war between us now, and the Mullah will kill me for not seeing you pass!'

'Rest easy,' said Halley; 'we are coming to kill the Mullah, if God please. His teeth have grown too long. No harm will come to thee unless the daylight shows thee as a face which is desired by the gallows for crime done. But what of the dead regiment?'

'I only kill within my own border,' said the man, immensely relieved. 'The Dead Regiment is below. The men must have passed through it on their journey—four hundred dead on horses, stumbling among their own graves, among the little heaps—dead men all, whom we slew.'

'Whew!' said Halley. 'That accounts for my cursing Carter and the Major cursing me. Four hundred sabres, eh? No wonder we thought there were a few extra men in the troop. Kurruk Shah,' he whispered to a grizzled native officer that lay within a few feet of him, 'hast thou heard anything of a dead Rissala in these hills?'

'Assuredly,' said Kurruk Shah with a grim chuckle. 'Otherwise, why did I, who have served the Queen for seven-and-twenty years, and killed many hill-dogs, shout aloud for quarter when the lightning revealed us to the watch-towers? When I was a young man I saw the killing in the valley of Sheor-Kôt there at our feet, and I know the tale that grew up therefrom. But how can the ghosts of unbelievers prevail against us who are of the Faith?

Strap that dog's hands a little tighter, Sahib. An Afghan is like an eel.'

'But a dead Rissala,' said Halley, jerking his captive's wrist. 'That is foolish talk, Kurruk Shah. The dead are dead. Hold still, *sag*.' The Afghan wriggled.

'The dead are dead, and for that reason they walk at night. What need to talk? We be men; we have our eyes and ears. Thou canst both see and hear them, down the hillside' said Kurruk Shah composedly.

Halley stared and listened long and intently. The valley was full of stifled noises, as every valley must be at night; but whether he saw or heard more than was natural Halley alone knows, and he does not choose to speak on the subject.

At last, and just before the dawn, a green rocket shot up from the far side of the valley of Bersund, at the head of the gorge, to show that the Goorkhas were in position. A red light from the infantry at left and right answered it, and the cavalry burnt a white flare. Afghans in winter are late sleepers, and it was not till full day that the Gulla Kutta Mullah's men began to straggle from their huts, rubbing their eyes. They saw men in green, and red, and brown uniforms, leaning on their arms, neatly arranged all round the crater of the village of Bersund, in a cordon that not even a wolf could have broken. They rubbed their eyes the more when a pink-faced young man, who was not even in the Army, but represented the Political Department, tripped down the hillside with two orderlies, rapped at the door of the Gulla Kutta Mullah's house, and told him quietly to step out and be tied up for safe transport. That same young man passed on through the huts, tapping here one cateran and there another lightly with his cane; and as each was pointed out, so he was tied up, staring hopelessly at the crowned heights around where the English soldiers looked down with incurious eyes. Only the Mullah tried to carry it off with curses and high words, till a soldier who was tying his hands said:—

'None o' your lip! Why didn't you come out when you was ordered, instead o' keepin' us awake all night? You're no better than my own barrack-sweeper, you white-'eaded old polyanthus! Kim up!'

Half an hour later the troops had gone away with the Mullah and his thirteen friends. The dazed villagers were looking ruefully at a pile of broken muskets and snapped swords, and wondering how in the world they had come so to miscalculate the forbearance of the Indian Government.

It was a very neat little affair, neatly carried out, and the men concerned were unofficially thanked for their services.

Yet it seems to me that much credit is also due to another regiment whose name did not appear in the Brigade Orders, and whose very existence is in danger of being forgotten.

The Bridge-Builders

THE least that Findlayson, of the Public Works Department, expected was a C.I.E.; he dreamed of a C.S.I.: indeed his friends told him that he deserved more. For three years he had endured heat and cold, disappointment, discomfort, danger, and disease, with responsibility almost too heavy for one pair of shoulders; and day by day, through that time, the great Kashi Bridge over the Ganges had grown under his charge. Now, in less than three months, if all went well, His Excellency the Viceroy would open the bridge in state, an archbishop would bless it, the first train-load of soldiers would come over it, and there would be speeches.

Findlayson, C.E., sat in his trolley on a construction-line that ran along one of the main revetments—the huge stone-faced banks that flared away north and south for three miles on either side of the river—and permitted himself to think of the end. With its approaches, his work was one mile and three-quarters in length; a lattice-girder bridge, trussed with the Findlayson truss, standing on seven-and-twenty brick piers. Each one of those piers was twenty-four feet in diameter, capped with red Agra stone and sunk eighty feet below the shifting sand of the Ganges' bed. Above them ran the railway-line fifteen feet broad; above that, again, a cart-road of eighteen feet, flanked with footpaths. At either end rose towers of red brick, loopholed for musketry and pierced for big guns, and the ramp of the road was being pushed forward to their haunches. The raw earth-ends were crawling and alive with hundreds upon hundreds of tiny asses climbing out of the yawning borrow-pit below with sackfuls of stuff; and the hot afternoon air was filled with the noise of hooves, the rattle of the drivers' sticks, and the swish and roll-down of the dirt. The river was very low, and on the dazzling white sand between the three centre piers stood squat cribs of railway-sleepers, filled within and daubed without with mud, to support the last of the girders as those were riveted up. In the little deep water left by the drought, an overhead-crane travelled to and fro along its spile-pier, jerking sections of iron into place, snorting and backing and grunting as an elephant grunts in the timber-yard. Riveters by the hundred swarmed about the lattice side-work and the iron roof of the railway-line, hung from invisible staging under the bellies of the girders, clustered round the throats of the piers, and rode on the overhang of the footpath-stanchions; their fire-pots and the spurts of flame that answered each hammer-stroke showing no more than pale yellow in the sun's glare. East and west and north and south the construction-trains rattled and shrieked up and down the embankments, the piled trucks of brown and white stone banging behind them till the side-boards were unpinned, and with a roar and a grumble a few thousand tons more material were thrown out to hold the river in place.

Findlayson, C.E., turned on his trolley and looked over the face of the country that he had changed for seven miles around. Looked back on the humming village of five thousand workmen; up-stream and down, along the vista of spurs and sand; across the river to the far piers, lessening in the haze; overhead to the guard-towers—and only he knew how strong those were—and with a sigh of contentment saw that his work was good. There stood his bridge before him in the sunlight, lacking only a few weeks' work on the girders of the three middle piers—his bridge, raw and ugly as original sin, but *pukka*—permanent—to endure when all memory of the builder, yea, even of the splendid Findlayson truss, had perished. Practically, the thing was done.

Hitchcock, his assistant, cantered along the line on a little switch-tailed Kabuli pony, who, through long practice, could have trotted securely over a trestle, and nodded to his chief.

'All but,' said he, with a smile.

'I've been thinking about it,' the senior answered. 'Not half a bad job for two men, is it?'

'One—and a half. 'Gad what a Cooper's Hill cub I was when I came on the works!' Hitchcock felt very old in the crowded experiences of the past three years, that had taught him power and responsibility.

'You *were* rather a colt,' said Findlayson. 'I wonder how you'll like going back to office work when this job's over.'

'I shall hate it!' said the young man, and as he went on his eye followed Findlayson's, and he muttered, 'Isn't it damned good?'

'I think we'll go up the service together,' Findlayson said to himself. 'You're too good a youngster to waste on another man. Cub thou wast; assistant thou art. Personal assistant, and at Simla, thou shalt be, if any credit comes to me out of the business!'

Indeed the burden of the work had fallen altogether on Findlayson and his assistant, the young man whom he had chosen because of his rawness to break to his own needs. There were labour-contractors by the half-hundred—fitters and riveters, European, borrowed from the railway workshops, with perhaps twenty white

and half-caste subordinates to direct, under direction, the
bevies of workmen—but none knew better than these
two, who trusted each other, how the underlings were
not to be trusted. They had been tried many times
in sudden crises—by slipping of booms, by breaking
of tackle, failure of cranes, and the wrath of the
river—but no stress had brought to light any man
among them whom Findlayson and Hitchcock would
have honoured by working as remorselessly as they
worked themselves. Findlayson thought it over from the
beginning: the months of office work destroyed at a blow
when the Government of India, at the last moment, added
two feet to the width of the bridge, under the impression
that bridges were cut out of paper, and so brought to ruin
at least half an acre of calculations—and Hitchcock, new
to disappointment, buried his head in his arms and wept;
the heart-breaking delays over the filling of the contracts
in England; the futile correspondences hinting at great
wealth of commission if one, only one, rather doubtful
consignment were passed; the war that followed the
refusal; the careful, polite obstruction at the other end
that followed the war, till young Hitchcock, putting one
month's leave to another month, and borrowing ten days
from Findlayson, spent his poor little savings of a year
in a wild dash to London, and there, as his own tongue
asserted and the later consignments proved, put the Fear
of God into a man so great that he feared only Parliament,
and said so till Hitchcock wrought with him across his
own dinner-table, and—he feared the Kashi Bridge and
all who spoke in its name. Then there was the cholera
that came in the night to the village by the bridge-works;
and after the cholera smote the smallpox. The fever they
had always with them. Hitchcock had been appointed a
magistrate of the third class with whipping powers, for
the better government of the community, and Findlayson

watched him wield his powers temperately, learning what to overlook and what to look after. It was a long, long reverie, and it covered storm, sudden freshets, death in every manner and shape, violent and awful rage against red tape half frenzying a mind that knows it should be busy on other things; drought, sanitation, finance; birth, wedding, burial, and riot in the village of twenty warring castes; argument, expostulation, persuasion, and the blank despair that a man goes to bed upon, thankful that his rifle is all in pieces in the gun-case. Behind everything rose the black frame of the Kashi Bridge—plate by plate, girder by girder, span by span—and each pier of it recalled Hitchcock, the all-round man, who had stood by his chief without failing from the very first to this last.

So the bridge was two men's work—unless one counted Peroo, as Peroo certainly counted himself. He was a Lascar, a Kharva from Bulsar, familiar with every port between Rockhampton and London, who had risen to the rank of serang on the British India boats, but wearying of routine musters and clean clothes had thrown up the service and gone inland, where men of his calibre were sure of employment. For his knowledge of tackle and the handling of heavy weights, Peroo was worth almost any price he might have chosen to put upon his services; but custom decreed the wage of the overhead-men, and Peroo was not within many silver pieces of his proper value. Neither running water nor extreme heights made him afraid; and, as an ex-serang, he knew how to hold authority. No piece of iron was so big or so badly placed that Peroo could not devise a tackle to lift it—a loose-ended, sagging arrangement, rigged with a scandalous amount of talking, but perfectly equal to the work in hand. It was Peroo who had saved the girder of Number Seven Pier from destruction when the new wire rope jammed in the eye of the crane, and the huge plate tilted in its slings, threatening to slide out sideways. Then the native workmen lost their heads with great shoutings, and Hitchcock's right arm was broken by a falling T-plate, and he buttoned it up in his coat and swooned, and came to and directed for four hours till Peroo, from the top of the crane, reported, 'All's well,' and the plate swung home. There was no one like Peroo, serang, to lash and guy and hold, to control the donkey-engines, to hoist a fallen locomotive craftily out of the borrow-pit into which it had tumbled; to strip and dive, if need be, to see how the concrete blocks round the piers stood the scouring of Mother Gunga, or to adventure up-stream on a monsoon night and report on the state of the embankment-facings. He would interrupt the field-councils of Findlayson and Hitchcock without fear, till his wonderful English, or his still more wonderful *lingua-franca*, half Portuguese and half Malay, ran out and he was forced to take string and show the knots that he would recommend. He controlled his own gang of tacklemen—mysterious relatives from Kutch Mandvi gathered month by month and tried to the uttermost. No consideration of family or kin allowed Peroo to keep weak hands or a giddy head on the pay-roll. 'My honour is the honour of this bridge,' he would say to the about-to-be-dismissed. 'What do I care for your honour? Go and work on a steamer. That is all you are fit for.'

The little cluster of huts where he and his gang lived centred round the tattered dwelling of a sea-priest—one who had never set foot on Black Water, but had been chosen as ghostly counsellor by two generations of sea-rovers, all unaffected by port missions or those creeds which are thrust upon sailors by agencies along Thames' bank. The priest of the Lascars had nothing to do with their caste, or indeed with anything at all. He ate the offerings of his church, and slept and smoked, and slept again, 'for,' said Peroo, who had haled him a thousand miles inland, 'he is a very holy man. He never cares what you eat so long as you do not eat beef, and that is good, because on land we worship Shiva, we Kharvas; but at sea on the Kumpani's boats we attend strictly to the orders of the Burra Malum (the first mate), and on this bridge we observe what Finlinson Sahib says.'

Findlayson Sahib had that day given orders to clear the scaffolding from the guard-tower on the right bank, and Peroo with his mates was casting loose and lowering down the bamboo poles and planks as swiftly as ever they had whipped the cargo out of a coaster.

From his trolley he could hear the whistle of the serang's silver pipe and the creak and clatter of the pulleys. Peroo was standing on the topmost coping of the tower, clad in the blue dungaree of his abandoned service, and as Findlayson motioned to him to be careful, for his was no life to throw away, he gripped the last pole, and, shading his eyes ship-fashion, answered with the long-drawn wail of the fo'c'sle look-out: *'Ham dekhta hai'* ('I am looking out'). Findlayson laughed, and then sighed. It was years since he had seen a steamer, and he was sick for home. As his trolley passed under the tower, Peroo descended by a rope, ape-fashion, and cried: 'It looks well now, Sahib. Our bridge is all but done. What think you Mother Gunga will say when the rail runs over?'

'She has said little so far. It was never Mother Gunga that delayed us.'

'There is always time for her; and none the less there has been delay. Has the Sahib forgotten last autumn's flood, when the stone-boats were sunk without warning—or only a half-day's warning?'

'Yes, but nothing save a big flood could hurt us now. The spurs are holding well on the west bank.'

'Mother Gunga eats great allowances. There is always

room for more stone on the revetments. I tell this to the Chota Sahib'—he meant Hitchcock—'and he laughs.'

'No matter, Peroo. Another year thou wilt be able to build a bridge in thine own fashion.'

The Lascar grinned. 'Then it will not be in this way—with stonework sunk under water, as the *Quetta* was sunk. I like sus-sus-pen-sheen bridges that fly from bank to bank, with one big step, like a gang-plank. Then no water can hurt. When does the Lord Sahib come to open the bridge?'

'In three months, when the weather is cooler.'

'Ho! ho! He is like the Burra Malum. He sleeps below while the work is being done. Then he comes upon the quarter-deck and touches with his finger, and says: "This is not clean! Dam jiboonwallah!"'

'But the Lord Sahib does not call me a dam jiboonwalah, Peroo.'

'No, Sahib; but he does not come on deck till the work is all finished. Even the Burra Malum of the *Nerbudda* said once at Tuticorin——'

'Bah! Go! I am busy.'

'I, also!' said Peroo, with an unshaken countenance. 'May I take the light dinghy now and row along the spurs?'

'To hold them with thy hands? They are, I think, sufficiently heavy.'

'Nay, Sahib. It is thus. At sea, on the Black Water, we have room to be blown up and down without care. Here we have no room at all. Look you, we have put the river into a dock, and run her between stone sills.'

Findlayson smiled at the 'we.'

'We have bitted and bridled her. She is not like the sea, that can beat against a soft beach. She is Mother Gunga—in irons.' His voice fell a little.

'Peroo, thou hast been up and down the world more

even than I. Speak true talk, now. How much dost thou
in thy heart believe of Mother Gunga?'

'All that our priest says. London is London, Sahib.
Sydney is Sydney, and Port Darwin is Port Darwin.
Also Mother Gunga is Mother Gunga, and when I come
back to her banks I know this and worship. In London I
did poojah to the big temple by the river for the sake of
the God within. . . . Yes, I will not take the cushions in
the dinghy.'

Findlayson mounted his horse and trotted to the shed
of a bungalow that he shared with his assistant. The place
had become home to him in the last three years. He had
grilled in the heat, sweated in the rains, and shivered
with fever under the rude thatch roof; the limewash
beside the door was covered with rough drawings and
formulae, and the sentry-path trodden in the matting
of the verandah showed where he had walked alone.
There is no eight-hour limit to an engineer's work, and
the evening meal with Hitchcock was eaten booted and
spurred: over their cigars they listened to the hum of the
village as the gangs came up from the river-bed and the
lights began to twinkle.

'Peroo has gone up the spurs in your dinghy. He's
taken a couple of nephews with him, and he's lolling
in the stern like a commodore,' said Hitchcock.

'That's all right. He's got something on his mind.
You'd think that ten years in the British India boats
would have knocked most of his religion out of him.'

'So it has,' said Hitchcock, chuckling. 'I overheard
him the other day in the middle of a most atheistical talk
with that fat old *guru* of theirs. Peroo denied the efficacy
of prayer; and wanted the *guru* to go to sea and watch a
gale out with him, and see if he could stop a monsoon.'

'All the same, if you carried off his *guru* he'd leave us
like a shot. He was yarning away to me about praying

to the dome of St. Paul's when he was in London.'

'He told me that the first time he went into the engine-room of a steamer, when he was a boy, he prayed to the low-press cylinder.'

'Not half a bad thing to pray to, either. He's propitiating his own Gods now, and he wants to know what Mother Gunga will think of a bridge being run across her. Who's there?' A shadow darkened the doorway, and a telegram was put into Hitchcock's hand.

'She ought to be pretty well used to it by this time. Only a *tar*. It ought to be Ralli's answer about the new rivets . . . Great Heavens!' Hitchcock jumped to his feet.

'What is it?' said the senior, and took the form. '*That's* what Mother Gunga thinks, is it?' he said, reading. 'Keep cool, young 'un. We've got all our work cut out for us. Let's see. Muir wires, half an hour ago: "*Floods on the Ramgunga. Look out.*" Well, that gives us—one, two—nine and a half for the flood to reach Melipur Ghaut and seven's sixteen, and a half to Latodi—say fifteen hours before it comes down to us.'

'Curse that hill-fed sewer of a Ramgunga! Findlayson, this is two months before anything could have been expected, and the left bank is littered up with stuff still. Two full months before the time!'

'That's why it happens. I've only known Indian rivers for five and twenty years, and I don't pretend to understand. Here comes another *tar*.' Findlayson opened the telegram. 'Cockran, this time, from the Ganges Canal: "*Heavy rains here. Bad.*" He might have saved the last word. Well, we don't want to know any more. We've got to work the gangs all night and clean up the river-bed. You'll take the east bank and work out to meet me in the middle. Get everything that floats below the bridge: we shall have quite enough river-craft coming down adrift anyhow, without letting the stone-boats ram the piers. What have you got on the east bank that needs looking after?'

'Pontoon, one big pontoon with the overhead crane on it. T'other overhead crane on the mended pontoon, with the cart-road rivets from Twenty to Twenty-three piers—two construction lines, and a turning-spur. The pile-work must take its chance,' said Hitchcock.

'All right. Roll up everything you can lay hands on. We'll give the gang fifteen minutes more to eat their grub.'

Close to the verandah stood a big night-gong, never used except for flood, or fire in the village. Hitchcock had called for a fresh horse, and was off to his side of the bridge when Findlayson took the cloth-bound stick and smote with the rubbing stroke that brings out the full thunder of the metal.

Long before the last rumble ceased every night-gong in the village had taken up the warning. To these were added the hoarse screaming of conchs in the little temples; the throbbing of drums and tomtoms; and from the European quarters, where the riveters lived, M'Cartney's bugle, a weapon of offence on Sundays and festivals, brayed desperately, calling to 'Stables.' Engine after engine toiling home along the spurs after her day's work whistled in answer till the whistles were answered from the far bank. Then the big gong thundered thrice for a sign that it was flood and not fire; conch, drum, and whistle echoed the call, and the village quivered to the sound of bare feet running upon soft earth. The order in all cases was to stand by the day's work and wait instructions. The gangs poured by in the dusk; men stopping to knot a loin-cloth or fasten a sandal; gang-foremen shouting to their subordinates as they ran or paused by the tool-issue sheds for bars and mattocks;

locomotives creeping down their tracks wheel-deep in the crowd, till the brown torrent disappeared into the dusk of the river-bed, raced over the pilework, swarmed along the lattices, clustered by the cranes, and stood still, each man in his place.

Then the troubled beating of the gong carried the order to take up everything and bear it beyond high-water mark, and the flare-lamps broke out by the hundred between the webs of dull iron as the riveters began a night's work racing against the flood that was to come. The girders of the three centre piers—those that stood on the cribs—were all but in position. They needed just as many rivets as could be driven into them, for the flood would assuredly wash out the supports, and the iron-work would settle down on the caps of stone if they were not blocked at the ends. A hundred crowbars strained at the sleepers of the temporary line that fed the unfinished piers. It was heaved up in lengths, loaded into trucks, and backed up the bank beyond flood-level by the groaning locomotives. The tool-sheds on the sands melted away before the attack of shouting armies, and with them went the stacked ranks of Government stores, iron-bound boxes of rivets, pliers, cutters, duplicate parts of the riveting-machines, spare pumps and chains. The big crane would be the last to be shifted, for she was hoisting all the heavy stuff up to the main structure of the bridge. The concrete blocks on the fleet of stone-boats were dropped overside, where there was any depth of water, to guard the piers, and the empty boats themselves were poled under the bridge downstream. It was here that Peroo's pipe shrilled loudest, for the first stroke of the big gong had brought back the dinghy at racing speed, and Peroo and his people were stripped to the waist, working for the honour and credit which are better than life.

'I knew she would speak,' he cried. '*I* knew, but the telegraph gave us good warning. O sons of unthinkable begetting—children of unspeakable shame—are we here for the look of the thing?' It was two feet of wire rope frayed at the ends, and it did wonders as Peroo leaped from gunnel to gunnel, shouting the language of the sea.

Findlayson was more troubled for the stone-boats than anything else. M'Cartney, with his gangs, was blocking up the ends of the three doubtful spans, but boats adrift, if the flood chanced to be a high one, might endanger the girders; and there was a very fleet in the shrunken channels.

'Get them behind the swell of the guard-tower,' he shouted to Peroo. 'It will be dead-water there; get them below the bridge.'

'*Achcha!* [Very good.] *I* know. We are mooring them with wire rope,' was the answer. 'Heh! Listen to the Chota Sahib. He is working hard.'

From across the river came an almost continuous whistling of locomotives, backed by the rumble of stone. Hitchcock at the last minute was spending a few hundred more trucks of Tarakee stone in reinforcing his spurs and embankments.

'The bridge challenges Mother Gunga,' said Peroo, with a laugh. 'But when *she* talks I know whose voice will be the loudest.'

For hours the naked men worked, screaming and shouting under the lights. It was a hot, moonless night; the end of it was darkened by clouds and a sudden squall that made Findlayson very grave.

'She moves!' said Peroo, just before the dawn. 'Mother Gunga is awake! Hear!' He dipped his hand over the side of a boat and the current mumbled on it. A little wave hit the side of a pier with a crisp slap.

'Six hours before her time,' said Findlayson, mopping

his forehead savagely. 'Now we can't depend on anything. We'd better clear all hands out of the river-bed.'

Again the big gong beat, and a second time there was the rushing of naked feet on earth and ringing iron; the clatter of tools ceased. In the silence, men heard the dry yawn of water crawling over thirsty sand.

Foreman after foreman shouted to Findlayson, who had posted himself by the guard-tower, that his section of the river-bed had been cleaned out, and when the last voice dropped Findlayson hurried over the bridge till the iron plating of the permanent way gave place to the temporary plank-walk over the three centre piers, and there he met Hitchcock.

'All clear your side?' said Findlayson. The whisper rang in the box of latticework.

'Yes, and the east channel's filling now. We're utterly out of our reckoning. When is this thing down on us?'

'There's no saying. She's filling as fast as she can. Look!' Findlayson pointed to the planks below his feet, where the sand, burned and defiled by months of work, was beginning to whisper and fizz.

'What orders?' said Hitchcock.

'Call the roll—count stores—sit on your hunkers—and pray for the bridge. That's all I can think of. Good-night. Don't risk your life trying to fish out anything that may go downstream.'

'Oh, I'll be as prudent as you are! 'Night. Heavens, how she's filling! Here's the rain in earnest!' Findlayson picked his way back to his bank, sweeping the last of M'Cartney's riveters before him. The gangs had spread themselves along the embankments, regardless of the cold rain of the dawn, and there they waited for the flood. Only Peroo kept his men together behind the swell of the guard-tower, where the stone-boats lay tied fore and aft with hawsers, wire-rope, and chains.

A shrill wail ran along the line, growing to a yell, half fear and half wonder: the face of the river whitened from bank to bank between the stone facings, and the far-away spurs went out in spouts of foam. Mother Gunga had come bank-high in haste, and a wall of chocolate-coloured water was her messenger. There was a shriek above the roar of the water, the complaint of the spans coming down on their blocks as the cribs were whirled out from under their bellies. The stone-boats groaned and ground each other in the eddy that swung round the abutments, and their clumsy masts rose higher and higher against the dim sky-line.

'Before she was shut between these walls we knew what she would do. Now she is thus cramped God only knows what she will do!' said Peroo, watching the furious turmoil round the guard-tower. 'Ohé! Fight, then! Fight hard, for it is thus that a woman wears herself out.'

But Mother Gunga would not fight as Peroo desired. After the first down-stream plunge there came no more walls of water, but the river lifted herself bodily, as a snake when she drinks in midsummer, plucking and fingering along the revetments, and banking up behind the piers till even Findlayson began to recalculate the strength of his work.

When day came the village gasped. 'Only last night,' men said, turning to each other, 'it was as a town in the river-bed! Look now!'

And they looked and wondered afresh at the deep water, the racing water that licked the throat of the piers. The farther bank was veiled by rain, into which the bridge ran out and vanished; the spurs up-stream were marked by no more than eddies and spoutings, and downstream the pent river, once freed of her guidelines, had spread like a sea to the horizon. Then hurried by, rolling in the water, dead men and oxen together, with

here and there a patch of thatched roof that melted when
it touched a pier.

'Big flood,' said Peroo, and Findlayson nodded. It
was as big a flood as he had any wish to watch. His
bridge would stand what was upon her now, but not
very much more; and if by any of a thousand chances
there happened to be a weakness in the embankments,
Mother Gunga would carry his honour to the sea with
the other raffle. Worst of all, there was nothing to do
except to sit still; and Findlayson sat still under his
macintosh till his helmet became pulp on his head, and
his boots were over-ankle in mire. He took no count of
time, for the river was marking the hours, inch by inch
and foot by foot, along the embankment, and he listened,
numb and hungry, to the straining of the stone-boats, the
hollow thunder under the piers, and the hundred noises
that make the full note of a flood. Once a dripping
servant brought him food, but he could not eat; and once
he thought that he heard a faint toot from a locomotive
across the river, and then he smiled. The bridge's failure
would hurt his assistant not a little, but Hitchcock was a
young man with his big work yet to do. For himself the
crash meant everything—everything that made a hard
life worth the living. They would say, the men of his own
profession—he remembered the half-pitying things that
he himself had said when Lockhart's big water-works
burst and broke down in bricks heaps and sludge,
and Lockhart's spirit broke in him and he died. He
remembered what he himself had said when the Sumao
Bridge went out in the big cyclone by the sea; and most
he remembered poor Hartopp's face three weeks later,
when the shame had marked it. His bridge was twice the
size of Hartopp's, and it carried the Findlayson truss as
well as the new pier-shoe—the Findlayson bolted shoe.
There were no excuses in his service. Government might

listen, perhaps, but his own kind would judge him by his
bridge, as that stood or fell. He went over it in his head,
plate by plate, span by span, brick by brick, pier by pier,
remembering, comparing, estimating, and recalculating,
lest there should be any mistake; and through the long
hours and through the flights of formulae that danced
and wheeled before him a cold fear would come to pinch
his heart. His side of the sum was beyond question; but
what man knew Mother Gunga's arithmetic? Even as he
was making all sure by the multiplication-table, the river
might be scooping pot-holes to the very bottom of any
one of those eighty-foot piers that carried his reputation.
Again a servant came to him with food, but his mouth was
dry, and he could only drink and return to the decimals in
his brain. And the river was still rising. Peroo, in a mat
shelter-coat, crouched at his feet, watching now his face
and now the face of the river, but saying nothing.

At last the Lascar rose and floundered through the
mud towards the village, but he was careful to leave an
ally to watch the boats.

Presently he returned, most irreverently driving before
him the priest of his creed—a fat old man, with a gray
beard that whipped the wind with the wet cloth that
blew over his shoulder. Never was seen so lamentable
a *guru*.

'What good are offerings and little kerosene lamps
and dry grain,' shouted Peroo, 'if squatting in the mud
is all that thou canst do? Thou hast dealt long with the
Gods when they were contented and well-wishing. Now
they are angry. Speak to them!'

'What is a man against the wrath of Gods?' whined
the priest, cowering as the wind took him. 'Let me go
to the temple, and I will pray there.'

'Son of a pig, pray *here*! Is there no return for
salt fish and curry powder and dried onions? Call

aloud! Tell Mother Gunga we have had enough. Bid
her be still for the night. I cannot pray, but I have
served in the Kumpani's boats, and when men did not
obey my orders I——' A flourish of the wire-rope colt
rounded the sentence, and the priest, breaking from his
disciple, fled to the village.

'Fat pig!' said Peroo. 'After all that we have done for
him! When the flood is down I will see to it that we get a
new *guru*. Finlinson Sahib, it darkens for night now, and
since yesterday nothing has been eaten. Be wise, Sahib.
No man can endure watching and great thinking on an
empty belly. Lie down, Sahib. The river will do what the
river will do.'

'The bridge is mine; I cannot leave it.'

'Wilt thou hold it up with thy hands, then?' said Peroo,
laughing. 'I was troubled for my boats and sheers *before*
the flood came. Now we are in the hands of the Gods.
The Sahib will not eat and lie down? Take these, then.
They are meat and good toddy together, and they kill all
weariness, besides the fever that follows the rain. I have
eaten nothing else to-day at all.'

He took a small tin tobacco-box from his sodden
waist-belt and thrust it into Findlayson's hand, saying,
'Nay, do not be afraid. It is no more than opium—clean
Malwa opium!'

Findlayson shook two or three of the dark-brown
pellets into his hand, and hardly knowing what he
did, swallowed them. The stuff was at least a good
guard against fever—the fever that was creeping upon
him out of the wet mud—and he had seen what Peroo
could do in the stewing mists of autumn on the strength
of a dose from the tin box.

Peroo nodded with bright eyes. 'In a little—in a
little the Sahib will find that he thinks well again. I
too will——' He dived into his treasure-box, resettled

the rain-coat over his head, and squatted down to
watch the boats. It was too dark now to see beyond
the first pier, and the night seemed to have given the
river new strength. Findlayson stood with his chin on
his chest, thinking. There was one point about one of
the piers—the Seventh—that he had not fully settled in
his mind. The figures would not shape themselves to the
eye except one by one and at enormous intervals of time.
There was a sound, rich and mellow in his ears, like the
deepest note of a double-bass—an entrancing sound upon
which he pondered for several hours, as it seemed. Then
Peroo was at his elbow, shouting that a wire hawser had
snapped and the stone-boats were loose. Findlayson saw
the fleet open and swing out fanwise to a long-drawn
shriek of wire straining across gunnels.

'A tree hit them. They will all go,' cried Peroo. 'The
main hawser has parted. What does the Sahib do?'

An immensely complex plan had suddenly flashed into
Findlayson's mind. He saw the ropes running from boat
to boat in straight lines and angles—each rope a line of
white fire. But there was one rope which was the master-
rope. He could see that rope. If he could pull it once,
it was absolutely and mathematically certain that the
disordered fleet would reassemble itself in the backwater
behind the guard-tower. But why, he wondered, was
Peroo clinging so desperately to his waist as he hastened
down the bank? It was necessary to put the Lascar aside,
gently and slowly, because it was necessary to save the
boats, and, further, to demonstrate the extreme ease of
the problem that looked so difficult. And then—but it was
of no conceivable importance—a wire rope raced through
his hand, burning it, the high bank disappeared, and with
it all the slowly dispersing factors of the problem. He was
sitting in the rainy darkness—sitting in a boat that spun
like a top, and Peroo was standing over him.

'I had forgotten,' said the Lascar slowly, 'that to those fasting and unused the opium is worse than any wine. Those who die in Gunga go to the Gods. Still, I have no desire to present myself before such great ones. Can the Sahib swim?'

'What need? He can fly—fly as swiftly as the wind,' was the thick answer.

'He is mad!' muttered Peroo under his breath. 'And he threw me aside like a bundle of dung-cakes. Well, he will not know his death. The boat cannot live an hour here even if she strike nothing. It is not good to look at death with a clear eye.'

He refreshed himself again from the tin box, squatted down in the bows of the reeling, pegged, and stitched craft, staring through the mist at the nothing that was there. A warm drowsiness crept over Findlayson, the Chief Engineer, whose duty was with his bridge. The heavy raindrops struck him with a thousand tingling little thrills, and the weight of all time since time was made hung heavy on his eyelids. He thought and perceived that he was perfectly secure, for the water was so solid that a man could surely step out upon it, and, standing still with his legs apart to keep his balance—this was the most important point—would be borne with great and easy speed to the shore. But yet a better plan came to him. It needed only an exertion of will for the soul to hurl the body ashore as wind drives paper; to waft it kite-fashion to the bank. Thereafter—the boat spun dizzily—suppose the high wind got under the freed body? Would it tower up like a kite and pitch headlong on the far-away sands, or would it duck about beyond control through all eternity? Findlayson gripped the gunnel to anchor himself, for it seemed that he was on the edge of taking the flight before he had settled all his plans. Opium has more effect cn the white man than the black.

Peroo was only comfortably indifferent to accidents. 'She cannot live,' he grunted. 'Her seams open already. If she were even a dinghy with oars we could have ridden it out; but a box with holes is no good. Finlinson Sahib, she fills.'

'*Achcha!* I am going away. Come thou also.'

In his mind Findlayson had already escaped from the boat, and was circling high in the air to find a rest for the sole of his foot. His body—he was really sorry for its gross helplessness—lay in the stern, the water rushing about its knees.

'How very ridiculous!' he said to himself, from his eyrie; 'that—is Findlayson—chief of the Kashi Bridge. The poor beast is going to be drowned, too. Drowned when it's close to shore. I'm—I'm on shore already. Why doesn't it come along?'

To his intense disgust, he found his soul back in his body again, and that body spluttering and choking in deep water. The pain of the reunion was atrocious, but it was necessary, also, to fight for the body. He was conscious of grasping wildly at wet sand, and striding prodigiously, as one strides in a dream, to keep foot-hold in the swirling water, till at last he hauled himself clear of the hold of the river, and dropped, panting, on wet earth.

'Not this night,' said Peroo in his ear. 'The Gods have protected us.' The Lascar moved his feet cautiously, and they rustled among dried stumps. 'This is some island of last year's indigo crop,' he went on. 'We shall find no men here; but have great care, Sahib; all the snakes of a hundred miles have been flooded out. Here comes the lightning, on the heels of the wind. Now we shall be able to look; but walk carefully.'

Findlayson was far and far beyond any fear of snakes, or indeed any merely human emotion. He saw, after he had rubbed the water from his eyes, with an immense clearness, and trod, so it seemed to himself, with world-encompassing strides. Somewhere in the night of time he had built a bridge—a bridge that spanned illimitable levels of shining seas; but the Deluge had swept it away, leaving this one island under heaven for Findlayson and his companion, sole survivors of the breed of man.

An incessant lightning, forked and blue, showed all that there was to be seen on the little patch in the flood—a clump of thorn, a clump of swaying creaking bamboos, and a gray gnarled peepul over-shadowing a Hindoo shrine, from whose dome floated a tattered red flag. The holy man whose summer resting-place it was had long since abandoned it, and the weather had broken the red-daubed image of his God. The two men stumbled, heavy-limbed and heavy-eyed, over the ashes of a brick-set cooking-place, and dropped down under the shelter of the branches, while the rain and river roared together.

The stumps of the indigo crackled, and there was a smell of cattle, as a huge and dripping Brahminee Bull shouldered his way under the tree. The flashes revealed the trident mark of Shiva on his flank, the insolence of head and hump, the luminous stag-like eyes, the brow crowned with a wreath of sodden marigold blooms, and the silky dewlap that nigh swept the ground. There was a noise behind him of other beasts coming up from the flood-line through the thicket, a sound of heavy feet and deep breathing.

'Here be more beside ourselves,' said Findlayson, his head against the tree-bole, looking through half-shut eyes, wholly at ease.

'Truly,' said Peroo thickly, 'and no small ones.'

'What are they, then? I do not see clearly.'

'The Gods. Who else? Look!'

'Ah, true! The Gods surely—the Gods.' Findlayson

smiled as his head fell forward on his chest. Peroo was eminently right. After the Flood, who should be alive in the land except the Gods that made it—the Gods to whom his village prayed nightly—the Gods who were in all men's mouths and about all men's ways? He could not raise his head or stir a finger for the trance that held him, and Peroo was smiling vacantly at the lightning.

The Bull paused by the shrine, his head lowered to the damp earth. A green Parrot in the branches preened his wet wings and screamed against the thunder as the circle under the tree filled with the shifting shadows of beasts. There was a Black-buck at the Bull's heels—such a buck as Findlayson in his far-away life upon earth might have seen in dreams—a buck with a royal head, ebon back, silvery belly, and gleaming straight horns. Beside him, her head bowed to the ground, the green eyes burning under the heavy brows, with restless tail switching the dead grass, paced a Tigress, full-bellied and deep-jowled.

The Bull crouched beside the shrine, and there leaped from the darkness a monstrous gray Ape, who seated himself man-wise in the place of the fallen image, and the rain spilled like jewels from the hair of his neck and shoulders.

Other shadows came and went behind the circle, among them a drunken Man flourishing staff and drinking-bottle. Then a hoarse bellow broke out from near the ground. 'The flood lessens even now,' it cried. 'Hour by hour the water falls, and their bridge still stands!'

'My bridge,' said Findlayson to himself. 'That must be very old work now. What have the Gods to do with my bridge!'

His eyes rolled in the darkness following the roar. A Crocodile—the blunt-nosed, ford-haunting Mugger of the Ganges—draggled herself before the beasts, lashing furiously to right and left with her tail.

'They have made it too strong for me. In all this night I have only torn away a handful of planks. The walls stand! The towers stand! They have chained my flood, and my river is not free any more. Heavenly Ones, take this yoke away! Give me clear water between bank and bank! It is I, Mother Gunga, that speak. The Justice of the Gods! Deal me the Justice of the Gods!'

'What said I?' whispered Peroo. 'This is in truth a Punchayet of the Gods. Now we know that all the world is dead, save you and I, Sahib.'

The Parrot screamed and fluttered again, and the Tigress, her ears flat to her head, snarled wickedly.

Somewhere in the shadow a great trunk and gleaming tusks swayed to and fro, and a low gurgle broke the silence that followed on the snarl.

'We be here,' said a deep voice, 'the Great Ones. One only and very many. Shiv, my father, is here, with Indra. Kali has spoken already. Hanuman listens also.'

'Kashi is without her Kotwal to-night,' shouted the Man with the drinking-bottle, flinging his staff to the ground, while the island rang to the baying of hounds. 'Give her the Justice of the Gods.'

'Ye were still when they polluted my waters,' the great Crocodile bellowed. 'Ye made no sign when my river was trapped between the walls. I had no help save my own strength, and that failed—the strength of Mother Gunga failed—before their guard-towers. What could I do? I have done everything. Finish now, Heavenly Ones!'

'I brought the death; I rode the spotted sickness from hut to hut of their workmen, and yet they would not cease.' A nose-slitten, hide-worn Ass, lame, scissor-legged, and galled, limped forward. 'I cast the death at them out of my nostrils, but they would not cease.'

Peroo would have moved, but the opium lay heavy upon him.

'Bah!' he said, spitting. 'Here is Sitala herself; Mata—
the small-pox. Has the Sahib a handkerchief to put over
his face?'

'Small help!' said the Crocodile. 'They fed me the
corpses for a month, and I flung them out on my
sand-bars, but their work went forward. Demons they
are, and sons of demons! And ye left Mother Gunga alone
for their fire-carriage to make a mock of. The Justice of
the Gods on the bridge-builders!'

The Bull turned the cud in his mouth and answered
slowly, 'If the Justice of the Gods caught all who made
a mock of holy things, there would be many dark altars
in the land, mother.'

'But this goes beyond a mock,' said the Tigress,
darting forward a griping paw. 'Thou knowest, Shiv,
and ye too, Heavenly Ones; ye know that they have
defiled Gunga. Surely they must come to the Destroyer.
Let Indra judge.'

The Buck made no movement as he answered, 'How
long has this evil been?'

'Three years, as men count years,' said the Mugger,
close pressed to the earth.

'Does Mother Gunga die, then, in a year, that she
is so anxious to see vengeance now? The deep sea was
where she runs but yesterday, and to-morrow the sea
shall cover her again as the Gods count that which men
call time. Can any say that this their bridge endures till
to-morrow?' said the Buck.

There was a long hush, and in the clearing of the
storm the full moon stood up above the dripping trees.

'Judge ye, then,' said the Mugger sullenly. 'I have
spoken my shame. The flood falls still. I can do no
more.'

'For my own part'—it was the voice of the great
Ape seated within the shrine—'it pleases me well to

watch these men, remembering that I also builded no small bridge in the world's youth.'

'They say, too,' snarled the Tiger, 'that these men came of the wreck of thy armies, Hanuman, and therefore thou hast aided——'

'They toil as my armies toiled in Lanka, and they believe that their toil endures. Indra is too high, but Shiv, thou knowest how the land is threaded with their fire-carriages.'

'Yea, I know,' said the Bull. 'Their Gods instructed them in the matter.'

A laugh ran round the circle.

'Their Gods! What should their Gods know? They were born yesterday, and those that made them are scarcely yet cold,' said the Mugger. 'To-morrow their Gods will die.'

'Ho!' said Peroo. 'Mother Gunga talks good talk. I told that to the padre-sahib who preached on the *Mombasa*, and he asked the Burra Malum to put me in irons for a great rudeness.'

'Surely they make these things to please their Gods,' said the Bull again.

'Not altogether,' the Elephant rolled forth. 'It is for the profit of my mahajuns—my fat money-lenders that worship me at each new year, when they draw my image at the head of the account-books. I, looking over their shoulders by lamplight, see that the names in the books are those of men in far places—for all the towns are drawn together by the fire-carriage, and the money comes and goes swiftly, and the account-books grow as fat as—myself. And I, who am Ganesh of Good Luck, I bless my peoples.'

'They have changed the face of the land—which is my land. They have killed and made new towns on my banks,' said the Mugger.

'It is but the shifting of a little dirt. Let the dirt dig in the dirt if it pleases the dirt,' answered the Elephant.

'But afterwards?' said the Tiger. 'Afterwards they will see that Mother Gunga can avenge no insult, and they fall away from her first, and later from us all, one by one. In the end, Ganesh, we are left with naked altars.'

The drunken Man staggered to his feet, and hiccuped vehemently in the face of the assembled Gods.

'Kali lies. My sister lies. Also this my stick is the Kotwal of Kashi, and he keeps tally of my pilgrims. When the time comes to worship Bhairon—and it is always time—the fire-carriages move one by one, and each bears a thousand pilgrims. They do not come afoot any more, but rolling upon wheels, and my honour is increased.'

'Gunga, I have seen thy bed at Prayag black with the pilgrims,' said the Ape, leaning forward, 'and but for the fire-carriage they would have come slowly and in fewer numbers. Remember.'

'They come to me always,' Bhairon went on thickly. 'By day and night they pray to me, all the Common People in the fields and the roads. Who is like Bhairon to-day? What talk is this of changing faiths? Is my staff Kotwal of Kashi for nothing? He keeps the tally, and he says that never were so many altars as to-day, and the fire-carriage serves them well. Bhairon am I—Bhairon of the Common People, and the chiefest of the Heavenly Ones to-day. Also my staff says——'

'Peace, thou!' lowed the Bull. 'The worship of the schools is mine, and they talk very wisely, asking whether I be one or many, as is the delight of my people, and ye know what I am. Kali, my wife, thou knowest also.'

'Yea, I know,' said the Tigress, with lowered head.

'Greater am I than Gunga also. For ye know who moved

the minds of men that they should count Gunga holy among the rivers. Who die in that water—ye know how men say—come to Us without punishment, and Gunga knows that the fire-carriage has borne to her scores upon scores of such anxious ones; and Kali knows that she has held her chiefest festivals among the pilgrimages that are fed by the fire-carriage. Who smote at Pooree, under the Image there, her thousands in a day and a night, and bound the sickness to the wheels of the fire-carriages, so that it ran from one end of the land to the other? Who but Kali? Before the fire-carriage came it was a heavy toil. The fire-carriages have served thee well, Mother of Death. But I speak for mine own altars, who am not Bhairon of the Common Folk, but Shiv. Men go to and fro, making words and telling talk of strange Gods, and I listen. Faith follows faith among my people in the schools, and I have no anger; for when the words are said, and the new talk is ended, to Shiv men return at the last.'

'True. It is true,' murmured Hanuman. 'To Shiv and to the others, mother, they return. I creep from temple to temple in the North, where they worship one God and His Prophet; and presently my image is alone within their shrines.'

'Small thanks,' said the Buck, turning his head slowly. 'I am that One and His Prophet also.'

'Even so, father,' said Hanuman. 'And to the South I go who am the oldest of the Gods as men know the Gods, and presently I touch the shrines of the new faith and the Woman whom we know is hewn twelve-armed, and still they call her Mary.'

'Small thanks, brother,' said the Tigress. 'I am that Woman.'

'Even so, sister; and I go West among the fire-carriages, and stand before the bridge-builders in many shapes, and

because of me they change their faiths and are very wise.
Ho! ho! I am the builder of bridges indeed—bridges
between this and that, and each bridge leads surely
to Us in the end. Be content, Gunga. Neither these
men nor those that follow them mock thee at all.'

'Am I alone, then, Heavenly Ones? Shall I smooth
out my flood lest unhappily I bear away their walls?
Will Indra dry my springs in the hills and make me
crawl humbly between their wharfs? Shall I bury me
in the sand ere I offend?'

'And all for the sake of a little iron bar with the
fire-carriage atop. Truly, Mother Gunga is always young!'
said Ganesh the Elephant. 'A child had not spoken more
foolishly. Let the dirt dig in the dirt ere it return to the
dirt. I know only that my people grow rich and praise me.
Shiv has said that the men of the schools do not forget;
Bhairon is content for his crowd of the Common People:
and Hanuman laughs.'

'Surely I laugh,' said the Ape. 'My altars are few beside
those of Ganesh or Bhairon, but the fire-carriages bring
me new worshippers from beyond the Black Water—the
men who believe that their God is toil. I run before them
beckoning, and they follow Hanuman.'

'Give them the toil that they desire, then,' said the
Mugger. 'Make a bar across my flood and throw the
water back upon the bridge. Once thou wast strong in
Lanka, Hanuman. Stoop and lift my bed.'

'Who gives life can take life.' The Ape scratched in
the mud with a long forefinger. 'And yet, who would
profit by the killing? Very many would die.'

There came up from the water a snatch of a love-song
such as the boys sing when they watch their cattle in the
noon heats of late spring. The Parrot screamed joyously,
sidling along his branch with lowered head as the song
grew louder, and in a patch of clear moonlight stood

revealed the young herd, the darling of the Gopis, the idol of dreaming maids and of mothers ere their children are born—Krishna the Well-beloved. He stooped to knot up his long wet hair, and the Parrot fluttered to his shoulder.

'Fleeting and singing, and singing and fleeting,' hiccuped Bhairon. 'Those make thee late for the council, brother.'

'And then?' said Krishna, with a laugh, throwing back his head. 'Ye can do little without me or Karma here.' He fondled the Parrot's plumage and laughed again. 'What is this sitting and talking together? I heard Mother Gunga roaring in the dark, and so came quickly from a hut where I lay warm. And what have ye done to Karma, that he is so wet and silent? And what does Mother Gunga here? Are the heavens full that ye must come paddling in the mud beast-wise? Karma, what do they do?'

'Gunga has prayed for a vengeance on the bridge-builders, and Kali is with her. Now she bids Hanuman whelm the bridge, that her honour may be made great,' cried the Parrot. 'I waited here, knowing that thou wouldst come, O my master!'

'And the Heavenly Ones said nothing? Did Gunga and the Mother of Sorrows out-talk them? Did none speak for my people?'

'Nay,' said Ganesh, moving uneasily from foot to foot; 'I said it was but dirt at play, and why should we stamp it flat?'

'I was content to let them toil—well content,' said Hanuman.

'What had I to do with Gunga's anger?' said the Bull.

'I am Bhairon of the Common Folk, and this my staff is Kotwal of all Kashi. I spoke for the Common People.'

'Thou?' The young God's eyes sparkled.

'Am I not the first of the Gods in their mouths

to-day?' returned Bhairon, unabashed. 'For the sake
of the Common People I said—very many wise things
which I have now forgotten—but this my staff——'

Krishna turned impatiently, saw the Mugger at his
feet, and kneeling, slipped an arm round the cold neck.
'Mother,' he said gently, 'get thee to thy flood again. The
matter is not for thee. What harm shall thy honour take
of this live dirt? Thou hast given them their fields new
year after year, and by thy flood they are made strong.
They come all to thee at the last. What need to slay them
now? Have pity, mother, for a little—and it is only for a
little.'

'If it be only for a little——' the slow beast began.

'Are they Gods, then?' Krishna returned with a laugh,
his eyes looking into the dull eyes of the Mugger. 'Be
certain that it is only for a little. The Heavenly Ones
have heard thee, and presently justice will be done. Go
now, mother, to the flood again. Men and cattle are thick
on the waters—the banks fall—the villages melt because
of thee.'

'But the bridge—the bridge stands.' The Mugger
turned grunting into the undergrowth as Krishna rose.

'It is ended,' said the Tigress, viciously. 'There is no
more justice from the Heavenly Ones. Ye have made
shame and sport of Gunga, who asked no more than
a few score lives.'

'Of *my* people—who lie under the leaf-roofs of the
village yonder—of the young girls, and the young men
who sing to them in the dark—of the child that will be
born, next morn—of that which was begotten to-night,'
said Krishna. 'And when all is done, what profit? To-
morrow sees them at work. Ay, if ye swept the bridge
out from end to end they would begin anew. Hear me!
Bhairon is drunk always. Hanuman mocks his people
with new riddles.'

'Nay, but they are very old ones,' the Ape said, laughing.

'Shiv hears the talk of the schools and the dreams of the holy men; Ganesh thinks only of his fat traders; but I—I live with these my people, asking for no gifts, and so receiving them hourly.'

'And very tender art thou of thy people,' said the Tigress.

'They are my own. The old women dream of me, turning in their sleep; the maids look and listen for me when they go to fill their lotahs by the river. I walk by the young men waiting without the gates at dusk, and I call over my shoulder to the white-beards. Ye know, Heavenly Ones, that I alone of us all walk upon the earth continually, and have no pleasure in our heavens so long as a green blade springs here, or there are two voices at twilight in the standing crops. Wise are ye, but ye live far off, forgetting whence ye came. So do I not forget. And the fire-carriage feeds your shrines, ye say? And the fire-carriages bring a thousand pilgrimages where but ten came in the old years? True. That is true to-day.'

'But to-morrow they are dead, brother,' said Ganesh.

'Peace!' said the Bull, as Hanuman leaned forward again. 'And to-morrow, beloved—what of to-morrow?'

'This only. A new word creeping from mouth to mouth among the Common Folk—a word that neither man nor God can lay hold of—an evil word—a little lazy word among the Common Folk, saying (and none know who set that word afoot) that they weary of ye, Heavenly Ones.'

The Gods laughed together softly. 'And then, beloved?' they said.

'And to cover that weariness they, my people, will bring to thee, Shiv, and to thee, Ganesh, at first greater

offerings and a louder noise of worship. But the word
has gone abroad, and, after, they will pay fewer dues
to your fat Brahmins. Next they will forget your altars,
but so slowly that no man can say how his forgetfulness
began.'

'I knew—I knew! I spoke this also, but they would
not hear,' said the Tigress. 'We should have slain—we
should have slain!'

'It is too late now. Ye should have slain at the
beginning, when the men from across the water had
taught our folk nothing. Now my people see their work,
and go away thinking. They do not think of the Heavenly
Ones altogether. They think of the fire-carriage and the
other things that the bridge-builders have done, and
when your priests thrust forward hands asking alms,
they give unwillingly a little. That is the beginning,
among one or two, or five or ten—for I, moving among
my people, know what is in their hearts.'

'And the end, Jester of the Gods? What shall the
end be?' said Ganesh.

'The end shall be as it was in the beginning, O
slothful son of Shiv! The flame shall die upon the
altars and the prayer upon the tongue till ye become
little Gods again—Gods of the jungle—names that the
hunters of rats and noosers of dogs whisper in the thicket
and among the caves—rag-Gods, pot Godlings of the tree,
and the village-mark, as ye were at the beginning. That
is the end, Ganesh, for thee, and for Bhairon—Bhairon
of the Common People.'

'It is very far away,' grunted Bhairon. 'Also, it is a lie.'

'Many women have kissed Krishna. They told him
this to cheer their own hearts when the gray hairs
came, and he has told us the tale,' said the Bull, below
his breath.

'Their Gods came, and we changed them. I took the

Woman and made her twelve-armed. So shall we twist all their Gods,' said Hanuman.

'Their Gods! This is no question of their Gods—one or three—man or woman. The matter is with the people. *They* move, and not the Gods of the bridge-builders,' said Krishna.

'So be it. I have made a man worship the fire-carriage as it stood still breathing smoke, and he knew not that he worshipped me,' said Hanuman the Ape. 'They will only change a little the names of their Gods. I shall lead the builders of the bridges as of old: Shiv shall be worshipped in the schools by such as doubt and despise their fellows: Ganesh shall have his mahajuns, and Bhairon the donkey-drivers, the pilgrims, and the sellers of toys. Beloved, they will do no more than change the names, and that we have seen a thousand times.'

'Surely they will do no more than change the names,' echoed Ganesh: but there was an uneasy movement among the Gods.

'They will change more than the names. Me alone they cannot kill, so long as maiden and man meet together or the spring follows the winter rains. Heavenly Ones, not for nothing have I walked upon the earth. My people know not now what they know; but I, who live with them, I read their hearts. Great Kings, the beginning of the end is born already. The fire-carriages shout the names of new Gods that are *not* the old under new names. Drink now and eat greatly! Bathe your faces in the smoke of the altars before they grow cold! Take dues and listen to the cymbals and the drums, Heavenly Ones, while yet there are flowers and songs. As men count time the end is far off; but as we who know reckon it is to-day. I have spoken.'

The young God ceased, and his brethren looked at each other long in silence.

'This I have not heard before,' Peroo whispered in his companion's ear. 'And yet sometimes, when I oiled the brasses in the engine-room of the *Goorkha*, I have wondered if our priests were so wise—so wise. The day is coming, Sahib. They will be gone by the morning.'

A yellow light broadened in the sky, and the tone of the river changed as the darkness withdrew.

Suddenly the Elephant trumpeted aloud as though a man had goaded him.

'Let Indra judge. Father of all, speak thou! What of the things we have heard? Has Krishna lied indeed? Or——'

'Ye know,' said the Buck, rising to his feet. 'Ye know the Riddle of the Gods. When Brahm ceases to dream, the Heavens and the Hells and Earth disappear. Be content. Brahm dreams still. The dreams come and go, and the nature of the dreams changes, but still Brahm dreams. Krishna has walked too long upon earth, and yet I love him the more for the tale he has told. The Gods change, beloved—all save One!'

'Ay, all save one that makes love in the hearts of men,' said Krishna, knotting his girdle. 'It is but a little time to wait, and ye shall know if I lie.'

'Truly it is but a little time, as thou sayest, and we shall know. Get thee to thy huts again, beloved, and make sport for the young things, for still Brahm dreams. Go, my children! Brahm dreams—and till He wakes the Gods die not.'

'Whither went they?' said the Lascar, awestruck, shivering a little with the cold.

'God knows!' said Findlayson. The river and the island lay in full daylight now, and there was never mark of hoof or pug on the wet earth under the peepul. Only a parrot screamed in the branches, bringing down showers of water-drops as he fluttered his wings.

'Up! We are cramped with cold! Has the opium died out? Canst thou move, Sahib?'

Findlayson staggered to his feet and shook himself. His head swam and ached, but the work of the opium was over, and, as he sluiced his forehead in a pool, the Chief Engineer of the Kashi Bridge was wondering how he had managed to fall upon the island, what chances the day offered of return, and, above all, how his work stood.

'Peroo, I have forgotten much. I was under the guard-tower watching the river; and then——Did the flood sweep us away?'

'No. The boats broke loose, Sahib, and' (if the Sahib had forgotten about the opium, decidedly Peroo would not remind him) 'in striving to retie them, so it seemed to me—but it was dark—a rope caught the Sahib and threw him upon a boat. Considering that we two, with Hitchcock Sahib, built, as it were, that bridge, I came also upon the boat, which came riding on horseback, as it were, on the nose of this island, and so, splitting, cast us ashore. I made a great cry when the boat left the wharf, and without doubt Hitchcock Sahib will come for us. As for the bridge, so many have died in the building that it cannot fall.'

A fierce sun, that drew out all the smell of the sodden land, had followed the storm, and in that clear light there was no room for a man to think of dreams of the dark. Findlayson stared upstream, across the blaze of moving water, till his eyes ached. There was no sign of any bank to the Ganges, much less of a bridge-line.

'We came down far,' he said. 'It was wonderful that we were not drowned a hundred times.'

'That was the least of the wonder, for no man dies before his time. I have seen Sydney, I have seen

London, and twenty great ports, but'—Peroo looked at the damp, discoloured shrine under the peepul—'never man has seen that we saw here.'

'What?'

'Has the Sahib forgotten; or do we black men only see the Gods?'

'There was a fever upon me.' Findlayson was still looking uneasily across the water. 'It seemed that the island was full of beasts and men talking, but I do not remember. A boat could live in this water now, I think.'

'Oho! Then it *is* true. "When Brahm ceases to dream, the Gods die." Now I know, indeed, what he meant. Once, too, the *guru* said as much to me; but then I did not understand. Now I am wise.'

'What?' said Findlayson over his shoulder.

Peroo went on as if he were talking to himself. 'Six—seven—ten monsoons since, I was watch on the fo'c'sle of the *Rewah*—the Kumpani's big boat—and there was a big *tufan*, green and black water beating; and I held fast to the life-lines, choking under the waters. Then I thought of the Gods—of Those whom we saw to-night'—he stared curiously at Findlayson's back, but the white man was looking across the flood. 'Yes, I say of Those whom we saw this night past, and I called upon Them to protect me. And while I prayed, still keeping my look-out, a big wave came and threw me forward upon the ring of the great black bow-anchor, and the *Rewah* rose high and high, leaning towards the left-hand side, and the water drew away from beneath her nose, and I lay upon my belly, holding the ring, and looking down into those great deeps. Then I thought, even in the face of death, if I lose hold I die, and for me neither the *Rewah* nor my place by the galley where the rice is cooked, nor Bombay, nor Calcutta, nor even London, will be any more

for me. "How shall I be sure," I said, "that the Gods to
whom I pray will abide at all?" This I thought, and the
Rewah dropped her nose as a hammer falls, and all the
sea came in and slid me backwards along the fo'c'sle and
over the break of the fo'c'sle, and I very badly bruised my
shin against the donkey-engine: but I did not die, and I
have seen the Gods. They are good for live men, but for
the dead—— They have spoken Themselves. Therefore,
when I come to the village I will beat the *guru* for talking riddles which are no riddles. When Brahm ceases to
dream, the Gods go.'

'Look up-stream. The light blinds. Is there smoke
yonder?'

Peroo shaded his eyes with his hands. 'He is a wise man
and quick. Hitchcock Sahib would not trust a rowboat. He
has borrowed the Rao Sahib's steam-launch, and comes
to look for us. I have always said that there should have
been a steam-launch on the bridge-works for us.'

The territory of the Rao of Baraon lay within ten miles
of the bridge; and Findlayson and Hitchcock had spent
a fair portion of their scanty leisure in playing billiards
and shooting Black-buck with the young man. He had
been bear-led by an English tutor of sporting tastes for
some five or six years, and was now royally wasting the
revenues accumulated during his minority by the Indian
Government. His steam-launch, with its silver-plated
rails, striped silk awning, and mahogany decks, was
a new toy which Findlayson had found horribly in the
way when the Rao came to look at the bridge-works.

'It's great luck,' murmured Findlayson, but he was
none the less afraid, wondering what news might be of
the bridge.

The gaudy blue and white funnel came downstream
swiftly. They could see Hitchcock in the bows, with a
pair of opera-glasses, and his face was unusually white.

Then Peroo hailed, and the launch made for the tail of the island. The Rao Sahib, in tweed shooting-suit and a seven-hued turban, waved his royal hand, and Hitchcock shouted. But he need have asked no questions, for Findlayson's first demand was for his bridge.

'All serene! 'Gad, I never expected to see you again, Findlayson. You're seven koss down-stream. Yes, there's not a stone shifted anywhere; but how are you? I borrowed the Rao Sahib's launch, and he was good enough to come along. Jump in.'

'Ah, Finlinson, you are very well, eh? That was most unprecedented calamity last night, eh? My royal palace, too, it leaks like the devil, and the crops will also be short all about my country. Now you shall back her out, Hitchcock. I—I do not understand steam-engines. You are wet? You are cold, Finlinson? I have some things to eat here, and you will take a good drink.'

'I'm immensely grateful, Rao Sahib. I believe you've saved my life. How did Hitchcock——'

'Oho! His hair was upon end. He rode to me in the middle of the night and woke me up in the arms of Morphus. I was most truly concerned, Finlinson, so I came too. My head-priest he is very angry just now. We will go quick, Mister Hitchcock. I am due to attend at twelve forty-five in the state temple, where we sanctify some new idol. If not so I would have asked you to spend the day with me. They are dam-bore, these religious ceremonies, Finlinson, eh?'

Peroo, well known to the crew, had possessed himself of the wheel, and was taking the launch craftily up-stream. But while he steered he was, in his mind, handling two feet of partially untwisted wire-rope; and the back upon which he beat was the back of his *guru*.

'They'

ONE view called me to another; one hill top to its fellow, half across the county, and since I could answer at no more trouble than the snapping forward of a lever, I let the county flow under my wheels. The orchid-studded flats of the East gave way to the thyme, ilex, and grey grass of the Downs; these again to the rich cornland and fig-trees of the lower coast, where you carry the beat of the tide on your left hand for fifteen level miles; and when at last I turned inland through a huddle of rounded hills and woods I had run myself clean out of my known marks. Beyond that precise hamlet which stands godmother to the capital of the United States, I found hidden villages where bees, the only things awake, boomed in eighty-foot lindens that overhung grey Norman churches; miraculous brooks diving under stone bridges built for heavier traffic than would ever vex them again; tithe-barns larger than their churches, and an old smithy that cried out aloud how it had once been a hall of the Knights of the Temple. Gipsies I found on a common where the gorse, bracken, and heath fought it out together up a mile of Roman road; and a little farther on I disturbed a red fox rolling dog-fashion in the naked sunlight.

As the wooded hills closed about me I stood up in the car to take the bearings of that great Down whose ringed head is a landmark for fifty miles across the low countries.

I judged that the lie of the country would bring me across some westward-running road that went to his feet, but I did not allow for the confusing veils of the woods. A quick turn plunged me first into a green cutting brim-full of liquid sunshine, next into a gloomy tunnel where last year's dead leaves whispered and scuffled about my tyres. The strong hazel stuff meeting overhead had not been cut for a couple of generations at least, nor had any axe helped the moss-cankered oak and beech to spring above them. Here the road changed frankly into a carpeted ride on whose brown velvet spent primrose-clumps showed like jade, and a few sickly, white-stalked blue-bells nodded together. As the slope favoured I shut off the power and slid over the whirled leaves, expecting every moment to meet a keeper; but I only heard a jay, far off, arguing against the silence under the twilight of the trees.

Still the track descended. I was on the point of reversing and working my way back on the second speed ere I ended in some swamp, when I saw sunshine through the tangle ahead and lifted the brake.

It was down again at once. As the light beat across my face my fore-wheels took the turf of a great still lawn from which sprang horsemen ten feet high with levelled lances, monstrous peacocks, and sleek round-headed maids of honour—blue, black, and glistening—all of clipped yew. Across the lawn—the marshalled woods besieged it on three sides—stood an ancient house of lichened and weather-worn stone, with mullioned windows and roofs of rose-red tile. It was flanked by semi-circular walls, also rose-red, that closed the lawn on the fourth side, and at their feet a box hedge grew man-high. There were doves on the roof about the slim brick chimneys, and I caught a glimpse of an octagonal dove-house behind the screening wall.

Here, then, I stayed; a horseman's green spear laid at
my breast; held by the exceeding beauty of that jewel in
that setting.

'If I am not packed off for a trespasser, or if this knight
does not ride a wallop at me,' thought I, 'Shakespeare and
Queen Elizabeth at least must come out of that half-open
garden door and ask me to tea.'

A child appeared at an upper window, and I thought
the little thing waved a friendly hand. But it was to call
a companion, for presently another bright head showed.
Then I heard a laugh among the yew-peacocks, and
turning to make sure (till then I had been watching
the house only) I saw the silver of a fountain behind a
hedge thrown up against the sun. The doves on the roof
cooed to the cooing water; but between the two notes I
caught the utterly happy chuckle of a child absorbed in
some light mischief.

The garden door—heavy oak sunk deep in the thick-
ness of the wall—opened further: a woman in a big
garden hat set her foot slowly on the time-hollowed
stone step and as slowly walked across the turf. I was
forming some apology when she lifted up her head and
I saw that she was blind.

'I heard you,' she said. 'Isn't that a motor car?'

'I'm afraid I've made a mistake in my road. I should
have turned off up above—I never dreamed——' I began.

'But I'm very glad. Fancy a motor car coming into the
garden! It will be such a treat——' She turned and made
as though looking about her. 'You—you haven't seen any
one, have you—perhaps?'

'No one to speak to, but the children seemed interested
at a distance.'

'Which?'

'I saw a couple up at the window just now, and
I think I heard a little chap in the grounds.'

'Oh, lucky you!' she cried, and her face brightened. 'I hear them, of course, but that's all. You've seen them and heard them?'

'Yes,' I answered. 'And if I know anything of children, one of them's having a beautiful time by the fountain yonder. Escaped, I should imagine.'

'You're fond of children?'

I gave her one or two reasons why I did not altogether hate them.

'Of course, of course,' she said. 'Then you understand. Then you won't think it foolish if I ask you to take your car through the gardens, once or twice—quite slowly. I'm sure they'd like to see it. They see so little, poor things. One tries to make their life pleasant, but——' she threw out her hands towards the woods. 'We're so out of the world here.'

'That will be splendid,' I said. 'But I can't cut up your grass.'

She faced to the right. 'Wait a minute,' she said. 'We're at the South gate, aren't we? Behind those peacocks there's a flagged path. We call it the Peacocks' Walk. You can't see it from here, they tell me, but if you squeeze along by the edge of the wood you can turn at the first peacock and get on to the flags.'

It was sacrilege to wake that dreaming house-front with the clatter of machinery, but I swung the car to clear the turf, brushed along the edge of the wood and turned in on the broad stone path where the fountain-basin lay like one star-sapphire.

'May I come too?' she cried. 'No, please don't help me. They'll like it better if they see me.'

She felt her way lightly to the front of the car, and with one foot on the step she called: 'Children, oh, children! Look and see what's going to happen!'

The voice would have drawn lost souls from the

Pit, for the yearning that underlay its sweetness, and
I was not surprised to hear an answering shout behind
the yews. It must have been the child by the fountain,
but he fled at our approach, leaving a little toy boat in
the water. I saw the glint of his blue blouse among the
still horsemen.

Very disposedly we paraded the length of the walk
and at her request backed again. This time the child
had got the better of his panic, but stood far off and
doubting.

'The little fellow's watching us,' I said. 'I wonder
if he'd like a ride.'

'They're very shy still. Very shy. But, oh, lucky
you to be able to see them! Let's listen.'

I stopped the machine at once, and the humid stillness,
heavy with the scent of box, cloaked us deep. Shears I
could hear where some gardener was clipping; a mumble
of bees and broken voices that might have been the
doves.

'Oh, unkind!' she said wearily.

'Perhaps they're only shy of the motor. The little
maid at the window looks tremendously interested.'

'Yes?' She raised her head. 'It was wrong of me to
say that. They are really fond of me. It's the only thing
that makes life worth living—when they're fond of you,
isn't it? I daren't think what the place would be without
them. By the way, is it beautiful?'

'I think it is the most beautiful place I have ever seen.'

'So they all tell me. I can feel it, of course, but
that isn't quite the same thing.'

'Then have you never——?' I began, but stopped
abashed.

'Not since I can remember. It happened when I
was only a few months old, they tell me. And yet
I must remember something, else how could I dream

about colours. I see light in my dreams, and colours, but I never see *them*. I only hear them just as I do when I'm awake.'

'It's difficult to see faces in dreams. Some people can, but most of us haven't the gift,' I went on, looking up at the window where the child stood all but hidden.

'I've heard that too,' she said. 'And they tell me that one never sees a dead person's face in a dream. Is that true?'

'I believe it is—now I come to think of it.'

'But how is it with yourself—yourself?' The blind eyes turned towards me.

'I have never seen the faces of my dead in any dream,' I answered.

'Then it must be as bad as being blind.'

The sun had dipped behind the woods and the long shades were possessing the insolent horsemen one by one. I saw the light die from off the top of a glossy-leaved lance and all the brave hard green turn to soft black. The house, accepting another day at end, as it had accepted an hundred thousand gone, seemed to settle deeper into its rest among the shadows.

'Have you ever wanted to?' she said after the silence.

'Very much sometimes,' I replied. The child had left the window as the shadows closed upon it.

'Ah! So've I, but I don't suppose it's allowed. . . . Where d'you live?'

'Quite the other side of the county—sixty miles and more, and I must be going back. I've come without my big lamp.'

'But it's not dark yet. I can feel it.'

'I'm afraid it will be by the time I get home. Could you lend me someone to set me on my road at first? I've utterly lost myself.'

'I'll send Madden with you to the cross-roads. We

are so out of the world, I don't wonder you were lost! I'll guide you round to the front of the house; but you will go slowly, won't you, till you're out of the grounds? It isn't foolish, do you think?'

'I promise you I'll go like this,' I said, and let the car start herself down the flagged path.

We skirted the left wing of the house, whose elaborately cast lead guttering alone was worth a day's journey; passed under a great rose-grown gate in the red wall, and so round to the high front of the house which in beauty and stateliness as much excelled the back as that all others I had seen.

'Is it so very beautiful?' she said wistfully when she heard my raptures. 'And you like the lead-figures too? There's the old azalea garden behind. They say that this place must have been made for children. Will you help me out, please? I should like to come with you as far as the cross-roads, but I mustn't leave them. Is that you, Madden? I want you to show this gentleman the way to the cross-roads. He has lost his way but—he has seen them.'

A butler appeared noiselessly at the miracle of old oak that must be called the front door, and slipped aside to put on his hat. She stood looking at me with open blue eyes in which no sight lay, and I saw for the first time that she was beautiful.

'Remember,' she said quietly, 'if you are fond of them you will come again,' and disappeared within the house.

The butler in the car said nothing till we were nearly at the lodge gates, where catching a glimpse of a blue blouse in a shrubbery I swerved amply lest the devil that leads little boys to play should drag me into child-murder.

'Excuse me,' he asked of a sudden, 'but why did you do that, Sir?'

'The child yonder.'

'Our young gentleman in blue?'

'Of course.'

'He runs about a good deal. Did you see him by the fountain, Sir?'

'Oh, yes, several times. Do we turn here?'

'Yes, Sir. And did you 'appen to see them upstairs too?'

'At the upper window? Yes.'

'Was that before the mistress come out to speak to you, Sir?'

'A little before that. Why d'you want to know?'

He paused a little. 'Only to make sure that—that they had seen the car, Sir, because with children running about, though I'm sure you're driving particularly careful, there might be an accident. That was all, Sir. Here are the cross-roads. You can't miss your way from now on. Thank you, Sir, but that isn't *our* custom, not with——'

'I beg your pardon,' I said, and thrust away the British silver.

'Oh, it's quite right with the rest of 'em as a rule. Good-bye, Sir.'

He retired into the armour-plated conning tower of his caste and walked away. Evidently a butler solicitous for the honour of his house, and interested, probably through a maid, in the nursery.

Once beyond the signposts at the cross-roads I looked back, but the crumpled hills interlaced so jealously that I could not see where the house had lain. When I asked its name at a cottage along the road, the fat woman who sold sweetmeats there gave me to understand that people with motor cars had small right to live—much less to 'go about talking like carriage folk.' They were not a pleasant-mannered community.

When I retraced my route on the map that evening I was little wiser. Hawkin's Old Farm appeared to be

the Survey title of the place, and the old County
Gazetteer, generally so ample, did not allude to it.
The big house of those parts was Hodnington Hall,
Georgian with early Victorian embellishments, as an
atrocious steel engraving attested. I carried my difficulty
to a neighbour—a deep-rooted tree of that soil—and
he gave me a name of a family which conveyed no
meaning.

A month or so later—I went again, or it may have
been that my car took the road of her own volition.
She over-ran the fruitless Downs, threaded every turn
of the maze of lanes below the hills, drew through the
high-walled woods, impenetrable in their full leaf, came
out at the cross-roads where the butler had left me, and
a little farther on developed an internal trouble which
forced me to turn her in on a grass way-waste that cut
into a summer-silent hazel wood. So far as I could make
sure by the sun and a six-inch Ordnance map, this should
be the road flank of that wood which I had first explored
from the heights above. I made a mighty serious business
of my repairs and a glittering shop of my repair kit, span-
ners, pump, and the like, which I spread out orderly upon
a rug. It was a trap to catch all childhood, for on such a
day, I argued, the children would not be far off. When I
paused in my work I listened, but the wood was so full
of the noises of summer (though the birds had mated)
that I could not at first distinguish these from the tread
of small cautious feet stealing across the dead leaves. I
rang my bell in an alluring manner, but the feet fled, and
I repented, for to a child a sudden noise is very real terror.
I must have been at work half an hour when I heard in the
wood the voice of the blind woman crying: 'Children, oh,
children! Where are you?' and the stillness made slow to
close on the perfection of that cry. She came towards me,
half feeling her way between the tree boles, and though

a child it seemed clung to her skirt, it swerved into the leafage like a rabbit as she drew nearer.

'Is that you?' she said, 'from the other side of the county?'

'Yes, it's me from the other side of the county.'

'Then why didn't you come through the upper woods? They were there just now.'

'They were here a few minutes ago. I expect they knew my car had broken down, and came to see the fun.'

'Nothing serious, I hope? How do cars break down?'

'In fifty different ways. Only mine has chosen the fifty first.'

She laughed merrily at the tiny joke, cooed with delicious laughter, and pushed her hat back.

'Let me hear,' she said.

'Wait a moment,' I cried, 'and I'll get you a cushion.'

She set her foot on the rug all covered with spare parts, and stooped above it eagerly. 'What delightful things!' The hands through which she saw glanced in the chequered sunlight. 'A box here—another box! Why you've arranged them like playing shop!'

'I confess now that I put it out to attract them. I don't need half those things really.'

'How nice of you! I heard your bell in the upper wood. You say they were here before that?'

'I'm sure of it. Why are they so shy? That little fellow in blue who was with you just now ought to have got over his fright. He's been watching me like a Red Indian.'

'It must have been your bell,' she said. 'I heard one of them go past me in trouble when I was coming down. They're shy—so shy even with me.' She turned her face over her shoulder and cried again: 'Children, oh, children! Look and see!'

'They must have gone off together on their own affairs,' I suggested, for there was a murmur behind us of lowered voices broken by the sudden squeaking giggles of childhood. I returned to my tinkerings and she leaned forward, her chin on her hand, listening interestedly.

'How many are they?' I said at last. The work was finished, but I saw no reason to go.

Her forehead puckered a little in thought. 'I don't quite know,' she said simply. 'Sometimes more—sometimes less. They come and stay with me because I love them, you see.'

'That must be very jolly,' I said, replacing a drawer, and as I spoke I heard the inanity of my answer.

'You—you aren't laughing at me,' she cried. 'I—I haven't any of my own. I never married. People laugh at me sometimes about them because—because—'

'Because they're savages,' I returned. 'It's nothing to fret for. That sort laugh at everything that isn't in their own fat lives.'

'I don't know. How should I? I only don't like being laughed at about *them*. It hurts; and when one can't see. . . . I don't want to seem silly,' her chin quivered like a child's as she spoke, 'but we blindies have only one skin, I think. Everything outside hits straight at our souls. It's different with you. You've such good defences in your eyes—looking out—before anyone can really pain you in your soul. People forget that with us.'

I was silent reviewing that inexhaustible matter—the more than inherited (since it is also carefully taught) brutality of the Christian peoples, beside which the mere heathendom of the West Coast nigger is clean and restrained. It led me a long distance into myself.

'Don't do that!' she said of a sudden, putting her hands before her eyes.

'What?'

She made a gesture with her hand.

'That! It's—it's all purple and black. Don't! That colour hurts.'

'But, how in the world do you know about colours?' I exclaimed, for here was a revelation indeed.

'Colours as colours?' she asked.

'No. *Those* colours which you saw just now.'

'You know as well as I do,' she laughed, 'else you wouldn't have asked that question. They aren't in the world at all. They're in *you*—when you went so angry.'

'D'you mean a dull purplish patch, like port wine mixed with ink?' I said.

'I've never seen ink or port wine, but the colours aren't mixed. They are separate—all separate.'

'Do you mean black streaks and jags across the purple?'

She nodded. 'Yes—if they are like this,' and zig-zagged her finger again, 'but it's more red than purple—that bad colour.'

'And what are the colours at the top of the—whatever you see?'

Slowly she leaned forward and traced on the rug the figure of the Egg itself.

'I see them so,' she said, pointing with a grass stem, 'white, green, yellow, red, purple, and when people are angry or bad, black across the red—as you were just now.'

'Who told you anything about it—in the beginning?' I demanded.

'About the colours? No one. I used to ask what colours were when I was little—in table-covers and curtains and carpets, you see—because some colours hurt me and some made me happy. People told me; and when I got older that was how I saw people.' Again she traced the outline of the Egg which it is given to very few of us to see.

'All by yourself?' I repeated.

'All by myself. There wasn't anyone else. I only found out afterwards that other people did not see the Colours.'

She leaned against the tree-bole plaiting and unplaiting chance-plucked grass stems. The children in the wood had drawn nearer. I could see them with the tail of my eye frolicking like squirrels.

'Now I am sure you will never laugh at me,' she went on after a long silence. 'Nor at *them*.'

'Goodness! No!' I cried, jolted out of my train of thought. 'A man who laughs at a child—unless the child is laughing too—is a heathen!'

'I didn't mean that, of course. You'd never laugh *at* children, but I thought—I used to think—that perhaps you might laugh about *them*. So now I beg your pardon. . . . What are you going to laugh at?'

I had made no sound, but she knew.

'At the notion of your begging my pardon. If you had done your duty as a pillar of the State and a landed proprietress you ought to have summoned me for trespass when I barged through your woods the other day. It was disgraceful of me—inexcusable.'

She looked at me, her head against the tree trunk— long and steadfastly—this woman who could see the naked soul.

'How curious,' she half whispered. 'How very curious.'

'Why, what have I done?'

'You don't understand . . . and yet you understood about the Colours. Don't you understand?'

She spoke with a passion that nothing had justified, and I faced her bewilderedly as she rose. The children had gathered themselves in a roundel behind a bramble bush. One sleek head bent over something smaller, and the set of the little shoulders told me that fingers were on lips. They, too, had some child's tremendous secret. I alone was hopelessly astray there in the broad sunlight.

'No,' I said, and shook my head as though the dead eyes could note. 'Whatever it is, I don't understand yet. Perhaps I shall later—if you'll let me come again.'

'You will come again,' she answered. 'You will surely come again and walk in the wood.'

'Perhaps the children will know me well enough by that time to let me play with them—as a favour. You know what children are like.'

'It isn't a matter of favour but of right,' she replied, and while I wondered what she meant, a dishevelled woman plunged round the bend of the road, loose-haired, purple, almost lowing with agony as she ran. It was my rude, fat friend of the sweetmeat shop. The blind woman heard and stepped forward. 'What is it, Mrs. Madehurst?' she asked.

The woman flung her apron over her head and literally grovelled in the dust, crying that her grandchild was sick to death, that the local doctor was away fishing, that Jenny the mother was at her wits' end, and so forth, with repetitions and bellowings.

'Where's the next nearest doctor?' I asked between paroxysms.

'Madden will tell you. Go round to the house and take him with you. I'll attend to this. Be quick!' She half supported the fat woman into the shade. In two minutes I was blowing all the horns of Jericho under the front of the House Beautiful, and Madden, in the pantry, rose to the crisis like a butler and a man.

A quarter of an hour at illegal speeds caught us a doctor five miles away. Within the half-hour we had decanted him, much interested in motors, at the door of the sweatmeat shop, and drew up the road to await the verdict.

'Useful things cars,' said Madden, all man and no

butler. 'If I'd had one when mine took sick she wouldn't have died.'

'How was it?' I asked.

'Croup. Mrs. Madden was away. No one knew what to do. I drove eight miles in a tax cart for the doctor. She was choked when we came back. This car 'd ha' saved her. She'd have been close on ten now.'

'I'm sorry,' I said. 'I thought you were rather fond of children from what you told me going to the cross-roads the other day.'

'Have you seen 'em again, Sir—this mornin'?'

'Yes, but they're well broke to cars. I couldn't get any of them within twenty yards of it.'

He looked at me carefully as a scout considers a stranger—not as a menial should lift his eyes to his divinely appointed superior.

'I wonder why,' he said just above the breath that he drew.

We waited on. A light wind from the sea wandered up and down the long lines of the woods, and the wayside grasses, whitened already with summer dust, rose and bowed in sallow waves.

A woman, wiping the suds off her arms, came out of the cottage next the sweetmeat shop.

'I've be'n listenin' in de back-yard,' she said cheerily. 'He says Arthur's unaccountable bad. Did ye hear him shruck just now? Unaccountable bad. I reckon t'will come Jenny's turn to walk in de wood nex' week along, Mr. Madden.'

'Excuse me, Sir, but your lap-robe is slipping,' said Madden deferentially. The woman started, dropped a curtsey, and hurried away.

'What does she mean by "walking in the wood"?' I asked.

'It must be some saying they use hereabouts. I'm from

Norfolk myself,' said Madden. 'They're an independent lot in this county. She took you for a chauffeur, Sir.'

I saw the Doctor come out of the cottage followed by a draggle-tailed wench who clung to his arm as though he could make treaty for her with Death. 'Dat sort,' she wailed—'dey're just as much to us dat has 'em as if dey was lawful born. Just as much—just as much! An' God he'd be just as pleased if you saved 'un, Doctor. Don't take it from me. Miss Florence will tell ye de very same. Don't leave 'im, Doctor!'

'I know, I know,' said the man; 'but he'll be quiet for a while now. We'll get the nurse and the medicine as fast as we can.' He signalled me to come forward with the car, and I strove not to be privy to what followed; but I saw the girl's face, blotched and frozen with grief, and I felt the hand without a ring clutching at my knees when we moved away.

The Doctor was a man of some humour, for I remember he claimed my car under the Oath of Æculapius, and used it and me without mercy. First we convoyed Mrs. Madehurst and the blind woman to wait by the sick bed till the nurse should come. Next we invaded a neat county town for prescriptions (the Doctor said the trouble was cerebro-spinal meningitis), and when the County Institute, banked and flanked with scared market cattle, reported itself out of nurses for the moment we literally flung ourselves loose upon the county. We conferred with the owners of great houses—magnates at the ends of overarching avenues whose big-boned womenfolk strode away from their tea-tables to listen to the imperious Doctor. At last a white-haired lady sitting under a cedar of Lebanon and surrounded by a court of magnificent Borzois—all hostile to motors—gave the Doctor, who received them as from a princess, written orders which we bore many miles at top speed, through a park, to a French nunnery, where we took over in exchange a pallid-faced and trembling Sister. She knelt at the bottom of the tonneau telling her beads without pause till, by short cuts of the Doctor's invention, we had her to the sweetmeat shop once more. It was a long afternoon crowded with mad episodes that rose and dissolved like the dust of our wheels; cross-sections of remote and incomprehensible lives through which we raced at right angles; and I went home in the dusk, wearied out, to dream of the clashing horns of cattle; round-eyed nuns walking in a garden of graves; pleasant tea-parties beneath shaded trees; the carbolic-scented, grey-painted corridors of the County Institute; the steps of shy children in the wood, and the hands that clung to my knees as the motor began to move.

I had intended to return in a day or two, but it pleased Fate to hold me from that side of the county, on many pretexts, till the elder and the wild rose had fruited. There came at last a brilliant day, swept clear from the south-west, that brought the hills within hand's reach—a day of unstable airs and high filmy clouds. Through no merit of my own I was free, and set the car for the third time on that known road. As I reached the crest of the Downs I felt the soft air change, saw it glaze under the sun; and, looking down at the sea, in that instant beheld the blue of the Channel turn through polished silver and dulled steel to dingy pewter. A laden collier hugging the coast steered outward for deeper water, and, across copper-coloured haze, I saw sails rise one by one on the anchored fishing-fleet. In a deep dene behind me an eddy of sudden wind drummed through sheltered oaks, and spun aloft the first dry sample of autumn leaves. When I reached the beach road the sea-fog fumed over the brickfields, and the tide was telling all the groins of

the gale beyond Ushant. In less than an hour summer
England vanished in chill grey. We were again the shut
island of the North, all the ships of the world bellowing
at our perilous gates; and between their outcries ran the
piping of bewildered gulls. My cap dripped moisture, the
folds of the rug held it in pools or sluiced it away in
runnels, and the salt-rime stuck to my lips.

Inland the smell of autumn loaded the thickened
fog among the trees, and the drip became a continuous
shower. Yet the late flowers—mallow of the wayside,
scabious of the field, and dahlia of the garden—showed
gay in the mist, and beyond the sea's breath there was
little sign of decay in the leaf. Yet in the villages the
house doors were all open, and bare-legged, bare-headed
children sat at ease on the damp doorsteps to shout
'pip-pip' at the stranger.

I made bold to call at the sweetmeat shop, where
Mrs. Madehurst met me with a fat woman's hospitable
tears. Jenny's child, she said, had died two days after
the nun had come. It was, she felt, best out of the way,
even though insurance offices, for reasons which she
did not pretend to follow, would not willingly insure
such stray lives. 'Not but what Jenny didn't tend to
Arthur as though he'd come all proper at de end
of de first year—like Jenny herself.' Thanks to Miss
Florence, the child had been buried with a pomp which,
in Mrs. Madehurst's opinion, more than covered the small
irregularity of its birth. She described the coffin, within
and without, the glass hearse, and the evergreen lining
of the grave.

'But how's the mother?' I asked.

'Jenny? Oh, she'll get over it. I've felt dat way with
one or two o' my own. She'll get over. She's walkin' in
de wood now.'

'In this weather?'

Mrs. Madehurst looked at me with narrowed eyes across the counter.

'I dunno but it opens de 'eart like. Yes, it opens de 'eart. Dat's where losin' and bearin' comes so alike in de long run, we do say.'

Now the wisdom of the old wives is greater than that of all the Fathers, and this last oracle sent me thinking so extendedly as I went up the road, that I nearly ran over a woman and a child at the wooded corner by the lodge gates of the House Beautiful.

'Awful weather!' I cried, as I slowed dead for the turn.

'Not so bad,' she answered placidly out of the fog. 'Mine's used to 'un. You'll find yours indoors, I reckon.'

Indoors, Madden received me with professional courtesy, and kind inquiries for the health of the motor, which he would put under cover.

I waited in a still, nut-brown hall, pleasant with late flowers and warmed with a delicious wood fire—a place of good influence and great peace. (Men and women may sometimes, after great effort, achieve a creditable lie; but the house, which is their temple, cannot say anything save the truth of those who have lived in it.) A child's cart and a doll lay on the black-and-white floor, where a rug had been kicked back. I felt that the children had only just hurried away—to hide themselves, most like—in the many turns of the great adzed staircase that climbed statelily out of the hall, or to crouch at gaze behind the lions and roses of the carven gallery above. Then I heard her voice above me, singing as the blind sing—from the soul:—

In the pleasant orchard-closes.

And all my early summer came back at the call.

> In the pleasant orchard-closes,
>   God bless all our gains say we—
> But may God bless all our losses,
>   Better suits with our degree.

She dropped the marring fifth line, and repeated—

> Better suits with our degree!

I saw her lean over the gallery, her linked hands white as pearl against the oak.

'Is that you—from the other side of the county?' she called.

'Yes, me—from the other side of the county,' I answered, laughing.

'What a long time before you had to come here again.' She ran down the stairs, one hand lightly touching the broad rail. 'It's two months and four days. Summer's gone!'

'I meant to come before, but Fate prevented.'

'I knew it. Please do something to that fire. They won't let me play with it, but I can feel it's behaving badly. Hit it!'

I looked on either side of the deep fireplace, and found but a half-charred hedge-stake with which I punched a black log into flame.

'It never goes out, day or night,' she said, as though explaining. 'In case any one comes in with cold toes, you see.'

'It's even lovelier inside than it was out,' I murmured. The red light poured itself along the age-polished dusky panels till the Tudor roses and lions of the gallery took colour and motion. An old eagle-topped convex mirror gathered the picture into its mysterious heart, distorting afresh the distorted shadows, and curving the gallery

lines into the curves of a ship. The day was shutting
down in half a gale as the fog turned to stringy scud.
Through the uncurtained mullions of the broad window I
could see valiant horsemen of the lawn rear and recover
against the wind that taunted them with legions of dead
leaves.

'Yes, it must be beautiful,' she said. 'Would you
like to go over it? There's still light enough upstairs.'

I followed her up the unflinching, wagon-wide staircase
to the gallery whence opened the thin fluted Elizabethan
doors.

'Feel how they put the latch low down for the sake
of the children.' She swung a light door inward.

'By the way, where are they?' I asked. 'I haven't
even heard them to-day.'

She did not answer at once. Then, 'I can only hear
them,' she replied softly. 'This is one of their rooms—
everything ready, you see.'

She pointed into a heavily-timbered room. There
were little low gate tables and children's chairs. A doll's
house, its hooked front half open, faced a great dappled
rocking-horse, from whose padded saddle it was but a
child's scramble to the broad window-seat overlooking
the lawn. A toy gun lay in a corner beside a gilt wooden
cannon.

'Surely they've only just gone,' I whispered. In the
failing light a door creaked cautiously. I heard the rustle
of a frock and the patter of feet—quick feet through a
room beyond.

'I heard that,' she cried triumphantly. 'Did you?
Children, oh, children! Where are you?'

The voice filled the walls that held it lovingly to the
last perfect note, but there came no answering shout
such as I had heard in the garden. We hurried on from
room to oak-floored room; up a step here, down three

steps there; among a maze of passages; always mocked
by our quarry. One might as well have tried to work
an unstopped warren with a single ferret. There were
bolt-holes innumerable—recesses in walls, embrasures of
deep slitten windows now darkened, whence they could
start up behind us; and abandoned fireplaces, six feet deep
in the masonry, as well as the tangle of communicating
doors. Above all, they had the twilight for their helper
in our game. I had caught one or two joyous chuckles
of evasion, and once or twice had seen the silhouette of
a child's frock against some darkening window at the
end of a passage; but we returned empty-handed to the
gallery, just as a middle-aged woman was setting a lamp
in its niche.

'No, I haven't seen her either this evening, Miss
Florence,' I heard her say, 'but that Turpin he says
he wants to see you about his shed.'

'Oh, Mr. Turpin must want to see me very badly.
Tell him to come to the hall, Mrs. Madden.'

I looked down into the hall whose only light was
the dulled fire, and deep in the shadow I saw them
at last. They must have slipped down while we were
in the passages, and now thought themselves perfectly
hidden behind an old gilt leather screen. By child's law,
my fruitless chase was as good as an introduction, but
since I had taken so much trouble I resolved to force them
to come forward later by the simple trick, which children
detest, of pretending not to notice them. They lay close,
in a little huddle, no more than shadows except when a
quick flame betrayed an outline.

'And now we'll have some tea,' she said. 'I believe
I ought to have offered it you at first, but one doesn't
arrive at manners somehow when one lives alone and is
considered—h'm—peculiar.' Then with very pretty scorn,
'Would you like a lamp to see to eat by?'

'The firelight's much pleasanter, I think.' We descended into that delicious gloom and Madden brought tea.

I took my chair in the direction of the screen ready to surprise or be surprised as the game should go, and at her permission, since a hearth is always sacred, bent forward to play with the fire.

'Where do you get these beautiful short faggots from?' I asked idly. 'Why, they are tallies!'

'Of course,' she said. 'As I can't read or write I'm driven back on the early English tally for my accounts. Give me one and I'll tell you what it meant.'

I passed her an unburned hazel-tally, about a foot long, and she ran her thumb down the nicks.

'This is the milk-record for the home farm for the month of April last year, in gallons,' said she. 'I don't know what I should have done without tallies. An old forester of mine taught me the system. It's out of date now for every one else; but my tenants respect it. One of them's coming now to see me. Oh, it doesn't matter. He has no business here out of office hours. He's a greedy, ignorant man—very greedy or—he wouldn't come here after dark.'

'Have you much land then?'

'Only a couple of hundred acres in hand, thank goodness. The other six hundred are nearly all let to folk who knew my folk before me, but this Turpin is quite a new man—and a highway robber.'

'But are you sure I shan't be——?'

'Certainly not. You have the right. He hasn't any children.'

'Ah, the children!' I said, and slid my low chair back till it nearly touched the screen that hid them. 'I wonder whether they'll come out for me.'

There was a murmur of voices—Madden's and a deeper note—at the low, dark side door, and a ginger-headed,

canvas-gaitered giant of the unmistakable tenant-farmer
type stumbled or was pushed in.

'Come to the fire, Mr. Turpin,' she said.

'If—if you please, Miss, I'll—I'll be quite as well
by the door.' He clung to the latch as he spoke like a
frightened child. Of a sudden I realised that he was in
the grip of some almost overpowering fear.

'Well?'

'About that new shed for the young stock—that was
all. These first autumn storms settin' in . . . but I'll come
again, Miss.' His teeth did not chatter much more than
the door latch.

'I think not,' she answered levelly. 'The new shed—
m'm. What did my agent write you on the 15th?'

'I—fancied p'raps that if I came to see you—ma—man
to man like, Miss. But——'

His eyes rolled into every corner of the room wide
with horror. He half opened the door through which he
had entered, but I noticed it shut again—from without
and firmly.

'He wrote what I told him,' she went on. 'You are
overstocked already. Dunnett's Farm never carried more
than fifty bullocks—even in Mr. Wright's time. And *he*
used cake. You've sixty-seven and you don't cake. You've
broken the lease in that respect. You're dragging the
heart out of the farm.'

'I'm—I'm getting some minerals—superphosphates—
next week. I've as good as ordered a truck-load already.
I'll go down to the station to-morrow about 'em. Then I
can come and see you man to man like, Miss, in the
daylight. . . . That gentleman's not going away, is he?'
He almost shrieked.

I had only slid the chair a little farther back, reaching
behind me to tap on the leather of the screen, but he
jumped like a rat.

'No. Please attend to me, Mr. Turpin.' She turned in her chair and faced him with his back to the door. It was an old and sordid little piece of scheming that she forced from him—his plea for the new cow-shed at his landlady's expense, that he might with the covered manure pay his next year's rent out of the valuation after, as she made clear, he had bled the enriched pastures to the bone. I could not but admire the intensity of his greed, when I saw him out-facing for its sake whatever terror it was that ran wet on his forehead.

I ceased to tap the leather—was, indeed, calculating the cost of the shed—when I felt my relaxed hand taken and turned softly between the soft hands of a child. So at last I had triumphed. In a moment I would turn and acquaint myself with those quick-footed wanderers. . . .

The little brushing kiss fell in the centre of my palm—as a gift on which the fingers were, once, expected to close: as the all-faithful half-reproachful signal of a waiting child not used to neglect even when grown-ups were busiest—a fragment of the mute code devised very long ago.

Then I knew. And it was as though I had known from the first day when I looked across the lawn at the high window.

I heard the door shut. The woman turned to me in silence, and I felt that she knew.

What time passed after this I cannot say. I was roused by the fall of a log, and mechanically rose to put it back. Then I returned to my place in the chair very close to the screen.

'Now you understand,' she whispered, across the packed shadows.

'Yes, I understand—now. Thank you.'

'I—I only hear them.' She bowed her head in her hands. 'I have no right, you know—no other right. I have neither borne nor lost—neither borne nor lost!'

'Be very glad then,' said I, for my soul was torn open within me.

'Forgive me!'

She was still, and I went back to my sorrow and my joy.

'It was because I loved them so,' she said at last, brokenly. '*That* was why it was, even from the first—even before I knew that they—they were all I should ever have. And I loved them so!'

She stretched out her arms to the shadows and the shadows within the shadow.

'They came because I loved them—because I needed them. I—I must have made them come. Was that wrong, think you?'

'No—no.'

'I—I grant you that the toys and—and all that sort of thing were nonsense, but—but I used to so hate empty rooms myself when I was little.' She pointed to the gallery. 'And the passages all empty. . . . And how could I ever bear the garden door shut? Suppose——'

'Don't! For pity's sake, don't!' I cried. The twilight had brought a cold rain with gusty squalls that plucked at the leaded windows.

'And the same thing with keeping the fire in all night. *I* don't think it so foolish—do you?'

I looked at the broad brick hearth, saw, through tears I believe, that there was no unpassable iron on or near it, and bowed my head.

'I did all that and lots of other things—just to make believe. Then they came. I heard them, but I didn't know that they were not mine by right till Mrs. Madden told me——'

'The butler's wife? What?'

'One of them—I heard—she saw. And knew. Hers! *Not* for me. I didn't know at first. Perhaps I was

jealous. Afterwards, I began to understand that it was
only because I loved them, not because—— . . . Oh, you
must bear or lose,' she said piteously. 'There is no other
way—and yet they love me. They must! Don't they?'

There was no sound in the room except the lapping
voices of the fire, but we two listened intently, and
she at least took comfort from what she heard. She
recovered herself and half rose. I sat still in my chair
by the screen.

'Don't think me a wretch to whine about myself like
this, but—but I'm all in the dark, you know, and *you*
can see.'

In truth I could see, and my vision confirmed me
in my resolve, though that was like the very parting of
spirit and flesh. Yet a little longer I would stay since it
was the last time.

'You think it is wrong, then?' she cried sharply,
though I had said nothing.

'Not for you. A thousand times no. For you it is
right. . . . I am grateful to you beyond words. For me
it would be wrong. For me only. . . . '

'Why?' she said, but passed her hand before her face
as she had done at our second meeting in the wood. 'Oh,
I see,' she went on simply as a child. 'For you it would
be wrong.' Then with a little indrawn laugh, 'and, d'you
remember, I called you lucky—once—at first. You who
must never come here again!'

She left me to sit a little longer by the screen, and
I heard the sound of her feet die out along the gallery
above.

The Bull that Thought

WESTWARD from a town by the Mouths of the Rhône, runs a road so mathematically straight, so barometrically level, that it ranks among the world's measured miles and motorists use it for records.

I had attacked the distance several times, but always with a Mistral blowing, or the unchancy cattle of those parts on the move. But once, running from the East, into a high-piled, almost Egyptian, sunset, there came a night which it would have been sin to have wasted. It was warm with the breath of summer in advance; moonlit till the shadow of every rounded pebble and pointed cypress wind-break lay solid on that vast flat-floored waste; and my Mr. Leggatt, who had slipped out to make sure, reported that the road-surface was unblemished.

'Now,' he suggested, 'we might see what she'll do under strict road-conditions. She's been pullin' like the Blue de Luxe all day. Unless I'm all off, it's her night out.'

We arranged the trial for after dinner—thirty kilometres as near as might be; and twenty-two of them without even a level crossing.

There sat beside me at table d'hôte an elderly, bearded Frenchman wearing the rosette of by no means the lowest grade of the Legion of Honour, who had arrived in a talkative Citroën. I gathered that he had spent much of his life in the French Colonial Service in Annam and Tonquin. When the war came, his years barring

him from the front line, he had supervised Chinese
wood-cutters who, with axe and dynamite, deforested the
centre of France for trench-props. He said my chauffeur
had told him that I contemplated an experiment. He was
interested in cars—had admired mine—would, in short,
be greatly indebted to me if I permitted him to assist as
an observer. One could not well refuse; and, knowing my
Mr. Leggatt, it occurred to me there might also be a bet
in the background.

While he went to get his coat, I asked the proprietor his
name. 'Voiron—Monsieur André Voiron,' was the reply.
'And his business?' 'Mon Dieu! He is Voiron! He is all
those things, there!' The proprietor waved his hands at
brilliant advertisements on the dining-room walls, which
declared that Voiron Frères dealt in wines, agricultural
implements, chemical manures, provisions and produce
throughout that part of the globe.

He said little for the first five minutes of our trip, and
nothing at all for the next ten—it being, as Leggatt had
guessed, Esmeralda's night out. But, when her indicator
climbed to a certain figure and held there for three
blinding kilometres, he expressed himself satisfied, and
proposed to me that we should celebrate the event at the
hotel. 'I keep yonder,' said he, 'a wine on which I should
value your opinion.'

On our return, he disappeared for a few minutes, and
I heard him rumbling in a cellar. The proprietor presently
invited me to the dining-room, where, beneath one frugal
light, a table had been set with local dishes of renown.
There was, too, a bottle beyond most known sizes, marked
black on red, with a date. Monsieur Voiron opened it, and
we drank to the health of my car. The velvety, perfumed
liquor, between fawn and topaz, neither too sweet nor too
dry, creamed in its generous glass. But I knew no wine
composed of the whispers of angels' wings, the breath of

Eden and the foam and pulse of Youth renewed. So I
asked what it might be.

'It is champagne,' he said gravely.

'Then what have I been drinking all my life?'

'If you were lucky, before the War, and paid thirty
shillings a bottle, it is possible you may have drunk one
of our better-class *tisanes*.'

'And where does one get this?'

'Here, I am happy to say. Elsewhere, perhaps, it
is not so easy. We growers exchange these real wines
among ourselves.'

I bowed my head in admiration, surrender, and joy.
There stood the most ample bottle, and it was not
yet eleven o'clock. Doors locked and shutters banged
throughout the establishment. Some last servant yawned
on his way to bed. Monsieur Voiron opened a window
and the moonlight flooded in from a small pebbled court
outside. One could almost hear the town of Chambres
breathing in its first sleep. Presently, there was a thick
noise in the air, the passing of feet and hooves, lowings,
and a stifled bark or two. Dust rose over the courtyard
wall, followed by the strong smell of cattle.

'They are moving some beasts,' said Monsieur Voiron,
cocking an ear. 'Mine, I think. Yes, I hear Christophe.
Our beasts do not like automobiles—so we move at night.
You do not know our country—the Crau, here, or the
Camargue? I was—I am now, again—of it. All France is
good; but this is the best.' He spoke, as only a Frenchman
can, of his own loved part of his own lovely land.

'For myself, if I were not so involved in all these
affairs'—he pointed to the advertisements—'I would
live on our farm with my cattle, and worship them
like a Hindu. You know our cattle of the Camargue,
Monsieur? No? It is not an acquaintance to rush upon
lightly. There are no beasts like them. They have a

mentality superior to that of others. They graze and they ruminate, by choice, facing our Mistral, which is more than some automobiles will do. Also they have in them the potentiality of thought—and when cattle think—I have seen what arrives.'

'Are they so clever as all that?' I asked idly.

'Monsieur, when your sportif chauffeur camouflaged your limousine so that she resembled one of your Army lorries, I would not believe her capacities. I bet him—ah—two to one—she would not touch ninety kilometres. It was proved that she could. I can give you no proof, but will you believe me if I tell you what a beast who thinks can achieve?'

'After the War,' said I spaciously, 'everything is credible.'

'That is true! Everything inconceivable has happened; but still we learn nothing and we believe nothing. When I was a child in my father's house—before I became a Colonial Administrator—my interest and my affection were among our cattle. We of the old rock live here—have you seen?—in big farms like castles. Indeed, some of them may have been Saracenic. The barns group round them—great white-walled barns, and yards solid as our houses. One gate shuts all. It is a world apart; an administration of all that concerns beasts. It was there I learned something about cattle. You see, they are our playthings in the Camargue and the Crau. The boy measures his strength against the calf that butts him in play among the manure-heaps. He moves in and out among the cows, who are—not so amiable. He rides with the herdsmen in the open to shift the herds. Sooner or later, he meets as bulls the little calves that knocked him over. So it was with me—till it became necessary that I should go to our Colonies.' He laughed. 'Very necessary. That is a good time in youth, Monsieur, when one does these things which shock our parents. Why is it always Papa who is so shocked and has never heard of such things—and Mamma who supplies the excuses? . . . And when my brother—my elder who stayed and created the business—begged me to return and help him, I resigned my Colonial career gladly enough. I returned to our own lands, and my well-loved, wicked white and yellow cattle of the Camargue and the Crau. My Faith, I could talk of them all night, for this stuff unlocks the heart, without making repentance in the morning. . . . Yes! It was after the War that his happened. There was a calf, among Heaven knows how many of ours—a bull-calf—an infant indistinguishable from his companions. He was sick, and he had been taken up with his mother into the big farmyard at home with us. Naturally the children of our herdsmen practised on him from the first. It is in their blood. The Spaniards make a cult of bull-fighting. Our little devils down here bait bulls as automatically as the English child kicks or throws balls. This calf would chase them with his eyes open, like a cow when she hunts a man. They would take refuge behind our tractors and wine-carts in the centre of the yard: he would chase them in and out as a dog hunts rats. More than that, he would study their psychology, his eyes in their eyes. Yes, he watched their faces to divine which way they would run. He himself, also, would pretend sometimes to charge directly at a boy. Then he would wheel right or left—one could never tell—and knock over some child pressed against a wall who thought himself safe. After this, he would stand over him, knowing that his companions must come to his aid; and when they were all together, waving their jackets across his eyes and pulling his tail, he would scatter them—how he would scatter them! He could kick, too, sideways like a cow. He knew his ranges as well as our gunners, and he was as quick on his feet

as our Carpentier. I observed him often. Christophe—the
man who passed just now—our chief herdsman, who
had taught me to ride with our beasts when I was
ten—Christophe told me that he was descended from
a yellow cow of those days that had chased us once into
the marshes. "He kicks just like her," said Christophe.
"He can side-kick as he jumps. Have you seen, too, that
he is not deceived by the jacket when a boy waves it? He
uses it to find the boy. They think they are feeling him.
He is feeling them always. He thinks, that one." I had
come to the same conclusion. Yes—the creature was a
thinker along the lines necessary to his sport; and he
was a humorist also, like so many natural murderers.
One knows the type among beasts as well as among men.
It possesses a curious truculent mirth—almost indecent
but infallibly significant——'

Monsieur Voiron replenished our glasses with the
great wine that went better at each descent.

'They kept him for some time in the yards to practise
upon. Naturally he became a little brutal; so Christophe
turned him out to learn manners among his equals in the
grazing lands, where the Camargue joins the Crau. How
old was he then? About eight or nine months, I think. We
met again a few months later—he and I. I was riding one
of our little half-wild horses, along a road of the Crau,
when I found myself almost unseated. It was he! He had
hidden himself behind a wind-break till we passed, and
had then charged my horse from behind. Yes, he had
deceived even my little horse! But I recognised him. I
gave him the whip across the nose, and I said: "Apis, for
this thou goest to Arles! It was unworthy of thee, between
us two." But that creature had no shame. He went away
laughing, like an Apache. If he had dismounted me, I do
not think it is I who would have laughed—yearling as
he was.'

'Why did you want to send him to Arles?' I asked.

'For the bull-ring. When your charming tourists leave us, we institute our little amusements there. Not a real bull-fight, you understand, but young bulls with padded horns, and our boys from hereabouts and in the city go to play with them. Naturally, before we send them we try them in our yards at home. So we brought up Apis from his pastures. He knew at once that he was among the friends of his youth—he almost shook hands with them—and he submitted like an angel to padding his horns. He investigated the carts and tractors in the yards, to choose his lines of defence and attack. And then—he attacked with an *élan*, and he defended with a tenacity and forethought that delighted us. In truth, we were so pleased that I fear we trespassed upon his patience. We desired him to repeat himself, which no true artist will tolerate. But he gave us fair warning. He went out to the centre of the yard, where there was some dry earth; he kneeled down and—you have seen a calf whose horns fret him thrusting and rooting into a bank? He did just that, very deliberately, till he had rubbed the pads off his horns. Then he rose, dancing on those wonderful feet that twinkled, and he said: "Now, my friends, the buttons are off the foils. Who begins?" We understood. We finished at once. He was turned out again on the pastures till it should be time to amuse them at our little metropolis. But, some time before he went to Arles—yes, I think I have it correctly—Christophe, who had been out on the Crau, informed me that Apis had assassinated a young bull who had given signs of developing into a rival. That happens, of course, and our herdsmen should prevent it. But Apis had killed in his own style—at dusk, from the ambush of a wind-break—by an oblique charge from behind which knocked the other over. He had then disembowelled him. All very possible, *but*—the murder accomplished—Apis went to the bank of a wind-break, knelt, and carefully, as he had in our yard, cleaned his horns in the earth. Christophe, who had never seen such a thing, at once borrowed (do you know, it is most efficacious when taken that way?) some Holy Water from our little chapel in those pastures, sprinkled Apis (whom it did not affect), and rode in to tell me. It was obvious that a thinker of that bull's type would also be meticulous in his toilette; so, when he was sent to Arles, I warned our consignees to exercise caution with him. Happily, the change of scene, the music, the general attention, and the meeting again with old friends—all our bad boys attended—agreeably distracted him. He became for the time a pure *farceur* again; but his wheelings, his rushes, his rat-huntings were more superb than ever. There was in them now, you understand, a breadth of technique that comes of reasoned art, and, above all, the passion that arrives after experience. Oh, he had learned, out there on the Crau! At the end of his little turn, he was, according to local rules, to be handled in all respects except for the sword, which was a stick, as a professional bull who must die. He was manoeuvred into, or he posed himself in, the proper attitude; made his rush; received the point on his shoulder and then—turned about and cantered toward the door by which he had entered the arena. He said to the world: "My friends, the representation is ended. I thank you for your applause. I go to repose myself." But our Arlesians, who are—not so clever as some, demanded an encore, and Apis was headed back again. We others from his country, we knew what would happen. He went to the centre of the ring, kneeled, and, slowly, with full parade, plunged his horns alternately in the dirt till the pads came off. Christophe shouts: "Leave him alone, you straight-nosed imbeciles! Leave him before you must." But they required emotion; for Rome has always debauched her loved Provincia with bread and circuses. It was given. Have you, Monsieur, ever seen a servant, with pan and broom, sweeping round the base-board of a room? In a half-minute Apis has them all swept out and over the barrier. Then he demands once more that the door shall be opened to him. It is opened and he retires as though—which, truly, is the case—loaded with laurels.'

Monsieur Voiron refilled the glasses, and allowed himself a cigarette, which he puffed for some time.

'And afterwards?' I said.

'I am arranging it in my mind. It is difficult to do it justice. Afterwards—yes, afterwards—Apis returned to his pastures and his mistresses and I to my business. I am no longer a scandalous old "sportif" in shirt-sleeves howling encouragement to the yellow son of a cow. I revert to Voiron Frères—wines, chemical manures, *et cetera*. And next year, through some chicane which I have not the leisure to unravel, and also, thanks to our patriarchal system of paying our older men out of the increase of the herds, old Christophe possesses himself of Apis. Oh, yes, he proves it through descent from a certain cow that my father had given his father before the Republic. Beware, Monsieur, of the memory of the illiterate man! An ancestor of Christophe had been a soldier under our Soult against your Beresford, near Bayonne. He fell into the hands of Spanish guerrillas. Christophe and his wife used to tell me the details on certain Saints' Days when I was a child. Now, as compared with our recent war, Soult's campaign and retreat across the Bidassoa——'

'But did you allow Christophe just to annex the bull?' I demanded.

'You do not know Christophe. He had sold him to the Spaniards before he informed me. The Spaniards pay in coin—douros of very pure silver. Our peasants mistrust our paper. You know the saying: "A thousand

francs paper; eight hundred metal, and the cow is yours."
Yes, Christophe sold Apis, who was then two and a half
years old, and to Christophe's knowledge thrice at least
an assassin.'

'How was that?' I said.

'Oh, his own kind only; and always, Christophe told
me, by the same oblique rush from behind, the same
sideways overthrow, and the same swift disembowel-
ment, followed by this levitical cleaning of the horns.
In human life he would have kept a manicurist—this
Minotaur. And so, Apis disappears from our country.
That does not trouble me. I know in due time I shall
be advised. Why? Because, in this land, Monsieur, not a
hoof moves between Berre and the Saintes Maries without the knowledge of specialists such as Christophe. The
beasts are the substance and the drama of their lives to
them. So when Christophe tells me, a little before Easter
Sunday, that Apis makes his début in the bull-ring of a
small Catalan town on the road to Barcelona, it is only
to pack my car and trundle there across the frontier with
him. The place lacked importance and manufactures, but
it had produced a matador of some reputation, who was
condescending to show his art in his native town. They
were even running one special train to the place. Now
our French railway system is only execrable, but the
Spanish——'

'You went down by road, didn't you?' said I.

'Naturally. It was not too good. Villamarti was the
matador's name. He proposed to kill two bulls for the
honour of his birthplace. Apis, Christophe told me, would
be his second. It was an interesting trip, and that little
city by the sea was ravishing. Their bull-ring dates from
the middle of the seventeenth century. It is full of feeling.
The ceremonial too—when the horsemen enter and ask
the Mayor in his box to throw down the keys of the

bull-ring—that was exquisitely conceived. You know, if
the keys are caught in the horseman's hat, it is considered
a good omen. They were perfectly caught. Our seats were
in the front row beside the gates where the bulls enter, so
we saw everything.

Villamarti's first bull was not too badly killed. The
second matador, whose name escapes me, killed his
without distinction—a foil to Villamarti. And the third,
Chisto, a laborious, middle-aged professional who had
never risen beyond a certain dull competence, was equally
of the background. Oh, they are as jealous as the girls
of the Comédie Française, these matadors! Villamarti's
troupe stood ready for his second bull. The gates opened,
and we saw Apis, beautifully balanced on his feet, peer
coquettishly round the corner, as though he were at
home. A picador—a mounted man with the long lance-
goad—stood near the barrier on his right. He had not
even troubled to turn his horse, for the capeadors—the
men with the cloaks—were advancing to play Apis—to
feel his psychology and intentions, according to the rules
that are made for bulls who do not think. . . . I did not
realise the murder before it was accomplished! The wheel,
the rush, the oblique charge from behind, the fall of horse
and man were simultaneous. Apis leaped the horse, with
whom he had no quarrel, and alighted, all four feet
together (it was enough), between the man's shoulders,
changed his beautiful feet on the carcass, and was away,
pretending to fall nearly on his nose. Do you follow me? In
that instant, by that stumble, he produced the impression
that his adorable assassination was a mere bestial blun-
der. Then, Monsieur, I began to comprehend that it was
an artist we had to deal with. He did not stand over the
body to draw the rest of the troupe. He chose to reserve
that trick. He let the attendants bear out the dead, and
went on to amuse himself among the capeadors. Now to

Apis, trained among our children in the yards, the cloak was simply a guide to the boy behind it. He pursued, you understand, the person, not the propaganda—the proprietor, not the journal. If a third of our electors of France were as wise, my friend! . . . But it was done leisurely, with humour and a touch of truculence. He romped after one man's cloak as a clumsy dog might do, but I observed that he kept the man on his terrible left side. Christophe whispered to me: "Wait for his mother's kick. When he has made the fellow confident it will arrive." It arrived in the middle of a gambol. My God! He lashed out in the air as he frisked. The man dropped like a sack, lifted one hand a little towards his head, and—that was all. So you see, a body was again at his disposition; a second time the cloaks ran up to draw him off, but, a second time, Apis refused his grand scene. A second time he acted that his murder was accident and—he convinced his audience! It was as though he had knocked over a bridge-gate in the marshes by mistake. Unbelievable? I saw it.'

The memory sent Monsieur Voiron again to the champagne, and I accompanied him.

'But Apis was not the sole artist present. They say Villamarti comes of a family of actors. I saw him regard Apis with a new eye. He, too, began to understand. He took his cloak and moved out to play him before they should bring on another picador. He had his reputation. Perhaps Apis knew it. Perhaps Villamarti reminded him of some boy with whom he has practised at home. At any rate Apis permitted it—up to a certain point; but he did not allow Villamarti the stage. He cramped him throughout. He dived and plunged clumsily and slowly, but always with menace and always closing in. We could see that the man was conforming to the bull—not the bull to the man; for Apis was playing him towards the centre of the ring, and, in a little while—I watched

his face—Villamarti knew it. But I could not fathom
the creature's motive. "Wait," said old Christophe. "He
wants that picador on the white horse yonder. When he
reaches his proper distance he will get him. Villamarti is
his cover. He used me once that way." And so it was, my
friend! With the clang of one of our own Seventy-fives,
Apis dismissed Villamarti with his chest—breasted him
over—and had arrived at his objective near the barrier.
The same oblique charge; the head carried low for the
sweep of the horns; the immense sideways fall of the
horse, broken-legged and half-paralysed; the senseless
man on the ground, and—behold Apis between them,
backed against the barrier—his right covered by the
horse; his left by the body of the man at his feet.
The simplicity of it! Lacking the carts and tractors
of his early parade-grounds he, being a genius, had
extemporised with the materials at hand, and dug himself
in. The troupe closed up again, their left wing broken by
the kicking horse, their right immobilised by the man's
body which Apis bestrode with significance. Villamarti
almost threw himself between the horns, but—it was
more an appeal than an attack. Apis refused him. He
held his base. A picador was sent at him—necessarily
from the front, which alone was open. Apis charged—he
who, till then, you realise, had not used the horn! The
horse went over backwards, the man half beneath him.
Apis halted, hooked him under the heart, and threw him
to the barrier. We heard his head crack, but he was dead
before he hit the wood. There was no demonstration
from the audience. They, also, had begun to realise this
Foch among bulls! The arena occupied itself again with
the dead. Two of the troupe irresolutely tried to play
him—God knows in what hope!—but he moved out to
the centre of the ring. "Look!" said Christophe. "Now
he goes to clean himself. That always frightened me."

He knelt down; he began to clean his horns. The earth
was hard. He worried at it in an ecstasy of absorption.
As he laid his head along and rattled his ears, it was
as though he were interrogating the Devils themselves
upon their secrets, and always saying impatiently: "Yes,
I know that—and *that*—and *that*! Tell me more—*more*!"
In the silence that covered us, a woman cried: "He digs a
grave! Oh, Saints, he digs a grave!" Some others echoed
this—not loudly—as a wave echoes in a grotto of the sea.

'And when his horns were cleaned, he rose up and
studied poor Villamarti's troupe, eyes in eyes, one by
one, with the gravity of an equal in intellect and the
remote and merciless resolution of a master in his art.
This was more terrifying than his toilette.'

'And they—Villamarti's men?' I asked.

'Like the audience, were dominated. They had ceased
to posture, or stamp, or address insults to him. They
conformed to him. The two other matadors stared. Only
Chisto, the oldest, broke silence with some call or other,
and Apis turned his head towards him. Otherwise he was
isolated, immobile—sombre—meditating on those at his
mercy. Ah!

'For some reason the trumpet sounded for the *bandil-
leras*—those gay hooked darts that are planted in
the shoulders of bulls who do not think, after their
neck-muscles are tired by lifting horses. When such
bulls feel the pain, they check for an instant, and, in
that instant, the men step gracefully aside. Villamarti's
bandillero answered the trumpet mechanically—like one
condemned. He stood out, poised the darts and stammered the usual patter of invitation. . . . And after? I
do not assert that Apis shrugged his shoulders, but
he reduced the episode to its lowest elements, as could
only a bull of Gaul. With his truculence was mingled
always—owing to the shortness of his tail—a certain

Rabelaisian abandon, especially when viewed from the rear. Christophe had often commented upon it. Now, Apis brought that quality into play. He circulated round that boy, forcing him to break up his beautiful poses. He studied him from various angles, like an incompetent photographer. He presented to him every portion of his anatomy except his shoulders. At intervals he feigned to run in upon him. My God, he was cruel! But his motive was obvious. He was playing for a laugh from the spectators which should synchronise with the fracture of the human morale. It was achieved. The boy turned and ran towards the barrier. Apis on him before the laugh ceased; passed him; headed him—what do I say?—herded him off to the left, his horns beside and a little in front of his chest; he did not intend him to escape into a refuge. Some of the troupe would have closed in, but Villamarti cried: "If he wants him he will take him. Stand!" They stood. Whether the boy slipped or Apis nosed him over I could not see. But he dropped, sobbing. Apis halted like a car with four brakes, struck a pose, smelt him very completely and turned away. It was dismissal more ignominious than degradation at the head of one's battalion. The representation was finished. Remained only for Apis to clear his stage of the subordinate characters.

'Ah! His gesture then! He gave a dramatic start—this Cyrano of the Camargue—as though he was aware of them for the first time. He moved. All their beautiful breeches twinkled for an instant along the top of the barrier. He held the stage alone! But Christophe and I, we trembled! For, observe, he had now involved himself in a stupendous drama of which he only could supply the third act. And, except for an audience on the razor-edge of emotion, he had exhausted his material. Molière himself—we have forgotten, my friend, to drink to the health of that great soul—might have been at a loss. And Tragedy is but a step behind Failure. We could see the four or five Civil Guards, who are sent always to keep order, fingering the breeches of their rifles. They were but waiting a word from the Mayor to fire on him, as they do sometimes at a bull who leaps the barrier among the spectators. They would, of course, have killed or wounded several people—but that would not have saved Apis.'

Monsieur Voiron drowned the thought at once, and wiped his beard.

'At that moment Fate—the Genius of France, if you will—sent to assist in the incomparable finale, none other than Chisto, the eldest, and I should have said (but never again will I judge!) the least inspired of all; mediocrity itself but, at heart—and it is the heart that conquers always, my friend—at heart an artist. He descended stiffly into the arena, alone and assured. Apis regarded him, his eyes in his eyes. The man took stance, with his cloak, and called to the bull as to an equal: "Now, Señor, we will show these honourable caballeros something together." He advanced thus against this thinker who at a plunge—a kick—a thrust—could, we all knew, have extinguished him. My dear friend, I wish I could convey to you something of the unaffected bonhomie, the humour, the delicacy, the consideration bordering on respect even, with which Apis, the supreme artist, responded to this invitation. It was the Master, wearied after a strenuous hour in the atelier, unbuttoned and at ease with some not inexpert but limited disciple. The telepathy was instantaneous between them. And for good reason! Christophe said to me: "All's well. That Chisto began among the bulls. I was sure of it when I heard him call just now. He has been a herdsman. He'll pull it off." There was a little feeling and adjustment, at first, for mutual distances and allowances.

'Oh, yes! And here occurred a gross impertinence of Villamarti. He had, after an interval, followed Chisto—to retrieve his reputation. My Faith! I can conceive the elder Dumas slamming his door on an intruder precisely as Apis did. He raced Villamarti into the nearest refuge at once. He stamped his feet outside it, and he snorted: "Go! I am engaged with an artist." Villamarti went—his reputation left behind for ever.

'Apis returned to Chisto saying: "Forgive the interruption. I am not always master of my time, but you were about to observe, my dear confrère . . . ?" Then the play began. Out of compliment to Chisto, Apis chose as his objective (every bull varies in this respect) the inner edge of the cloak—that nearest to the man's body. This allows but a few millimetres clearance in charging. But Apis trusted himself as Chisto trusted him, and, this time, he conformed to the man, with inimitable judgment and temper. He allowed himself to be played into the shadow or the sun, as the delighted audience demanded. He raged enormously; he feigned defeat; he despaired in statuesque abandon, and thence flashed into fresh paroxysms of wrath—but always with the detachment of the true artist who knows he is but the vessel of an emotion whence others, not he, must drink. And never once did he forget that honest Chisto's cloak was to him the gauge by which to spare even a hair on the skin. He inspired Chisto too. My God! His youth returned to that meritorious beef-sticker—the desire, the grace, and the beauty of his early dreams. One could almost see that girl of the past for whom he was rising, rising to these present heights of skill and daring. It was his hour too—a miraculous hour of dawn returned to gild the sunset. All he knew was at Apis' disposition. Apis acknowledged it with all that he had learned at home, at Arles and in his lonely murders on our grazing-grounds.

He flowed round Chisto like a river of death—round his knees, leaping at his shoulders, kicking just clear of one side or the other of his head; behind his back hissing as he shaved by; and once or twice—inimitable!—he reared wholly up before him while Chisto slipped back from beneath the avalanche of that instructed body. Those two, my dear friend, held five thousand people dumb with no sound but of their breathings—regular as pumps. It was unbearable. Beast and man realised together that we needed a change of note—a *détente*. They relaxed to pure buffoonery. Chisto fell back and talked to him outrageously. Apis pretended he had never heard such language. The audience howled with delight. Chisto slapped him; he took liberties with his short tail, to the end of which he clung while Apis pirouetted; he played about him in all postures; he had become the herdsman again—gross, careless, brutal, but comprehending. Yet Apis was always the more consummate clown. All that time (Christophe and I saw it) Apis drew off towards the gates of the *toril* where so many bulls enter but—have you ever heard of one that returned? *We* knew that Apis knew that as he had saved Chisto, so Chisto would save him. Life is sweet to us all; to the artist who lives many lives in one, sweetest. Chisto did not fail him. At the last, when none could laugh any longer, the man threw his cape across the bull's back, his arm round his neck. He flung up a hand at the gate, as Villamarti, young and commanding but *not* a herdsman, might have raised it, and he cried: "Gentlemen, open to me and my honourable little donkey." They opened—I have misjudged Spaniards in my time!—those gates opened to the man and the bull together, and closed behind them. And then? From the Mayor to the Guarda Civile they went mad for five minutes, till the trumpets blew and the fifth bull rushed out—an unthinking black Andalusian. I suppose some one killed him. My friend, my very dear friend, to whom I have opened my heart, I confess that I did not watch. Christophe and I, we were weeping together like children of the same Mother. Shall we drink to Her?'